The Stealth Genius

The Stealth Genius

E.E. "Doc" Murdock

H.O.T. Press
Publishing fine books since 1983

H.O.T. Press
Los Angeles, California
www.hotpresspublishing.com

ISBN: 0-923178-43-0
ISBN-13: 978-0-923178-43-7

Books by E.E. "Doc" Murdock

Novels

- **Death as Concept**
- **The Storyteller of Cottage H**
- **The Robots of Cottage H**
- **God's Messenger – God's Victim**: A *Bildungsroman* Stockholm Syndrome Novel
- **The Pain Artist:** An American Hikikomori
- **My Vietnam War**
- **A Psalm for Cock Robin**: A Harp and His (Dead) Mother Mystery
- **Crueltown**: A Drew Steele Los Angeles-Las Vegas Mystery
- **The End of the Civil War**: A Drew Steele Civil War Mystery
- **Who Owns Arizona**: A Drew Steele Civil War Mystery

Textbooks/How-To Books

- **How to Write Fiction: Tools and Techniques**
- **Self Management: A Guide to More Effective Study**
- **Computers Today**
- **Computers the Easy Way**
- **Windows the Easy Way**
- **DOS the Easy Way**
- **HyperCard the Easy Way**
- **dBASE the Easy Way**

History/Political Books

- **From Washington & Adams to Trump & Biden:** The Stories behind the Story of Every Presidential Election, With Special Focus on the *Volatile* Presidential Election of 2020
- **From Washington & Adams to Hillary & Trump:** The Stories behind the Story of Every Presidential Election, With Special Focus on the *Volatile* Presidential Election of 2016

Acknowledgments

I am indebted to the members of the Ojai Writing Workshop who provided valuable feedback as I worked through the many drafts of this book. I would also like to acknowledge the help of all my students at California State University, Long Beach who taught me so much. And of course, without Zoe, this book would not exist.

This one is especially for Zoe.

One

The counselor storms out of his glassed-in office at the back of the study hall. He goes to the front of the room and stands there glaring at us.

Uh oh, somebody is in trouble.

He looks at the sheet of paper he's holding and calls out, "Curt Smith."

Oh no. Smith is the name we've been using since Mom and I got to this country. How could my name be on that piece of paper? I've worked hard to play the role of an anonymous fourteen-year-old freshman at this high school, and I've learned to speak English just like a normal American kid.

The counselor looks all of us over, waiting. It means he doesn't know which boy I am. If I keep my head down and continue drawing my picture of an imaginary super robot, he might think the boy he's looking for isn't here.

"All right now, Curt, I know you're in study hall this period. You aren't in any trouble. I just need to discuss . . . something with you."

I'd better respond. Otherwise, he might get suspicious about why I'm not answering. I raise my hand, a little.

"Ah, there you are, Curt. Come into my office."

Just quietly follow him into his office. Act innocent. Act shy.

All the other boys are staring at me. Pretend not to notice.

The counselor leads me into his office and points at the gray metal chair that's in front of his desk. He closes his office door

I sit in the chair, trying to act calm and unconcerned.

He sits behind his beat-up gray metal desk and looks at the sheet of paper.

He's shaking his head. What does that head-shaking mean? Is there something on that paper he doesn't like? The paper has rows of printing on it, so it must be some kind of list. I must be on that list.

But he seems calmer now, so maybe he hasn't found out about me. This must be something related to my school work.

Looking him over, he's not a tall man, but he has a big chest and thick wrists. He's losing his hair. He's probably been in this office for many years, and it's not even a real office, only a glassed-in box in the back corner of the boys' study hall.

He holds up the sheet of paper and points to one line of print. "Look at this, Curt"

I can't read it from this distance.

"It's the results of that test you took, the test all entering freshmen take. Do you remember taking that test?"

Of course I remember taking that test. A lot of easy multiple-choice questions. Remain non-committal. Say nothing. Just nod.

"I'll cut to the chase, young man. The test gives us an indication of your IQ. It indicates you have the highest IQ of any student. And not just among the entering freshmen that took the test this year. Your score indicates you have a higher IQ than any student in this large high school." He shakes the sheet of paper at me. "How do you explain that?"

He's waiting for me to say something. But what? I took the test along with all the other incoming students. I had fun trying to figure out all the right answers. Now I realize that was a mistake. I should have intentionally missed enough questions to appear average.

"Uh, well, sir, I kind of . . . well, what I mean is nobody ever told me anything like that before."

Maybe that will work, but be careful.

"Come on now, boy. What do you think you're pulling? I looked up your first term grades. Mostly Cs."

So that's why he's mad at me. Does he realize I'm intentionally getting Cs to avoid attracting attention? Mom says we only have one rule now that we've found this town where she finally got a permanent job: don't attract attention. She says if they find out how we illegally got into this country, they'd send us back to Germany.

In this school's library, I've read newspaper stories that say the Russian are now in control of the part of Germany we came from. Mom says if we get sent back there, the Russians would imprison us, maybe send us to Siberia.

"Are you listening to me, young man? Come on now, you must have had some indication that you had superior intelligence. Genius level intelligence."

He's calling me a genius. I have to say something.

"Well, not really, sir. I mean I guess I sort of noticed some things were . . . easy for me."

That's enough. Don't say anything else.

He again points to that one line of print on the paper. "None of your teachers in elementary school ever mentioned this level of intelligence?"

He's waiting for a response.

"Uh, not really."

Has he been checking up on me? He can't know I'd never been in a school before we came to this city, not in Germany, and not in any of the towns we stopped in. But could he somehow know about the reading award I got at that local elementary school I briefly attended when we first got here? Just in case, better mention it. "Uh, I did get an award for reading the most books in the elementary school I went to. They were keeping track of who checked out the most books from the school library."

He's leaning forward, staring at me. "So, you read a lot of books."

I just shrug and continue to look down so he doesn't think I'm challenging him.

"Tell me son, have you always been an avid reader? Did you start reading at a very young age?"

Has he been in touch with my mother? Back in Germany, she was always bragging that I started reading newspapers when I was still a toddler. No, if this counselor had contacted her, she would have told me. And now he'd be asking me why she has so much trouble with the English language.

He's waiting. Don't let him start speculating about your silence. "Well, I guess I just wanted to see what was in those books."

"And what about your grades? Did you get all A's in elementary school?"

"Well, sir, grades in the elementary school I went to were just satisfactory or not satisfactory. My grades were always, uh, satisfactory."

"Right, right. There've been PhD dissertations written about the pros and cons of that kind of grading system. And here you're showing us an example of the problem. Instead of being in that kind of educational system, you could have been getting special schooling to take advantage of your superior intelligence."

Say nothing. Look down at the cracks in the wooden floor. A lot of years of accumulated dirt in those cracks.

"Well, son, unfortunately, in this public high school, we have a policy against advanced placements. Egalitarianism and all that. But if your parents can afford it, I think they should see about placing you in a more, uh, specialized school."

I can't tell him I have only one parent, and she works two jobs just so we can get by. No way she could afford a special school. She barely makes enough to pay the rent on our tiny one-bedroom apartment in the bad part of town. And wouldn't a special school want to see my elementary school records? Better divert him away from that. "Oh, okay, I'll talk to them about that."

"Good, good. See that you do. I'd hate to see your talents wasted in this . . . I mean in this kind of public school setting. And then there's college. With your high level of intelligence, you'll want to go to a top college. It takes good grades to get into them. And don't forget there's a war going on over there in Korea. Who knows how long that war will be going on. If you're a college student, you won't get drafted and sent over there."

Don't respond to that. I know there's an America war going on over there in far-away Korea, but with no TV at home, it's hard to get any information about it.

But he's waiting for me to say something. "Well, if that war ends, I expect there will be another one before long."

Now he's glaring at me. "Why'd you say that, boy? You mean because of the Cold War? You think it's wrong for us to keep Russia and China at bay? Do you think you're smarter than our military planners?"

Another mistake. I've got to be constantly on my guard. "Uh, no. It's just something I heard the history teacher say, that there will always be wars and rumor of wars."

"Oh yes, that. Well . . ."

Now he seems nervous, maybe even confused. He looks down at some papers on his desk.

I get up from the chair and partly turn as if I'm leaving. I hope he'll take it as the moment to let me go, as if I have school-work to get back to.

He seems a little surprised that I did that. Does he realize I'm subtly taking charge of the situation?

He just frowns and waves me away.

I go out and carefully close his office door. On the way back to my desk, all of the other boys are staring at me. I avoid making eye contact with any of them.

Now that I'm back at my desk, only one boy is still staring at me. An Asian-looking boy. He could be of Japanese heritage.

I ignore him and stare at the drawing that's on my desk. I've got to figure out how to solve this situation. Mom says we're relatively safe here in this Midwestern city, as long as no one ever finds out we came here illegally from Germany. Even now, six years since the end of the war, the people in this country are still angry at German people.

But I don't see why I should have to be German anyhow. Mom didn't like the main man who was in charge back there. Crazy Hitler, she called him. Just about my only childhood memories of Germany are of scary big airplanes in the sky and the sound of bombs hitting the cities far away. I never saw a single Russian, but Mom said they were coming, and that they would hurt us. Our hurried escape from our small town is now mostly a fast-moving blur of brief memories. I remember a Catholic priest was involved, and then we were crowded together with a lot of other people in the back of a big smelly truck.

After that, we were put on a big ship with a lot of more people. We had to stay hidden down in the in the bottom of that ship, mostly in the dark. Some of the people were afraid our ship would get sunk by a submarine attack, but that didn't happen. When we got let off that ship, we were in a noisy city with lots of cars and the smell of food cooking. I found out later it was the island of Cuba.

After a while, Mom found us passage on a smaller boat that took us to the United States. On that boat, I mainly remember the smell of everybody but me getting sick. They made me be the one to use buckets full of sea water to wash away the throw-up.

We landed in a place with palm trees and busy streets. Mom told me we were in Florida. After that, I remember dirty motels in a sequence of small towns. They now all kind of merge together. Every day, while Mom went out to find day jobs in each new town, I tried to stay anonymous. To learn English, I read books in bookstores and listened to people talking. But in every town, sooner or later, Mom would get afraid, and we'd have to move on to another place.

Eventually, she said we were running out of money. She was having trouble finding jobs because she couldn't quite figure out English. I tried to teach her, but she thought English was hard language to learn.

Finally, when we came to this city in what the Americans call the Midwest, she got a job at a motel out by the highway where none of the maids spoke much English, and the boss didn't require anybody to have identification papers.

Now that we've finally found a town where we might be able to stay for a while, did I mess up everything by doing too well on that test? Why didn't I realize that test might draw attention to me? How can I fix this?

Two

At the end of the hour, I leave the study hall, and the Japanese-looking boy falls into step next to me.

He says, "What was that about with the counselor?"

Better not ignore him. It might make him even more curious. "Oh, nothing," I say. "He just wanted to go over one of my test scores with me."

"Oh yeah? Then why was he so angry?"

"He wasn't angry. He was just in a hurry. There was just some kind of mix up on a test I took."

"Just a mix-up, eh? It felt like there was somethin' else going on."

"No, just a test mix up."

"Maybe so, maybe not. But there's somethin' about you. Where are you from?"

Why did he say that? Does he suspect I'm not from this country? No, his face just seems to show curiosity. "My family recently moved here from down South."

He shakes his head. "No, it's not that. You don't have a Southern accent. In fact, you speak very formally. There's somethin' else."

"Well, we lived in a lot of different parts of the country. Maybe that's what you're noticing."

"No, somethin' else. Maybe you're like me. In some way."

"Like you?"

"Aw, you don't know about me, do you? Aw hell, I might as well tell ya. You'll find out sooner or later. The students in this school think I don't belong here. Soon as they find out my name, Haru Yoshida, they hate me for being Japanese. And they found out I came from the big Japanese relocation camp upstate. It was where my family got locked up during the war, locked up just because we had a Japanese name. My people have been in this country for over a hundred years, but they locked us up anyway. And then, after they took us out of California, the people back there stole all the stuff my dad left in his store. Just took it. When my dad heard about that, he joined up in the U.S. Army. They took him out of the camp and sent him off to war in Europe He got killed over there. I think he wanted to get himself killed. My mother doesn't believe that, but I do."

How should I respond to this boy? He's dressed a lot like me. Polished shoes, but worn-out clothes. Even if he is poor like me and not accepted in this country, I can't let that influence me. It's better if I don't have any friends.

As we continue to walk down the hallway, he goes completely silent. Is he thinking about being locked up in that government camp? In the school library, I read about the U.S. government locking up anybody of Japanese ancestry that was living on the West Coast of this country. Hard to believe they did that to their own citizens, but I'm not sure what this Japanese boy wants me to say about it. The government of Germany did a lot worse things to its citizens, but I can't say that to him. But I should say something so he doesn't get too curious. "I read about that. Internment camps."

"Read about it, eh? Ha! Did you read about how we were locked up in barracks? Like big shacks. Freezing cold all winter, boiling hot all summer. And mud all around for weeks every time it rained. The camp was surrounded by barbed wire and guards with guns. Did you know that? Guns. Pointed in at us. We were prisoners, no matter what they say now. Land of the free? We weren't free. They locked us up for no reason except we had a Japanese name. Did you read about that?"

It's a sad story, but you'd better not get too involved with him. Just continue to play the role of an ordinary American boy.

"Doesn't seem right."

"Not right? That's for sure. A lot of people say that now, but did anybody speak up back then? And what have they done for me and my mom since the war ended? There's nothing left for us back there in California now, so we're stuck here."

"I'm sorry you had a hard time, Haru."

He seems surprised that I said that, but as we continue on down the hallway, he doesn't say anything more until, "Hey, here's something. Maybe it's why I wanted to talk to you. When we were locked up, I knew it was because the free people outside wanted us to be locked up. I was just a kid, but I hated everybody out there. But you know what? For some reason, I don't feel like you're one of those outsiders. You don't have that mean feel to ya."

We arrive at my class, and I knew I should get away from him quickly. "Well, nice to meet you, Haru, but I had better get in here to my class."

Now he seems sad. "Yeah, I gotta get to my next class too. Maybe we can talk later."

I hurry into the classroom and find a place in the back row, as usual.

What could that Japanese boy have seen in me? I've been very careful to seem ordinary, and I'm sure I don't have any kind of German accent left. I suspect he's just been through a hard time, and he needed somebody to talk to, somebody he thought would understand. At any rate, I'd better make sure I stay away from him from now on.

Now, it's time to think about this history class. It's the one class that somewhat interests me, especially when the teacher talks about European history.

Three

The history teacher arrives late, and for a change, he seems fairly happy. He's the school basketball coach, and he almost always starts the class by talking about basketball. This time, he's talking about the big win his team got on Friday.

But then, as soon as he's done talking about basketball, for some reason, he launches into a long rant about how much harder things were "back in his day." He want us to know he had to hike for miles to get to school, sometimes in knee-deep snow. He says kids these days don't realize how easy they have it.

His self-involved rambling gives me time to think about what the counselor told me. He called me a genius. As I told that counselor, I always knew things came easy for me, but is that what being a genius means? More likely, it's only what they call somebody who scores really high on a certain type of test. Therefore, that test is the problem. That school entry test. If I hadn't scored so high on that test, the counselor wouldn't have noticed me. What if he starts telling my teachers I'm a genius? They'd start paying a lot more attention to me, and that could ruin everything. Tomorrow, in study hall, I'd better go back into the counselor's office and try to convince him not to tell anyone. If he asks why I wouldn't want people to know how smart I am, I'll tell him I'm doing the best I can in my classes, and the best I can get is Cs. It wouldn't be fair for my teachers to start putting pressure on me to do better just because of one test. I'll tell him that test must have been some kind of fluke, that I was just making lucky guesses.

The history teacher finally starts talking about history. He's naming all the wars the United States has been involved in, saying we all should be really proud that we haven't ever lost even a single war.

I wonder what he would think if he knew where I came from.

When the bell finally rings, it means the school day is over so I can go do my usual thing, reading in the school library until it closes for the day.

When I get to the library, I go straight to the fiction section. I'll read just about any kind of book, but lately I've been reading fictional books, especially books about the future.

I find a book about robots. Standing next to the bookshelf, I quickly read it. In the book, the robot was made to be very much like us humans, but it didn't want to be human; it preferred to do robot jobs, which were easy and didn't involve any human-type worries. To me, robots are in a class above humans; they think clearly, and they never get lonely or sad.. They just do what needs to be done.

Looking through the books on the shelf, I realize I've already read all the books this library has about the future. I've already read Heinlein's *Red Planet,* and Arthur C. Clarke's *Prelude to Space*. They were interesting, but kind of slow. I love to read, but once I see where the story is going, I get impatient. I don't know why I'm so impatient. It's not just stories in books; a lot of things in the world also seem to move in slow motion.

I spot a book on the fiction shelf I haven't read. It's titled *The Story of an Unknown Man* by an author named Anton Chekhov.

I take it to a reading table, and it turns out not to be a book about the future; it's about a nobleman in Russia posing as a servant to a government official that was trying to steal state secrets. It takes me longer than usual to finish reading it, almost an hour. It's not the kind of book I normally read, but the writer did a good job of portraying the people in the story and developing the conflicts between them.

I wasn't all that interested in the story, but the writing itself felt different from the kind of writing I'm used to; the author tells the story as if from inside the mind of the main character. In addition to telling the events of the story, the character shares his most personal thoughts, what he's dreaming about, and what he's wishing for. Interesting.

To find out more about him, I go to the library's encyclopedia and look him up. Turn's out he's Russian, and he's been dead for a long time.

There are no more books by Chekhov on the fiction shelf, but the encyclopedia also listed some other dead Russian authors including one named Fyodor Dostoevsky, and I find a book by him titled *The Gambler.*

Sitting back down to read it, I learn it's about a young man who becomes a gambler to try to win money in order to impress a girl. It doesn't take me long to finish reading it, but just like the Chekhov story, this book is also interesting because of the interesting people the author creates. And once again, the author created a character who shares his innermost thoughts. A great way to tell a story, I think.

The only other book by Dostoevsky in the school library is a book of his short stories. Once I've finished it, I think I like his short stories even better than his novel because he develops the characters very quickly and brings the important events of the story to a head within a few pages.

I think I'm going to like reading these dead Russian authors, but it makes me wonder if these old books are still popular in Russia today. If so, would that say something about what it means to be Russian? It might even say something about how they were able to defeat the Nazis when no other country could, and why there were willing to sacrifice the lives of millions of their people in order to do it. That's something I should think more about later. I wonder it there are any books that might talk about that. The only thing I know about the Russians is that my mother was so afraid of them we ran away before their army could get to our town. What had she heard about them that was so bad? I should ask her about that.

Back on the bookshelf, I find a book by another Russian author named Leo Tolstoy. It's titled *The Death of Ivan Ilyich.*

But before I can get it back to the table to read it, the librarian comes to tell me, in her usual grumpy way, that she wants to close up.

I need at least one more book to read at home tonight, so I say, "I'm looking for a certain type of book. It's related to a class assignment."

"What assignment?" she demands.

"For my . . . history class."

She's scowling at me.

I quickly add, "The history of science."

I don't know why I said that. Will she wonder why the history teacher would have us reading about the history of science?

But she doesn't seem suspicious, and she leads me to another section of the library. She pulls a book off the shelf. "Here's one, but you'll have to check it out. I'm closing up."

I check out that book, along with the Tolstoy book, and leave the library.

As I walk home, I'm still trying to come up with a plan on how to talk to the counselor tomorrow. Maybe if he accepts my claim that my extraordinary test score was a fluke, he won't tell anybody else about it. Hopefully, he'll forget about it, and forget about me too.

Four

As soon as it starts to get light outside, I get dressed and head for school. I want to be there when the library opens to try to find some more books by Russian authors. The Tolstoy book I read last night was really interesting. The author's main character was a man striving to improve his lot in life. He has a fairly pleasant life, but he wants to achieve higher status. When he feels a pain in his side, he sees doctors, and realizes he's going to die. In my mind, that's where the story really started. Faced with his own death, Ivan Ilyich realizes he's not prepared for it. Because he's lived what he thinks of as a good life, he believes he should not have to die. But as he sinks into pain and suffering, he begins to doubt that he's lived such a good life after all. He thinks about the kind of life he's been living, and for the first time, he begins to feel sympathy for those around him.

I think Tolstoy was saying we never know how long we have in this life, so we should always be thinking about how we are living it.

Last night, after I finished reading that Tolstoy book, I was awake for a long time thinking about how I've been living my own life. Have I been wasting my time lately reading science fiction books and drawing pictures of imaginary robots? I've read all kinds of other books too, but I've never gotten into books about science or math or other deeper subjects like that. The school counselor said my exceptionally high intelligence meant I had the potential to do great things in life. At the time, I didn't think much about what he was saying because I was mainly worried it might result in people finding out that Mom and I came here illegally from Germany.

Now, after lying awake thinking about what Tolstoy was saying, I'm wondering if I should have taken what that counselor was telling me more seriously.

He said I should aspire to greater things. At the time, I just wondered if maybe he was feeling regret about how he was living his own life, wishing he could go back to when he was my age and do more important things in his own life, but maybe he wasn't thinking anything like that; maybe he was really was thinking, because of my high intelligence, that I was on the wrong track.

I'm not faced with death like Ivan Ilyich was, but I could have died during the war in Germany. A lot of civilians did. Or, I could have died while we were on the run escaping from there. We saw a lot of dead people on the side of the road, maybe from random bombings or from strafing by fighter airplanes. If I would have died back there in Germany, none of this life I'm living here in the United States would have happened. Tolstoy would probably have told me I shouldn't wait until I'm old and ready to die to start thinking about the kind of life I'm leading. So, what kind of life I should I be leading? The counselor thinks I should become a top student and try to get into a top college, but because we don't have much money, and because of my illegal status in this country, I can't see how that could be possible.

Another thing: faced with death, Ivan Ilyich, began to pay more attention to other people. By doing that, he learned more about himself. So, when I arrive at school, instead of going right in, I decide to stop and watch the other students arrive. The first two students to arrive are girls. They're giggly and excited, their heads close together, whispering. What are they giggling about? And why do they cover their mouths with their hands when they laugh? I doubt if their thoughts are about how they are living their lives. They're probably thinking—like Ivan Ilyich before he got sick—about their day-to-day lives, their clothes, and their positions in their society. They're probably also thinking about boys.

In contrast to those two giggling girls, I see a sad-looking boy whose eyes are cast down. What could he have to be so sad about at his age?

He seems to be dressed pretty well. Better than me, that's for sure. Is he having girl trouble? From the look of him, it doesn't seem likely he would even know how to get a girlfriend. Maybe he's having trouble at home. Sometimes I overhear kids complaining about their parents not letting them do the things they want to do. Oddly, they don't seem to have a clue about how to manage their own parents.

I never have those kinds of problems at home. But then, I hardly ever get see my mother because she works two jobs. From early in the morning until late afternoon she works as a maid at the motel, and then she goes to an office building to do janitor work until well into the night. And even on her days off, to make a little extra money, she fills in for others at the motel. I feel sorry for her, so I try to be the way she wants me to be. No use doing things that would cause her trouble. For a while, I tried to figure out a way to help her by getting some money of my own. I tried to find an after-school job at the local businesses, but they all said I was too young. One weekend, I walked to the country club to see if anybody would hire me as a golf caddie. The manager said I could hang around and hope some of the golfers would hire me to fetch their practice golf shots, but the other caddies, skinny old guys who smoked or chewed tobacco, chased me off. I guess they didn't want to take the chance that some of the golfers might want to hire a kid to carry their golf clubs.

So these days after school, with nothing else to do, I just lie on my living room couch/bed reading the books I get from the school library. If that's all I can do, I should start reading more important books. Maybe science books.

I wonder what the other students do with their time away from school. Yesterday, the counselor implied I'm different from the other students. Back in Germany, I did feel different from the other kids. I preferred to stay by myself, reading and thinking and wandering alone in the woods. And since we arrived in this country, I've had to avoid making friends. When we were traveling from Florida to here, stopping only briefly in all those towns, I kept to myself while I learned English.

But in his story, Tolstoy was suggesting there were important things to be learned from seeing how other people live their lives. And being sympathetic with them. From now on, I'll pay more attention to the other students, and to adults too. I'll be the observer, watching and learning.

Watching the students arriving, it seems like they are either mostly happy or mostly sad. Does that mean there basic types of students, basic types of people? No, that's too simple; I'll have to watch for more examples to confirm any such hypotheses.

And what about me? I don't think I'm either overly happy or sad. I'm just what I am. But what do the other students think of me? If I was over there where they are, observing me, how would I describe the person they're seeing?

Serious looking, I guess. When I was little, Mom sometimes commented on that: she'd say, "*Worüber denkt mein kleiner Junge jetzt so ernsthaft nach?*" That meant, "What is my little boy thinking about so seriously now?"

I didn't know how to answer that question. I just always thought there were a lot of things to think about.

Right now, if any of those students looked at me, they'd see a skinny kid, wearing worn-out clothes. They might even realize my clothes came from thrift stores, clothes that smell like somebody else no matter how many times I wash them.

And are they able to tell that my mother cuts my hair? Too short, I think, as compared with the other kids, but I'm not about to complain about something like that. She has enough trouble just getting by without me complaining about a little thing like a bad haircut.

Overall, I don't think the other students can tell much about me. Certainly not from my facial expressions because I try not to show much. Partly, that's because of Mom's rule about not attracting attention, but also because I don't see the point in it.

When most of the students have arrived, I know I'd better hurry inside. I've never been late to a class. That would only attract attention, and I sure don't want that.

Five

I make it to my first class on time and take my usual place at the back of the room. I thought I was going to like this English class so I could learn more about writing, but the woman who teaches it seems to care less about writing than about grammar and punctuation. Most days, she just has us write down the sentences she dictates to us so she can check our punctuation. I've read so many books, I can already do that correctly.

Once, she did have us write an essay about our most memorable incident. I didn't want to reveal any of my memorable incidents, which would be about war or traveling, so made up a story about seeing a boy get injured by a car when he ran into the street after his dog. I wrote that the most memorable part of the experience was hearing the really loud thump it made when the car hit the boy. In the essay, I wrote that the sound scared me.

I thought I wrote that essay pretty well. But not too well, of course—designed, I hoped, to get a grade of C. She did give me a C on that essay, but she didn't say a word about the essay itself; she only criticized the intentional spelling mistakes I'd made and said I had used a semicolon wrong: she said I should never use a semicolon after a dependent clause when it comes before an independent clause. I'll remember that from now on, but it seems like there might sometimes be exceptions to that rule.

Today, she is again reading to us from a book, telling us to copy down what we hear and focus on the punctuation. I do what I always do, get the punctuation mostly right, but make a few intentional mistakes.

During the rest of my other morning classes, it try to somewhat pay at least vague attention to what the teacher is lecturing about, but I can't stop thinking about Tolstoy's story and how I should be living my life.

That makes me wonder what good is it doing me to sit through these classes learning nothing?

The school day drags on, but finally, it's time for PE class. I do like that class. The only physical education we get is running because the teacher is also the track coach, but I like to run. Every day, he leads us outside to run around the dirt track that's next to the school. He berates us to try to catch whoever is ahead of us. I may not be as fast as some of the older boys, but I'm fairly fast, and at least I get to go outdoors during the school day and get some exercise in the fresh air.

After PE class, it's lunchtime. I hurry through the cafeteria line, loading up my tray with as much food as I think I can get away with because I know it will be the only food I'm going to get today. At the cashier, I have a low-income family ticket so I don't have to pay. As always, I take my tray to my usual place, as far away from everyone else as possible.

After lunch is math class. It should be an interesting class, but it's boring because I already know the rules of algebra he's teaching. I wonder why he's so focused on teaching rules. Does it say something about the kind of person he is?

The other students seem to be having trouble learning those simple rules. I wonder why.

Although the class is usually really boring, sometimes the teacher gives us word problems to solve, and at least they give me something to think about. Today he gives us a problem involving two trains that are heading for a collision. That math is easy to solve, but what if we added some complexity, such as determining the speed of the trains as compared to a bird flying back and forth between them? That would make it an infinite series problem, which I've read about.

While the other students take their guesses at how to solve the problem, I think about the one time my mother took us to a train station to see about getting us onto a passenger train heading west. But the tickets would have cost too much money, so we went back to hitchhiking.

We hitchhiked from Florida all through the South and into the Midwest, stopping for a day or two in many different towns while she looked for work. It's surprisingly easy for a woman and a young boy to get rides, and we didn't have any real problems, except for one time a man tried to get Mom to stop at a motel with him. I used my new English skills to tell the man we were in too much of a hurry to get to my father who was in the military. I said he had a tendency to get really angry if we were delayed. The man immediately stopped and told us to get out of his car.

When math class is over, and it's finally time for afternoon study hall, I head there quickly and don't even sit down at my assigned desk; I go straight back to the counselor's office. When he allows me in, I say, "I want to thank you for informing me about my test score, but I need to tell you there must have been some kind of mistake. You see, sir, I really have been trying as hard as I can in all of my classes. Therefore, there must have been some kind of mistake on that test. I remember that I had to guess at a lot of the questions. I think maybe I just got lucky in all my guesses."

The counselor frowns and shakes his head.

Uh oh, he's not going for it.

"Well, son, a person might get lucky guessing some questions, but not to the degree that you could achieve the top score in the entire school. You might have thought you were guessing, but your guesses were clearly guided."

"Thank you for saying that, sir. Maybe I'm just better at taking that kind of test than I thought. Anyhow, I've decided that from now on, I'm going to study a lot harder and try to get better grades. Instead of playing around, I'm going to spend all my spare time in the library, reading."

"I'm glad to hear it, son. As I told you before, with your capabilities, you have the potential to do great things in life. That is . . . what I mean is, if you do as well in school as I think you're capable of, it will undoubtedly lead to greater things thereafter."

His eyes are getting teary. I wonder why. I'd better quickly get to the reason I came into his office. "However, sir, I'd like to ask you to do me a big favor. I'd prefer that you don't tell anybody about my high score on that test. What I mean is, I want to be measured by my achievements, not by a score on a test."

He again seems surprised, but he says, "Well, I wasn't planing on telling anybody about it. However, there are periodic student evaluations. Your test score will be seen by your teachers. Assuming they ask for it."

"Geez, sir, I hope they don't expect me to get As or anything. I mean, I hope they don't put a lot of pressure on me do better than I can."

He starts to say something, but I quickly go on. "But I will start trying a lot harder. Now that you have confidence in me, I think I can do better."

Don't say anything else. Let him come up with a solution.

"Tell you what, son. Your test score is already in the system, along with all the others. How about if I just let the score stand on it's own and don't make a big deal about it? I mean, I don't necessarily need to point out to anybody that it was the highest score in the entire school."

I guess I have to be satisfied with that. "All right, sir. Whatever you think is best. And like I said, I will try harder from now on and not waste my time so much."

"Good, good. Now before you go, did you talk to your parents about getting you into some kind of special school?"

"Yes, sir, I did. They said they would look into it right away."

"I'm glad to hear that. I hope they find a better, uh, setting for a student of your abilities."

"Thank you for all you're doing for me, sir. I really appreciate it."

I quickly leave his office before he can say anything else.

Several of the students are again watching me as I sit down, but I ignore them, and they soon go back to their studies.

All except for the Haru. He's smiling at me as if there's something between us. I'd better ignore him and open the history of science book I picked up from the library yesterday. I should start reading books about more important subjects, like science.

The first couple of chapters that are about the origins of scientific thought in Egypt, Babylon, Greece, and Rome. They had little of what we could call real science back then, but some of their rulers and priests were starting to wonder about the nature of things, and they wrote about that.

The next chapter is about the development of the scientific method. It says that in 1600, William Gilbert became Queen Elizabeth's Physician in Ordinary, and he became known for his research on magnetism. He demonstrated that a magnet floating on wood in tub would align itself to the north. On that basis, he concluding that the earth is magnetic. He also coined the Latin word "electricitas," which eventually evolved into the modern English word "electricity."

The book says that at about that same time, in Italy, Galileo was studying gravity and the properties of pendulums. He invented a telescope and began studying celestial objects. He not only observed the craters of the moon, but he also studied Venus, Jupiter, and Saturn, and wrote about his findings.

That gets me to wondering how a person, like Galileo, would be able to discover all those things when nobody else could. He was described as a genius. I wonder if he got called a genius at an early age.

After the bell rings and I'm walking to my last class of the day, history, I'm still thinking about Galileo being called a genius and what the counselor said about me being a genius and having the capability to achieve great things.

No, I'd better not start thinking like that. For now, I need to keep on playing the role of an ordinary American high school student. The most important thing is not being found out.

Six

In history class, my last class of the day, the teacher is lamenting the loss his basketball team just suffered. The loss was to the dreaded cross-town rival high school, and he's saying that made it even worse.

When he finally stops lamenting, he abruptly announces a surprise assignment: he tells us to write an essay on who we think was the most important person in the second world war.

I expect most of the other students will write about General Eisenhower. I read a book about him, so I could write about how he ordered the allied invasion of Europe by landing troops on the French mainland at the Normandy beaches in 1944. Also, in the newspapers they have in the school library, I read a story about the US losing the war in Korea, and Eisenhower wanting to use atomic bombs to win it. Although the newspaper say Eisenhower is likely to be the next US president, the military is resisting his idea of using atomic bombs in Korea because of how the Chinese might react.

I've been curious about the atomic bomb ever since I heard about it. I read that it was invented only seven years ago, using an entirely new approach to bomb-making that was made possible partly by using theories devised by Albert Einstein, who the newspapers describe as a German Jew. At the time the atomic bomb was dropped on Japan, nobody made much of the fact that it was a new type of bomb, only that it was the biggest bomb ever.

Thinking about atomic bombs makes me think about Truman, the only president to have ever ordered the dropping of atomic bombs on humans. I should write about him.

I read a book about him that said he was born on a farm in Missouri, but later moved to Independence, Missouri where he got interested in playing the piano.

To humanize him, I start my essay with that. I write about where he grew up and that he didn't go to a college. Instead, he tried to get into the military, but couldn't because of his poor eyesight, so he enlisted in the Missouri National Guard. When World War One began, his reserve unit was sent to France where he served as an artillery officer.

After that war was over, Truman returned to Missouri where he opened a men's clothing store. But it soon went bankrupt. Nevertheless, he had made friends with some of his customers who were influential local politicians, and despite Truman not having a college degree and no legal training, they got him appointed as a county judge.

In 1933, the country was in a depression, and President Hoover wasn't very popular. Truman's politician friends were Democrats, so they supported the nomination of Franklin D. Roosevelt, the wealthy governor of New York, to run for president against Hoover, and they got Truman nominated to be a US Senator on the Democratic ticket.

Roosevelt easily beat Hoover, and when the wave of New Deal Democrats were also swept into office, Truman ended up getting elected as a Senator.

I realize I'm going on too long about Truman himself instead of answering the question about who was the most important person in the war, so I skip forward to Truman being picked to be President Roosevelt's vice-president in the next election. That happened while the war in Europe was going on. Hitler had ordered the invasion of Russia, and that wasn't going very well for the Germans.

I remember my mother telling me about that at the time. She didn't like Hitler and was happy he was losing, but afraid of what the Russians might do to us if they invaded. Obviously, I can't reveal anything about what the war felt like to me as a child in Germany, but now, trying to write about the war from the American perspective reminds me of how different it was for us over there.

We lived in a small remote village in southern Germany, and all I knew about the war was that my father had to go away to fight in it, and one day, my mother told me he had been killed in Russia.

Glancing at the clock on the all, I know I'd better hurry and get back to my writing before the hour is up. I write that Truman was suspicious of what the Russians would do in Europe after the war was over, so he said the US should support Germany in order to weaken Russia. However, the US military didn't want to support Hitler in any way, so that didn't happen.

I stop writing again. I wish I could remember more about what Mom said about Hitler. I'll have to tell her about this assignment and ask her what she remembers about him and about the war. It feels odd now that I've never asked her about that.

Thinking about Hitler makes it seem like *he* was actually the most important person in World War Two. After all, he was the one that started it, and just about everything that happened in that war was because of him.

I look up at the history teacher. He's sitting as his desk, writing something. He has dark hair and dark eyes. Could he be Jewish? He might be. If he is, he probably wouldn't like me writing something that implies Hitler was a great man, which of course he wasn't, even though he had a devastating impact on the world. No, I'd better stick to writing about Truman.

I write that Truman didn't have all that much to do as vice-president, but Roosevelt's health wasn't very good, so everybody knew it was possible he could die, meaning Truman would end up as president.

And that's exactly what happened. Not long after Roosevelt got reelected for a fourth term, he did die, and Truman became president. The war in Europe was winding down, and it looked like the Russians were going to invade Germany.

But the Japanese were still fighting to the last man on their outlying islands. The US air force was relentlessly bombing Tokyo and all the other Japanese cities and ports, pretty much destroying the entire country.

But the Japanese still wouldn't give up. Everybody was expecting the US military would soon invade the Japanese home island.

Soon after Truman was sworn in as president, than they told him about a new weapon that was being developed out in the New Mexico desert. They said it was called an "atomic" bomb, and it was supposed to be really powerful. Truman was ready to use it on Japan, but others said it was too dangerous. They said it worked by starting a chain reaction type of explosion, and nobody could predict how long the chain reaction would go on. Some top scientists said that once the chain reaction got started, it might keep on going and destroy the world. But they went ahead and tested it anyhow out there in the desert, and as it turned out, the chain reaction did eventually stop. The test proved the bomb was really powerful, more powerful than they had expected.

Hearing that the new bomb wasn't going to destroy the world, Truman was ready to drop it on Japan. Many of the scientists were against using the A-bomb against civilians, but Truman was ready to do exactly that. He only had one child, a girl, so he didn't have any close relatives over there fighting in the war. That could have influenced his decision. Also, the book I read said he was a strong supporter of locking up US citizens of Japanese heritage, like Haru, in internment camps, so maybe deep-down, Truman hated the Japanese, and that also influenced his decision.

By that time, the United States had only built two atomic bombs. Some of Truman's advisors recommended dropping one of them on a strictly military target, which would show the Japanese how powerful this new bomb was. They thought it would be enough to scare the Japanese into giving up.

But Truman wouldn't go for that idea. He didn't think that kind of demonstration would convince the Japanese of how powerful this new weapon really was. After all, most of Japan had already been devastated by non-stop bombing. Perhaps a million Japanese people had been killed, and they still weren't willing to give up.

Truman said dropping the bomb on civilians would teach those Japanese leaders how far we were willing to go to put an end to the war.

So, that's what they did. They dropped an atomic bomb on the Japanese town of Hiroshima, a remote seaside town that was chosen because it had mostly escaped any prior bombing. It instantly killed many, many Japanese civilians, including many thousands of children and babies in their cribs.

Contrary to what Truman thought, dropping that atomic bomb on Japanese civilians didn't make the Japanese government give up. In fact, it just made them angry and more willing to keep on fighting. So, three days later, Truman ordered the military to drop the one remaining atomic bomb they had on another Japanese city. It again killed huge numbers of Japanese citizens in the town of Nagasaki.

In addition to the dead and injured from the initial dropping of the two A-bombs, many more Japanese people were to die later from a mysterious illness that turned out to be radiation poisoning, something nobody knew anything about at that time.

But even after the US military had dropped two atomic bombs on Japanese cities, the Japanese government still wouldn't give up. In fact, it made them even more angry at the United States.

However, when the Russians heard about the powerful new bomb the United States had developed on Japan, they immediately declared war on Japan. When the Japanese saw that the whole world was now against them, they finally realized they had to surrender.

That's as far as I get before the bell rings, and the teacher says time is up.

I quickly add a concluding line summarizing why Truman was the most important person in the war because he ended it, and I insert a couple of intentional spelling mistakes to make sure I don't get a very good grade on it. I turn in my paper and leave the room.

Walking down the hallway, I'm thinking that I didn't write that essay very well. Instead of being about what person most influenced the war, my essay was mostly just about Truman himself. I could do better.

But then, I can't start thinking like that; I don't want to do better. I can't let what the counselor said influence my performance in my classes. The only rule is don't attract attention.

I don't expect the other students will write very well-organized papers, given that it was an unexpected in-class assignment. I'm glad I thought to add those spelling mistakes. Teachers seem to take spelling errors seriously. Hopefully, I'll only get a C on it.

Seven

After leaving History class, I immediately go up to the school library. I head straight for the science section, but I don't know what I should be looking for, so I just start pulling books off the shelf, almost at random and reading them while standing there.

Turns out, science is a lot more interesting than I might have thought, so I take several of the books to a table and start reading them, one after the other.

It seems like no time has passed at all before the librarian comes to say she's ready to close up. I have her check out the books I haven't finished. I put them in my locker so I can read them tomorrow in study hall.

As I leave the school building by the side door, I see three older students heading for the school's band building. They don't look like musicians. They look more like the type of boys I've heard other students describe as "hoods."

Now I see they're not going to the band building; they're going around back of it. What's back there?

My first thought is that I should ignore this. I should just go home and start reading the science books I just got from the school library.

But then I think about what I did here this morning, studying students as they arrived at school and attempting to categorize them. I should do the same with these three. But these students are of a completely different type from any I saw this morning; they have a put-on tough look—what they call "ducktail" haircuts, low-slung jeans, and white T-shirts. One of them even has a pack of cigarettes rolled up in the sleeve of his short-sleeved T-shirt. Pretty brazen when teenagers aren't even supposed to be able to buy cigarettes.

I peek around the edge of the building, making sure they don't see me.

Of course. I should have predicted it: they're smoking cigarettes back there. But while they smoke, they're also pointing at things up in the sky, then laughing, then exchanging dollar bills. They must be betting on something. But what? Cloud formations? Flying birds? Why would they be betting on things as random as that? Do they get some kind of thrill from risking money?

These boys are nothing like the innocent-looking students I was analyzing this morning. Should I join them? This could be my chance to learn more about a different type of person. But how would they react to me butting in? Could they be violent? Well, if I really am some kind of genius, maybe it's a necessary part of the learning process.

I come out from my hiding place and walk right up to them. "Hi there, fellas. Can I borrow a cigarette?"

The tallest of them says, "Get lost, kid. This is a private party."

"Right, I can see that. But what's the money all about? Are you betting on things?"

He hangs his cigarette out of the corner of his mouth and takes a step closer to me. He's trying to look threatening, but he's not very good at it. He says, "Didn't I say get lost?"

I do a quick little confident laugh to show him I'm not afraid, even if I am smaller than him. I say, "I like betting too. Do it all the time. Tell you what. See that bird up there on that phone line? I've got a five-dollar bill in my pocket that says that bird will soon take off and fly right toward the afternoon sun." I don't have any money in my pocket at all. But the bird is facing in that direction—not likely it will take off in any other direction. Will they see through my bet? And what if I lose the bet? Will they beat me up when they find out I don't actually have any money? I got hit a few times in the elementary school I went to briefly when we first got to this town, but then I learned how to be more invisible. And I soon saw that school bullies don't actually want to hurt you badly; they only want to best you, to be the dominant one. If you don't fight back, they'll only hit you a few times.

The same boy says, "You're on, kid." He looks at the other boys and smirks.

Pretty soon, the bird does take off, and of course, it does head more or less toward the afternoon sun.

I laugh and demand my five bucks. And a cigarette.

They give me a cigarette, which I put behind my ear. I hold out my hand for the money.

They begrudgingly pool their money and hand over five crumpled one-dollar bills.

I say, "Thanks, guys," and walk away.

One of them yells at me: "Get your ass back here, kid. You've got to give us a chance to win back our money."

I wave back over my shoulder and say, "Sorry, guys. Gotta go. I'll be back tomorrow. We can do this again then."

I hurry out from behind the building, practically running.

The boys follow me, yelling.

Luckily, a few of the teachers are just leaving the school building, and that causes the boys to stop following me.

I keep moving, and when I look back, I see that they're still watching me. Well, I may have made some enemies, but at least they're not going to chase me.

So, my first test interaction with that type of student worked out pretty well. What should I try next? Now that I've got five bucks in my pocket, maybe I should go downtown and find something to spend it on.

I start walking toward downtown, but I don't get far before I realize I'm not doing the smart thing; I should just take the money home and give it to Mom. She'd really appreciate that.

But she won't be home until late tonight. Maybe I should at least go downtown and look around a bit. It's not far to walk, and I've never really looked around down there. I have been there often to read books in the bookstore, just like I did in every town we stopped in on our way here. And when we first arrived in this town, Mom said I would need some better clothes before I went to a school for the first time in my life, so she took me to a down-town thrift store.

She bought me some used boy clothes that day, but she was very insecure about not knowing how to speak English, so she never wanted to go downtown again.

As I continue to walk toward downtown, I'm thinking back to what I just did back there. I interacted with some older students. And I gambled. All new for me. I've never had much interaction with other people. Not with kids, not with adults. So, why did I do that? It must have been more than just wanting to learn. I've always preferred being by myself with my thoughts, so, what changed? Is it because that counselor told me I'm a genius? If so, what am I going to do next?

I pass two girls sitting on a bus stop bench. They stare at me as I pass.

Why are they looking at me? Usually nobody notices me. Is there something different about me now?

Walk on past. Don't make eye contact.

Hurrying on down the sidewalk, I remember I have a cigarette behind my ear. That's probably what they were staring at, a fourteen-year-old boy brave enough to walk around with a cigarette behind his ear.

As soon as I'm well past them, I throw the cigarette into the bushes.

But why am I going downtown? What will I do when I get there? Wander around? Look at things? Is that what a genius would do? Who knows? Maybe I just want to see if anything looks different to me now.

When I get downtown, I decide to look at all the stores.

One of stores is selling jewelry. I wonder why people think they need to wear jewelry. Do they think it makes them a different person?

Another is selling fancy, expensive watches. I guess there's a need for that if people need to be somewhere on time. But why are they so expensive? Are they like jewelry?

The next store identifies itself as a "gift shop." I have no idea why there would be a whole store just for that. Do that many people like buying gifts for each other?

Another store is selling furniture, but the sign says it's "home decor," which of course means people buy furniture for more than just to sit on. It also means that store is not for poor people like Mom and me. In fact, none of these stores are for poor people.

Another store is selling clothes. A lot more people in that one. I wonder why so many people are shopping for clothes. Once they have the clothes they need to wear in each season, why do they need more? Maybe sometimes they want to change the way they look. I'll have to think more about that.

These stores seem to be telling me I don't understand why people do the things they do, and I'm not sure books are going to explain it to me. All the more reason to be down here analyzing things.

I come to the big corner Woolworth drug store. Should I go in? Why? I'm not going to buy anything.

Well, why not? Just walk through and look at things, see what they can tell me.

I go in and walk past the lunch counter. Pretty busy for this time of day. These people may be eating their evening meal here, sitting on a stool in a drug store. Kind of surprising.

I walk past their displays of candy and gum. A lot of different kinds. A mother is trying to pull her little girl away, but the child wants some candy. The display is obviously designed to attract the attention of children, and it's working.

Another glass case contains cigarettes. Twenty-five cents a pack. Pretty expensive. I guess that's why they are in a glass case that has to be opened, to keep kids from trying to grab a pack.

Not much else to see in this store, so I go back out the other door and head on down the street. Not many people on the street now. They're probably all heading home for supper.

I stop in front of a store that's selling radios and TVs. In the window, front and center, is a TV that they say is a brand type of TV that shows in color. But the picture on the display model is obviously a color poster, and the sign says "Coming Soon."

That will not only take a new type of TV set; it will also require new broadcast equipment, a major change in the TV broadcast industry. I'll have to read about that.

I turn off into a side street. The stores on this street are not quite as fancy. There's a Chinese restaurant, and a bar next door. I'm too young to be allowed in the bar, and the windows are painted over, so I can't see inside. I can see inside the Chinese restaurant, but I'm not interested—why would I spend my money on restaurant food when I can get food for free at the school cafeteria? I don't eat much anyhow.

I come to another business with the front window painted over like that bar, but the sign says "POOL." Seems like I've heard about pool. It's a game. Is that what's inside, a place to play the pool game? Might as well find out.

I go in, and right away, I'm struck by the smell of the place: cigarette smoke and human sweat.

A row of green-felt-covered tables fill the long narrow room. The room is relatively dark, but each table has a fairly bright light hanging over it. The tables are all surrounded by men, all older than me, some a lot older. The men are striking colorful balls with the point end of special sticks, and the place is filled with the clicking sound of the balls running into each other. I can see they're trying to knock the balls into the holes that are spaced around the edges of the tables.

A few young men, maybe in their twenties, are gathered around the front table. They're very intent on watching what is going on. I think I see why: the two players seem to be playing for money. Bills are stacked at the far end of the table, so I assume the winner of the game gets to collect the money.

One of the players, a tall guy, seems to be better than the other guy at getting the balls into the holes. It's obviously a game of skill, not luck. I'd like to try the game, but it probably costs money to play. I do have those five one-dollar bills in my pocket, so I could play if I wanted to. But no, I should save the money and give it to Mom.

Even though there are still balls left on the table, the tall guy apparently just won the game because he's collecting the money. He notices me watching and says, "Hey, kid, wanna play?"

I hold up both of my hands and say, "No thanks."

He lets out the kind of laugh that's not really a laugh and says, "No money, eh?"

I hesitate, and then say, "I've got money. It's just that I haven't played this game before."

He does his little non-laugh laugh again and says, "*Está Bien*. How 'bout if I give you a head start?"

A head start? What kind of head start could he give me? And why did he throw in a couple of Spanish words. Other than those few words, he doesn't talk with an accent like the Mexican workers I met out at the motel where Mom works.

I say, "What kind of head start?"

"I could spot ya a couple of balls. With that big an advantage, you're sure to win. C'mon, it'll only cost ya a buck."

So he wants to play me for money. Okay, if I'm supposed to be so smart, let's see how he reacts if I challenge him.

I mimic his little non-laugh laugh and say, "How about you spot me five balls and we play for five bucks?"

That gets the attention of some of the others. They come closer to watch.

The tall pool player turns to the other guys and says, "Well, looky here, boys, I think we got ourselves a hustler. Whatta ya say, Esteban, should I take him on?"

The guy he called Esteban, a short stocky guy with a sagging mustache, says, "*Chivo expiatorio.*"

I wonder what that means. I'll have to get a Spanish-English dictionary sometime and try to figure out what they were saying.

The tall pool player pulls a wad of bills out of his pocket, selects a five-dollar bill, and puts it on the end of the table. Okay, *estafador*, put some money where your mouth is."

I realize I'm committed now. But maybe with a five ball head start, I could win the money and have twice as much to surprise Mom with. Knocking the balls into the holes doesn't look all that hard.

I put my five crumpled-up one-dollar bills on the table next to his money.

"Okay, let's go," he says. "I break."

"All right, just tell me the rules."

"You don't know how to play eight ball?"

"No."

He looks at his friends and winks. "Okay, kid, assuming this isn't a put-on, I'll explain the game to ya. Pretty simple. Look at the balls." He points. "Striped balls'n solid balls. Whichever one you get in first, from then on, you go after that type. Once you knock 'em all in, you go for the black eight-ball."

I get it. I can see there are only seven balls of each type. Him giving me a five ball head start really is a big advantage. "So, I only have to knock in two of my balls, then I get to go for the eight ball?"

"Right."

"Okay. Sounds simple enough."

Pan gestures to his other pal and says, "Rack em up, Diego."

After the Diego guy organizes the balls on the table into a triangle shape, the pool player uses his stick to hit the white ball into them. That spreads the balls all over the table, and a striped ball goes into one of the holes. Then, he carefully and systematically continues, knocking in all the other striped balls, and without any trouble at all, he knocks in the eight-ball." He turns to me, grinning.

I say, "Okay, is it my turn now?"

The other guys laugh.

The pool player shakes his head. "Nope, the game is over. *Terminado*."

"But I never got my turn."

"That's right, kid. That's how the game is played. First one knocks in all his balls and gets the eight ball, wins."

I get it. Him giving me a five ball advantage was no advantage at all because if he can immediately knock in all of the required balls, I'll never get a turn.

I should just forget about my five dollars and get out of here. But he made knocking in the balls looks so easy, I have to give it a try. "Okay, how about this time, I get to go first."

"Fine with me. Ya got another five bucks?"

"Not with me. But I can get it."

"Sorry, kid, no money, no play." He turns to his pals. "*Está bien, quién es el siguiente?*"

He's speaking Spanish again. I think he's asking who wants to play him next.

But they all shake their heads

I say, "Tell you what, how about you spot me the five balls and I get to break."

He smiles, but shakes his head again. "No money, no play."

"Okay then, let's play for a hundred."

That stops him. He narrows his eyes. "A hundred bucks? Maybe ya really are a hustler."

"A hustler? I don't know what that is."

"It means you're an expert, just claming to not know how to play."

"No, I really am telling you the truth. I've never played this game before."

He stares at me, and then finally says, "Okay, kid. A hundred it is. But if I do play ya, you and me are gonna have a little talk."

"A little talk? About what?"

"No big deal. I might need a little somethin' from you. A favor, let's call it. C'mon, let's play."

"Okay, but this time, I break."

"Fine, kid. Go for it."

"And I get to use your stick."

That surprises him. "My pool cue? No way. It's custom made. Cost me a bundle."

"So, you're afraid you'll lose if I get to use a good pool cue."

Again, he stares at me for a long moment, and then says, "You're on."

After the Diego guy again gets the balls organized on the table, the poll player hands me his cue and says, "Go for it, kid."

I wave his pool cue around for a bit, just to get the feel of it.

That seems to irritate him. He says, "Come on, kid. *Darse prisa.* We ain't got all night. Go ahead and break."

I line up the white ball exactly the way he did it and give it a smack right toward the triangle assembly of balls.

It does manage to hit the balls, but it doesn't spread them out very much, and none of the balls go into any of the pockets. His pals laugh.

The pool player doesn't laugh, but he is grinning. "Now, it's my turn, kid."

He takes back his pool cue and knocks in a striped ball. He continues to knock in other striped balls, but this time, he doesn't manage to get all the striped balls into pockets.

I think that means it's my turn now. I still have a chance to win the hundred dollars.

He hands me his pool cue.

I take it and say, "So, I have to knock in two solid-colored balls?"

"*Correcto.* And then the eight ball."

I look over the table. The yellow ball that's numbered "one" is pretty close to a middle hole. All I have to do it knock the white ball into that yellow ball, and it should go right into that hole.

But when I do it, the yellow ball catches the felt edge of the hole and bounces right back out.

His friends laugh again. They're beginning to irritate me. I think that's what they're trying to do, but I can't let them get to me. I still have a chance to win. See if they laugh then.

The pool player takes back his pool cue and in short order, systematically finishes off all the striped balls, and then the eight ball.

The pool player turns to me. "Okay, kid. You owe me a hundred."

"I don't have a hundred. Actually, I don't have any money at all."

He stares at me. He doesn't seem all that angry, only puzzled. "I figured there was no way you had that much money on you, kid. So, what're you up to?"

"I just wanted to play. Turns out, it's harder than it looks."

The pool player leans on his pool cue and shakes his head. "Well, I'd say you'd better get on home and ask your Dad for the money."

"Don't have one of those."

"What?"

"I don't have a dad. I never did have one. At least not since I can remember."

Now he stares at the floor. Is he thinking about what I just said?

Finally, he looks up at me. "All right, kid. No big deal. I never had a dad either. How 'bout your ma? She must have some money."

"I'm afraid not. She works as a maid at a motel. She barely makes enough to pay our rent."

"So, with no money to pay off, you walk in here and started making hundred-dollar bets on a game you don't know how to play."

His two friends come closer. They look threatening. Are they going to beat me up now?

"Yes, I'm afraid that's true. Are you and your friends going to beat me up now?"

"Is that what usually happens to you when you try a stunt like this?"

"I've never tried anything like this before."

"¡No me digas! Ain't you the interesting one. So, why'd ya decide try it today?"

"I'm not sure. Things just feel kind of . . . changed for me today.

"Changed, eh?" He waves his friends away, but they don't go far.

"I'm not sure where you're comin' from, kid. But I can't keep on callin' ya kid. What's your name?"

"Curt. What's yours?"

"Pánfilo. But you can call me Pan."

"So, are you Jamaican?"

"No. My grandfather brought me and my mother here from Puerto Rico when I was little. He was the one that named me. Why'd you say Jamaican?"

"I just assumed you were named for Pánfilo de Narváez. He was a Spanish soldier that came to Jamaica in 1510."

"How the hell would you know that?"

"Oh. Well, I like to read. A lot."

"Read a lot, do ya? And you remember a thing like that? Well, reader, you may know some things from books, but you still owe me a hundred bucks And like I said, I might need somethin' from you. Tell you what, you do the little favor for me, and I'll cancel the hundred you owe me."

A little favor? Not likely. A hundred dollars is a lot of money. No way he's going to forget about it if it's only a *little* favor. "A little favor? Like what?"

He suddenly grabs the front of my shirt. "Listen kid, you admit you owe me, right?"

I try to push his hand away, but his grip is too strong. "Hey, let go of my shirt, Pan. This is the only going-out shirt I've got. I'll do your little favor. Just tell me what it is."

He lets go of my shirt and brushes it down. "No big deal, Curt. Call it an errand."

"An errand. Now?"

"In a couple of hours. Ya know where the Starlight Motel is? Not too far. That way." He points.

"I'll find it."

"Good. Meet us there after it gets dark. And you'd better be there, or we'll be comin' after ya. *¿Consíguelo?*"

"I'll be there."

I hurry out of the pool room, wondering what kind of little favor he might want from me at that motel. Before I agree to do it, I'd better make him tell me exactly what it is. He might be up to something illegal. Still, it might be something interesting enough to check out. I'll decide when I get there.

Eight

To kill time until I'm supposed to meet Pan at that motel, I go to the park and watch the ducks swim around in the pond. Interesting how they busily live out their lives, apparently totally involved in what they're doing. They look for food, and they interact with other ducks. In that, they are not unlike us humans; we too intake food and interact with each other. Of course, our activities are more complex because we have more complex brains, but we do have the same basic needs that any other mammal has. I wonder if there are books in the library about the concept of what makes us human. And what about the concept of concepts? I wonder how much of our thinking is involved in forming concepts. And what exactly is a concept? It's like a joke: what is the concept of a concept? More things to look up in the library.

It's starting to get dark. I better hurry and find the Starlight Motel.

I soon find the motel, but I don't see Pan or his friends anywhere. I sit on the bench out front to wait.

After a while, without them showing up, I'm beginning to wonder if maybe they were just playing a trick on me. Maybe they're still back at the pool hall, getting a big laugh out of imaging me out here wandering around in the dark. If they don't show up pretty soon, I'll just go home and forget about this.

The Starlight Motel seems kind of run down, but it does have a colorful neon sign with red letters and a glowing green palm tree. I don't know why they put a palm tree on their sign; there are no palm trees in this town, and the name of the motel doesn't have anything to do with a beach or the tropics.

I'm tired of sitting here listening to the buzzing of the neon sign. I might as well leave. But maybe I should first look for Pan out behind the motel.

I go around to the motel's back parking lot, but I still don't see him. I'm about ready to give up and leave when I see him. He's frantically waving at me from the back edge of the parking lot. He's standing next to an old white van. Esteban and Diego are with him, and it almost looks like they're hiding back there. What are they up to?

I go to them and say, "I almost couldn't find you guys. Are you hiding?"

Pan grabs my arm and pulls me behind the van. He says, "Never mind about that." He points at the back of the motel. "See that room? The one with the number fifteen on the door? We need you to get us in there."

He seems nervous. I wonder why. "Why do you want to get into that room?"

"We just need to—"

Esteban gets between me and Pan. He seems angry as he says something to Pan in Spanish, pointing back at me with his thumb.

Diego doesn't look happy either. He's shaking his head. Pan says something to Esteban in Spanish, who also shakes his head.

I don't understand what they are saying in Spanish, but it's obvious Pan is saying something they don't like. This situation is getting weird. It would probably be smart for me to just get the heck out of here.

I start to edge away, but Esteban notices and grabs my arm. What is it with these guys thinking they can keep on grabbing my arm? "You know, Pan, I think I'd better be getting home. Tell this guy to let go of my arm."

But Esteban doesn't let loose of my arm, and he and Pan start arguing in Spanish again.

Pan gets in Esteban's face and says "*¡Déjalo ir!*"

Esteban hesitates, but then he finally does let loose of my arm.

As I rub my aching arm, Pan puts his arm over my shoulder and whispers, "It's no big deal, Curt. Just go knock on that door. Number fifteen." He points. "That's all you have to do, and your part is done. The hundred dollar debt is wiped out."

"And what do I say when somebody opens the door?"

"You say you have to get in there."

"What if they ask me what I want?"

"Tell 'em you're lookin' for your father."

"My father?"

"Right. That's all you have to do. Just make sure you keep that door open 'til we get there."

This doesn't sound good. "All right now, Pan, what are you guys really up to?"

"Damn it, kid. Stop asking so many damn questions. Just get them to open the door and keep it open long enough for us to get in, and your job is done."

"Okay, okay, fine." I figure I might as well find out what's going on in that motel room. Once I see what's going on over there, I can just leave. My debt to Pan will be over, and I'll never have to see him again.

As I head across the parking lot toward the motel, I keep wondering why they don't just go knock on that door themselves. Whatever is in there, I'd better be on my guard.

When I get to room fifteen, I hesitate and look back. Pan and his pals are still mostly hidden behind that van, peeking around the back end of it. I could just walk away right now, and be done with them.

But now I'm curious. What could be inside a motel room that's so important? I tap lightly on the door.

There's no response.

I try the door handle, but it's locked.

I rap on the door again, a bit harder this time.

After a few moments, someone inside opens the door a crack. A dark eye is staring out at me. "Yeah?"

A gruff male voice.

I say, "I'm looking for my father."

The door opens a crack wider. All I can see is that it's dark and smoky inside the room.

"Looking for your old man? Why?"

"Uh, my mother's sick. She needs him. Right away."

"Oh, for Christ's sake. Okay, you can get him, but be quick about it."

He opens the door and lets me in.

The room is larger than I thought it would be. There are a bunch of round tables covered with green felt. Men are seated around every table, and they're playing some kind of card game. I'm almost about to go in and look around, pretending to look for my father, when I remember I'm supposed to keep the door open long enough for Pan and his pals to get in. I guess they want to get in on the card game. I stay in the doorway and lean forward, pretending to look for my supposed father through the smoke. I glance at the man who opened the door. He's a big guy, not especially tall, but really husky and tough looking.

But now, I see that he has a gun on his side a large black gun in a tan holster. Oh no, he's a guard. This "little task" Pan gave me is not as simple as he made it out to be.

I'd better tell this guard guy I don't see my father and get the heck out of here.

But before I can do anything, Pan and his two palls rush in. They're wearing nylon stockings over their faces, and they're holding pistols.

Guns! What the hell? They're going to rob this place.

Pan pushes me aside and slams the door shut. Esteban takes the gun away from the guard and pushes him back against the wall.

Pan yells, really loud, "Put all the money on the tables, assholes, and don't move!" He waves his pistol at them. Then he says something in Spanish to Esteban, but I only understand the English words, "Money box."

Esteban rushes toward the back of the room.

Pan stays close to me. I think he's making sure I don't try to escape. What does he think I'm going to do? Call the police? All I want to right now is get out of this room and go home. I can't believe I let myself get caught up in this.

Diego goes to the tables and starts threatening the card players. He makes them take out all of their money, and he stuffs it into a large white bag. It looks like a pillow case.

The robbing doesn't take very long: Pan and his two pals have gathered up the money and are back out the door in minutes.

I try to follow them, but the guard grabs my arm and says, "Oh no you don't. You're stayin' right here."

Now I've done it. I'm stuck inside this room with a bunch of angry men staring at me. I hold out both of my hands and say, as loud as I can, "I didn't know what they were going to do. They just told me to knock on the door."

The guard says "Yeah, sure." He forces me to sit down in one of the many chairs. He shakes his finger in my face and says, "Stay, put, kid."

He turns away and yells, "Did anybody call the cops?"

Somebody says, "Yeah, they're on the way."

That causes all of the card players to run out the door, which leaves playing cards spread across the green felt tables and all over on the floor. When the cops get here, it's going to be obvious that it was a card game and everybody left in a big hurry.

That leaves only me, the guard, and one other thin nervous-looking man whose holding a metal box. He opens it to show the guard it's empty.

The guard says, "Jesus! They got it all?"

The guy with the metal box looks like he's going to cry.

They both look at me. Uh oh, what are they going to do to me?

And what will the cops think of what I did? Will they believe me when I tell them I didn't know what Pan and his pals were going to do?

The two men go to stand by the door. I can't hear what they're saying, but I suspect they're getting their stories straight before the cops get here.

I hear sirens approaching, and soon, two uniformed cops come into the room, followed by another man who's wearing a rumpled brown suit. The two uniformed cops stand aside for him; he must be the policeman in charge. He calls the two card-room men over and says, "I'm Officer Flynn. Somebody reported a robbery."

"Well, officer," says the guard, "a bunch of us friends got together here for a poker night. All of a sudden some guys in masks broke in and took all our money."

Officer Flynn frowns and looks around the room. "You've got a bunch of professional-looking poker tables here. You must have a lot of friends."

The card-room men just shrug, and the man called Ed says, "Excuse me, sir, I have to go to the restroom."

Officer Flynn shakes his head. "No you don't. Go sit in one of the chairs and don't move.

The nervous man does what the officer said and puts his head in his hands.

He must really be scared. He's afraid he's going to be arrested for whatever they were doing here.

The guard doesn't seem as nervous. He's just standing there with his hands on his hips.

Officer Flynn turns to him. "Okay, you say the robbers were masked. What kind of masks?"

The guard mimics pulling something down over his face. "Nylon stockings. You know, like bank robbers in the movies wear. They were real pros. In and outta here really fast."

Officer Flynn says, "Real pros, eh? Maybe you have an idea of who they might be? Through the masks, I mean."

The guard shakes his head.

"Okay, then tell me this. How many of those *real professional* robbers were there?"

The guard says, "Uh, maybe four. Yeah, at least four."

The man seems very unsure of himself, and he's confused about the details. I know it was only Pan and his two pals. I guess having robbers wave guns in your face can make you overestimate how many robbers there were.

The two uniformed cops are staying pretty close to the door. They're grinning as if they think this situation is funny.

I'm starting to wonder when Officer Flynn is going to get around to me, and then, as if my thought made it happen, he turns to me. "And what's this kid doing here?"

The guard says, "He's the one that got me to open the door, officer. Claimed he was looking for his father. It's what allowed the robbers in."

Officer Flynn stares at me.

I try not to act nervous, even though I am. I didn't really do anything wrong. I didn't know what Pan and his pals were going to do. But the longer the officer stares at me, the more sure I am that he's going to throw me in jail. I'm the only one he's got, so he'll have to make an example of me. I'd better say something quick. I point at the door and say, "Some guys told me to knock on the door. I had no idea what they were up to."

He continues to stare at me. I guess there's no reason why he should believe me. Maybe I should have known what they were going to do. So, why didn't I? It must be because Pan was so friendly. How could such a friendly guy who was named for a famous Spanish explorer be a robber? That's a dumb thought. What's wrong with me? How did I get myself into this mess?

Officer Flynn is still staring at me. Does he want me to say more? Maybe I'd better. "Maybe I should have known they were up to no good, officer, but I guess I just thought they wanted to get in on whatever was going on in here."

For some reason, that seems to satisfy him. He turns back to the card-room men. "All right, you two. I suppose you know you could be arrested for running an illegal poker game. Are you sure you want to file charges against these so-called big-time professional robbers?"

The guard says, "Well, something should be done. They *are* robbers. And they had guns."

Flynn says, "I understand that, and we will be looking for them." He points to the guard's empty holster. "I see you had a gun too."

"Well, I . . . "

The nervous man jumps up out of his chair. "No, no, officer. We don't need to press charges. Nobody got hurt. Let's just drop the whole thing."

That causes the two uniformed officers to laugh right out loud.

Officer Flynn says, "Up to you. But I'll tell you this, if we come back here in the future, we'd better not find you hosting a poker game for your so-called friends."

"No, sir. We won't ever be here again."

With that, Officer Flynn grabs my arm and pulls me up out of the chair. "As for you, young man, you're coming with me."

"Am I under arrest?"

"Don't you think you should be?"

"If you say so, but I really didn't know what they were going to do."

Officer Flynn doesn't respond to that, but he keeps a tight hold on my arm as he pulls me out of the room.

The old white van that was parked way at the back of the parking lot it gone. It must have been their escape vehicle.

One of the uniformed cops says, "Should we take him in our car?"

Officer Flynn shakes his head. "I've got him. You men can go back to the station."

Officer Flynn leads me to his car. It's a plain black car with no police markings. But it does have a spotlight and a tall whip-like antenna.

Instead of putting me in the back seat, he puts me in front. I guess he wants to lecture me on the way to the police station.

But no, we just sit there in the dark parking lot, even after the other cops have driven away.

He's going to question me right here. I guess he'll want me to tell him who the robbers were. Well, why shouldn't I tell? Pan made me part of his robbery plan without telling me what he was getting me into, and then he left me there to get arrested. Besides, he and his friends have probably already left the city. They'd be stupid to stick around after this. Maybe Pan will go back to Puerto Rico.

"Well?" says Officer Flynn.

"Uh, like I already told you, officer. I didn't know what they were going to do. They just wanted me to open the door."

"And why would you do that? Are they friends of yours?"

"No, sir. I just met the three of them. At the downtown pool hall."

"And you became friends, eh? Just like that?"

"No, not really. You see, I started playing pool against a guy name Pan. For money. He said he was born in Puerto Rico. He called his two friends Esteban and Diego. That's all I know. Pan was too good at pool, so I ended up owing him money. He said he had a little task for me as a way to pay of the debt ."

"By committing a robbery."

"No, sir, he just said I'd be doing him a favor if I'd knock on the motel door and get them to open it. I didn't know what was in that room, and I didn't know what they were going to do. I thought they just wanted to get in."

"And you didn't think about why they couldn't do that themselves?"

"I guess they though a kid would have a better chance of getting in."

"And you didn't think why that might be?"

He's got me there. Why did I go along with it? Down deep, I sort of knew they were up to no good. So why did I go along with it? Has something in me changed that much in the last two days that I'm so overly curious I'm not thinking straight?

"Well?"

"I don't know, officer. I guess I was just curious about what was going on in that room."

"Curious, eh. Are you always so curious."

"No. Well, yes, I guess so, but not normally about thing like I got into today. Today, after school, I guess I wanted to try some new things."

"Try some new things, eh. Why today?"

Should I tell him the truth, that all this started when the counselor told me I was a genius.

Officer Flynn interrupts my thoughts. "So, are you a good pool player?"

"No, sir. In fact, I'd never played pool before. I didn't even know how the game was played."

"I see. So, despite not knowing how to play pool, you take on a good player. For money. Now why would you do that?"

I guess I have to tell him the truth. I'm probably going to jail no matter what I say. "Well, you see, officer, it all started at school. The counselor brought me into his office and told me I was a genius. He said I had the highest admissions test score of anybody in the whole school. I guess, after that, I got it into my head that I should start . . . uh, trying some new things."

"A genius, eh? And now, sitting here in a police car, do you feel like a genius?"

"Right, right. I see your point. I guess I made some bad decisions."

"You sure did. And what do you think your parents are going to think about this?"

"I only have a mother, sir. I sure wish I could avoid telling her. She works hard for us. I should have thought about that before I went along with what Pan wanted."

"That's right, you sure should have. Now here's what's going to happen. Tomorrow, we'll be asking around at that pool hall. We'll find out who they are, and we'll get them. I assume you won't be going anywhere near that place again, will you?"

"No, sir. I mean, yes, sir. You're right, sir. I won't ever go there again."

"Okay. Well, fasten your seat belt. Let's go."

"Are you taking me to jail?"

"Don't you think you should be in jail?"

He's got me there. If you can get thrown in jail for letting curiosity lead you into making stupid mistakes, I guess I'd deserve it.

Nine

As Officer Flynn drives us out of the motel parking lot, all I can think about it how my poor mother is going to take this. She works such long hours every day I hardly ever get to see her. I haven't even gotten a chance to tell her what the counselor told me about being a genius. And now, I've made such a mess of things, she'll probably have to pay what little money she has to bail me out of jail, and then we might have to quickly leave this town.

When I get to the jail, I probably shouldn't even call her. I should just plead guilty to whatever they want to charge me with.

But what if they find out where I came from? Then, they'd probably track down my mother and throw us both out of this country.

Damn, how could I have been so dumb? A genius? I'm not even a little bit smart. *Ein dummer.*

And this should just about end my school career too. And all because I let what that counselor told me made me think differently, that I really was a genius. What am I supposed to do now, tell my fellow inmates in jail that I'm a genius? No way. From now on I'm not going to tell anybody anything like that. I can only hope the school counselor doesn't tell anybody either.

My attention is brought back when Officer Flynn stops the car. But we're not at police headquarters; we're parked in front of the big downtown public library.

"Listen, son, I think I believe you. You had nothing to do with that robbery, but you made a mistake trusting those yahoos. A big mistake. I have a daughter your age, a little older, so I know kids sometimes don't think things through before they act, so I'm not going to take you to jail. But I am going to sentence you. I'm going to sentence you to do what you should have been doing on your own.

From now on, you're not going to be hanging around in pool halls, you're going to spend a least a couple of hours every day after school studying here at this library. I know the people who run this place. They'll be making sure you're here. And you won't be reading novels or newspapers or anything like that. You'll be reading important books. Learning important stuff. Got it?"

"Yes, sir. You are right, sir, that's exactly what I should have been doing with my time."

"All right, then. I'll tell my friends here at the library to expect you here tomorrow afternoon after you get out of school. And you'll be here every school day after that. Right?"

"Yes, sir. I mean, you are right, sir. I'll be here. Like you said, it's what I should have been doing anyhow."

"Good. Do you live far from here?"

"Not far at all, sir. Are you letting me go?"

"I am, but remember, I'm putting you on probation. You could still be charged with aiding and abetting a robbery. This library sentence is no joke. You'll be here every school day, or you'll be seeing me again."

"Yes, sir. I'll be here. Studying. I want to do it."

"Okay, see that you do. Now get out."

I quickly get out of his car and start walking home in the darkness. I sure am glad he didn't drive me home. I'm not sure what time it is, but Mom should just be getting home from her second job, and I wouldn't want her to see me getting out of a police car.

But what if she's already home? How will I explain why I'm getting home so late? I've never lied to her, but what else can I do?

I stop walking and look up at the sky. It's cloudy, with only a few stars peeking out. For some reason, that makes me sad. Maybe I should just tell her the truth, tell her how dumb I've been.

No, I can't do that. She doesn't deserve that. She works so hard, and now I've let her down. I can't throw that in her face.

I should start walking again. I should hurry home to make sure I get there before she does, but now I'm not sure I even deserve to go home. All of a sudden, the stupid things I've been doing today hits me, and it feels like I'm going to cry.

But no, I can't cry. What am I, a baby?

I start walking again. Officer Flynn said I'd made a big mistake, but he said it in a kind way, and then he let me go. Why was he being so nice to me? I didn't deserve to be let go. I didn't deserve any kindness.

I start walking faster, trying to deny the fact that tears are streaming down my face. Dumb, dumb, dumb. After all Mom went through to get us here to a safer town, why did I have to start acting so dumb?

I shake my head, hard. All right now, stop this stupid sniveling and start thinking like a smart person. I've got to hurry and get home before Mom does. She works hard to take care of us, to take care of me; one more thing to prove how stupid I've been, how I don't deserve such kindness.

Okay, that's it. I'll wipe away these stupid tears, and start acting right. Tomorrow, I'll go to school as if nothing is out of the ordinary, and then, after school, I'll go to the downtown library just like Officer Flynn said I should. I'll read important books there and start acting the way an actual smart person should. And I won't be telling anybody I'm a genius. If I really do have to be a genius, I'll be a secret one.

Ten

At school, none of the other students are looking at me. I hope that means nobody has heard about the trouble I got into last night.

In study hall, Haru does look at me, but then he always does. I know he wants me to be his friend, and I wish I could do that—after all, we do have some things in common. But I know I can't let anybody get too close.

After study hall lets out, he catches up to me and tries to talk to me, but I read one of my science book as I walk and tell him I've got to finish reading this chapter before I get to my history class.

He's not happy that I won't talk to him, and I feel bad abut that. But he's smart, and there's no telling what he might be able to learn about me if we became friends. Hopefully, now that I've rebuffed him again, he'll leave me alone.

When I get to my history class, my last class of the day, the teacher starts by passing back out essays about who was the most important figure in World War Two. My paper has a big bat F at the top of it, plus a note that says, "SEE ME."

Glancing around at the papers of the other students, I can see they mostly got Bs and Cs. So, why did he give me an F? He couldn't have failed me based on my ability to write an essay; other than a few intentional spelling errors, I don't think I did that bad a job on it.

The teacher begins the class by launching into a long-winded explanation about how unfair it is that the town's private Catholic high school gets to recruit their basketball players from anywhere in the city, or even from surrounding rural areas, whereas he has to make do with players who live in our area of the city.

When he finally starts talking about history, he refers the class to the textbook's section on prewar history, a time when many countries in Africa, Asia, and the Middle East were fighting to gain their independence from their European rulers. He reads from the part of the textbook that says before World War Two, the Europeans ruled over nearly a third of the world's population. From what he's reading, it sounds like the textbook is out of date and hasn't yet been undated to describe what happened after the war.

All of the other students have opened their textbooks and are following along with what he's reading. I hope he doesn't notice I don't have a textbook. If he does notice, I'll just say I forgot it today. There's no way he could know I didn't rent the required textbook this term. No use spending the money on a history textbook when I've probably already read everything that's likely to be in it.

When the bell finally rings, I go forward to ask him why I got an F on my paper.

He jerks my paper out of my hands and shakes it at me. "I told you to write an essay about the most important figure in the war, not a fiction about President Truman."

"A fiction?"

"That's right. A fiction. You made up a bunch of half truths about our president's personal history that had nothing to do with the war, and then you implied he wanted to use our atomic bombs to kill innocent people. Let me tell you something, young man, the Japanese were not innocent. I was on a ship in that war, and by the time we relieved our fighting men on Peleliu Island, the Japanese had killed six thousand of them. Our soldiers were half starved by the time we got them off that damn island, so don't you dare try to tell me the Japanese people were innocent."

I can see he's really angry, and I'm pretty sure anything I say to defend myself will just make things worse. I wonder why he never mentioned in class his involvement in the war.

He again shakes my paper at me and says, "Well, what do you have to say for yourself?"

"It's just what I read, sir. In a book."

That seems to make him even angrier. "A book? What kind of book would print that kind of crap? I don't believe they'd say those things about our great president. But you are a pretty good writer, if you'd learn how to spell, so I'm going to give you another chance. Write an essay about the real most important figure in World War Two, somebody like Eisenhower or MacArthur. I'll even let you write it at home and bring it in tomorrow. Now get out of here."

He hands me back my paper and turns away.

Now that school is out for the day, I leave the building and immediately head downtown to start my studying "probation" at the downtown public library.

But as I walk, I can't stop thinking about how angry the history teacher was. I should have known better that to write about the current American president; it's only been six years since the end of the war, and the Americans won, so I guess they want to feel like they did it in a proper way. I should have realized a man his age would have played some part in the war.

Maybe I should do what he said and write an essay about Eisenhower or MacArthur.

But wouldn't that be just operating at a low level? The counselor thinks I should be operating at higher level than that, and I should. Maybe I should write the essay I thought about writing in the first place, about the actual most important person in the war, the person who started it all, Hitler. He has to really be the most important person in the war: there wouldn't even have been a war if it weren't for him.

Oddly, even though I lived the early years of my life in Germany, I really don't know much about Hitler. All we ever heard about him was propaganda, and Mom said we shouldn't believe any of it. Maybe the big downtown library has a book about him.

The downtown bookstore has a lot of brand new books about the war, and I've read all of them, but I know they don't have a single book about Hitler.

But maybe I shouldn't write an essay about Hitler. Given the history teacher's attitude toward me, that might be taking a chance. Since he was in the US Navy, I probably should do the smart thing and write about some US naval hero.

One book I read at the bookstore talked about naval battles, including a big battle at Midway in which Admiral Nimitz, a US Navy admiral, defeated the Japanese. I could write about him.

But I don't know anything about him other than he won that big battle, and besides, would that one battle mean he could be considered the most famous person in the war?

Eleven

As I near the downtown library, I 'm wondering why Officer Flynn said my probation had to be at this library. Maybe he thinks they have more books than the school library. That's probably true, but could there have been another reason?

At the library, I go up the wide stone stairs and through the big double doors. Inside, there's what seems to be a main desk, and a young woman is behind it. Am I supposed to check in there? I can see that she's probably not all that much older than me, but of course she must be, to be the librarian. She's very pretty, for a librarian. I probably shouldn't think like that, but the only librarian I know is the one at the school library, and she's really old.

I go up to the desk, and not knowing what else to do, say, "Uh, hi. I'm Curt."

She stares at me blankly. "Yes, and?"

"Well, Officer Flynn told me to come here today to—"

"Oh, right. You're the boy who . . . well, never mind about that. My dad told me to help you get started."

"Your father?"

"That's right. I'm Julie Flynn. I guess I'm supposed to be your sort of probation officer." She does a little chuckle.

Unsure of how I'm supposed to respond to that, I just say, "Okay."

She leans across the desk closer to me and whispers, "I'm just kidding you, Curt. Actually, my dad is actually a pretty nice guy, once you get to know him. He only wants what's best for you." She stops talking, but she's still smiling. Apparently she wants me to say something.

"Uh, nice to meet you, Julie. Your dad wants me to learn new things. To read important books."

"Yes, that's what he told me. He said you might be a real live genius."

"Well, that was only because of a test I took at school. But I really do want to learn new things. I mean, so you don't really have to be my . . . uh, probation person."

"All right, Curt, it's a deal. Now, let's start with *what* you want to learn."

What do I want to learn? At the school library, and at the bookstore downtown, I read a lot of books, but not on any particular subject. I'm not sure where to begin.

She holds up her hand, still smiling. "You don't have to decide right away. Why don't you go to the card catalog and see what strikes your interest." She points.

I turn to look where she's pointing and see what she's referring to. It's a long cabinet made out of wood, much bigger than the little one at the school library.

She says, "After you decide what books you want to read, come back here, and I'll help you find them."

I thank her and head for the card catalog. Not knowing where to look first, I start in the first file drawer. It's alphabetical, by titles and the last names of book authors. How is that supposed to help me decide what I want to learn about?

Before I can even start looking through the cards, Julie is there next to me. She says, "I just realized what I told you isn't going to help. Sorry, it's a habit. We always send people to the card catalog. But you aren't looking for a specific book. Tell me what categories you're looking for."

I'm not sure what categories I should mention. I liked reading about history, but would that count as "important"?

Before I can decide what to say, she says, "Better yet, let me show you what we have. Follow me."

She leads me past some tables, where people are sitting reading, and into the back part of the library where long rows of metal shelves hold lots of books, a lot more than in the school library. She points to the little white card that's on the end of the first shelf. It has the numbers 0-099 on it. She says, "The numbers refer to the Dewey Decimal System, categories of book topics. But maybe you know that."

"Yes, it's the same at the school library."

"Right. All libraries use it. This shelf contains general reference books."

The next shelf we come to is numbered 100-199.

She says, "This shelf contains books on philosophy and psychology."

She does her little chuckle again, but I'm not sure why. Remembering my earlier idea about grouping people as happy or sad, I'd put her in the happy category.

I say, "Philosophy? I'm not even sure what philosophy is. As a subject for books, I mean."

She frowns. "You mean, what exactly is philosophy? Well, that's a good question. Not so easy to define. But I've got to get back to the desk. Why don't you go down this row and pull out a few philosophy books. If you really are a genius, like my dad said, you'll figure it out."

She leaves, and I'm left on my own. I've never had a class in school that even mentioned philosophy as a subject. I have a general idea of what the word means, like in the question, what was Hitler's philosophy? But what are all these books about, and if I read some of them, would they count as important? Well, it's something new for me, so I'd like to learn about it.

The first book I pull off the shelf lists philosophers by name and briefly describes what they were famous for. That isn't going to help me learn what philosophy is. The next book I pull out is a reference guide to branches of modern philosophy. Also not likely to tell me what philosophy is. It seems like all the books on this shelf assume you already know what philosophy is.

Finally, I find a book with a title that is the same as my question, "What Is Philosophy?" I take that one to a small table that's at the end of the row. It seems like a good place to read, hidden way back here.

I sit down and open the book to the first chapter. It says "Perhaps questions about philosophy should only be asked late in life."

Now that's funny: here I am, a fourteen-year-old high school freshman, reading about a subject that the author says should only be thought about later in life. Oddly, that makes me want to learn about it even more.

The author goes on to say such a questioner may be thinking about what they have been doing with their life.

So, is that what philosophy is, questioning what you've been doing with your life? That sounds a lot like what Tolstoy was saying in his book, but I don't think he was a philosopher.

Or maybe he was.

But could questioning your life be enough to fill so many books?

Thinking about it, maybe it could. But does anybody really do that? Do people actively question what they are doing with their life? Or do they just live their lives, going through their days thinking about what they're currently doing. Probably, but maybe questioning your life is something a genius *should* be thinking about. Asking such a question last night probably would have kept me out of trouble. It probably would have kept me from even going into that pool hall.

Okay, let's start with that: what am I doing with my life? Just going along, I guess. Getting by. When we were escaping through Germany, we were just trying to keep from getting killed. Then, when we got to this country, we were just trying not to get caught, moistly by trying not to be noticed.

Now that we've found a place we can stay for a while, I spend most of my time reading and going to school, but I'm still mostly trying not to be noticed too much.

So, is that what a genius should be doing, reading and learning, or should a real live genius be making his mark in the world. I think that's what the school counselor was suggesting. I'll have to think more about that later. Right now, I should go back to reading about what philosophy is.

The book goes on to finally give me at least a partial answer: it says the term "philosophy," in the broadest sense, refers to seeking wisdom.

It says people study philosophy in order to understand fundamental truths, both about themselves and about the world they live in.

Now that *does* seem like something that would fill up an entire long shelf of books. In fact, it seems like something that should be taught in every school. So why isn't it? Don't they want young students to think about things like that?

The book goes on to say philosophy studies the nature of reality, of what exists. Now that's a big subject for sure, but is it referring to reality as we perceive it individually, or to the "real" reality, if there is such a thing. But can we ever know what that is? While scientists, like astronomers try to answer that question with science, philosophers seem to be trying to get at it by thinking. So, which is the best approach, thinking, or by using scientific instruments to observe, like astrophysicists use astrophysics to try to learn about the reality of the universe.

Astrophysics? Now where did I get that word? I must have run across the word somewhere in my reading, but I don't really know what it is. I know it has something to do with astronomy, observing the planets and the stars, but the "physics" part must mean it's more than that. Maybe I need a dictionary with me as I read.

I get up and go back to the front desk.

Julie is not there, only an older woman. When I ask her where to find a dictionary, she directs me to a very large book on a stand that's near the card catalogue.

I look up the word "astrophysics," and it says it's a branch of science that applies the laws of physics to understand the universe and our place in it. Now there's a field of study that seems big enough for a genius.

Before I go back to my little study table, I look up astrophysics in the card catalog. It directs me to a bookshelf that has science books. I go down that row until I find a book titled "Fundamentals of Astrophysics." I take it back to my study table and open it up to the first chapter. It says astrophysics is the science of learning about the physical processes of the cosmos.

It says astronomers gather information about the cosmos using telescopes, and then use physics to better understand how it all works.

Okay, that's pretty much what the dictionary told me. To do that, I guess a person would first have to learn about physics. Obviously, that would be a long-term course of study, maybe leading to a college degree. In fact, studying any kind of science feels like a big, long-term course of study. Maybe that's where I'm heading, but right now I just want to learn. I should build a foundation of basics about everything, and then expand into specific subjects, like physics, or something like that.

I close the astrophysics book and switch back to reading about philosophy.

After reading for quite a while, I notice my school notebook on the table. Interesting that after all this reading, I haven't written down anything. I didn't even think about taking notes. And now that we found this city, and I'm in a school, for the first time in my life, I realize I've never taken a single note in my classes there either. But somehow I always manage to remember it all, word for word. Should that kind of memory have told me I was a genius? I just took it for granted that you should be able to remember what you heard or what you read. Other students must not be able to do that; otherwise, why would they be taking notes?

I'm ready to go back to reading, but then I remember the essay I'm supposed to write about the most important person in the war. I'd better do that before I get too lost in this philosophy stuff.

I go back to the card catalog and look for books on Hitler. There are only a two books listed. I find them both on the shelf. It surprises me that they haven't already been checked out. Aren't people in this country interested in the man that plunged the world into war? I take the books back to my little study table, and open the one with the newest publication date. It briefly describes the kind of politician Hitler was, and then it describes how he ordered the invasion of Germany's neighboring countries.

It's interesting to read the author's perspective on the war: he suggests Hitler had successfully built a great war machine and was spreading the war all over the globe when Japan ruined everything by bringing the United States into the war.

I can tell that this book was published when the war in Europe was barely over because it mostly portrays Hitler as a very evil person, which I guess he was, but I'd like to learn more about him as a person.

I open the other book. This one describes Hitler's youth and how he got started in politics. That gives me a good idea for my essay: I'll write about how Hitler started out as an unknown, and then, step by step, rose to be the kind of autocratic leader who could lead a country into war. That, of course, would explain how he ended up as the most important person in World War Two. He caused it.

I open my notebook, but before I start writing my essay, shouldn't I stop to think about how my history teacher will react to this? What will he think if I don't write about an American hero, as he recommended, and instead, write about this country's greatest enemy?

Well, he's probably not going to give me a good grade anyhow, no matter what I write, so I might as well write about something that interests me.

I start my writing with the fact that Hitler was born in 1889 in Austria. When he was still a toddler, his family moved to Germany for a while before they moved back to Austria and lived on a farm where they kept bees. He went to a state school there, and he took singing lessons. The book says he sang in the church choir and considered becoming a priest.

That's interesting. It doesn't sound at all like the person the world thinks of, the evil tyrant that started a war and ordered the killing of millions. Maybe I shouldn't write things in my essay that make him seen too nice, or at least too normal. But it's what this book says about him, so it must be true. Why shouldn't I write something if it's true?

That makes me wonder what it would be like to always tell the truth, no matter what people think. That might be something important to think about.

But I'd better put that off until later. Right now, I'd better get back to writing.

I write about how Hitler wanted to become an artist, even though it was against his father's wishes. And at the same time, he was already showing signs of becoming a nationalist; he and his friends pledged their loyalty to their powerful neighboring country, Germany.

After finishing school, he left to study art in Vienna. But he had no profession or trade, so therefore no way to support himself. He was entirely dependent on what little money his mother sent him.

I stop writing to think about that. I too am totally dependent on my mother, and I don't seem to be heading toward any kind of profession either. So far, thinking of myself as a genius also doesn't seem to be leading me toward any obvious way to make money. Maybe I should focus my studies on things that will lead toward making money. Something else to think about later.

I go back to writing, describing how when Hitler was eighteen, his mother died, and he was forced to try to make it on his own. He wasn't so good at that. He just about starved, living in homeless shelters until he finally found work as a laborer. He still wanted to be an artist, and he continued painting, making a little money out on the streets selling watercolor pictures of Vienna's tourist sights.

Now I seem to be writing too much about Hitler himself instead of why he might be considered to be the most important figure in the war. I did the same thing when I wrote my essay on Truman, and my history teacher didn't like it.

So, should I keep on with this, or start over?

It seems to me that in order to understand why Hitler became the tyrant who started a war, we need to understand what type of person he was.

Anyhow, I don't think I'd enjoy writing an essay that was only facts, even if that is what my teacher wants. If there's one thing I know about myself, it's that I'm impatient. Sooner or later, I always decide there's no point of doing anything if I'm not learning something new. If that's what made me a genius, I guess I should keep on doing that.

I go back to writing that it was in Vienna that Hitler first became exposed to anti-Jewish attitudes. The book suggests that he might have had some trouble with Jewish merchants in Vienna when he was out on the streets trying to sell his art, but the book says others doubt that and instead think the anti-Jewish programs he instituted later were done strictly for political purposes, because he needed scapegoats.

Eventually, Hitler got drafted into the German Army and was sent to fight in World War One. Because he was thin and quick, he served as a dispatch runner. He was wounded when a shell exploded nearby, and he was sent to an Army hospital. But as soon as he recovered, he was sent right back to the front where he was temporarily blinded by a mustard gas attack. He was still hospitalized for that when Germany surrendered.

When he got out of the hospital, he liked to go to German beer halls and talk loudly how being a soldier in the war as the greatest expedience of his life. He also started complaining that Germany could have won the war, if they hadn't been "stabbed in the back" by the Jews. However, he was still officially in the Army, and he received an assignment to infiltrate the National Socialist German Workers Party, known as the Nazis. But instead of infiltrating the Nazis, Hitler eventually became a willing participant. The book says he might have actually been the person who designed the party's swastika banner.

After Hitler finished his required time with the Army, he began working full-time for the Nazi Party. As he developed his public speaking ability, he eventually rose to become party chairman. He was becoming known for his vitriolic beer hall speeches and his scapegoating of the Jews.

Well, I realize I'm doing it again. So far, nothing I've written has anything to do with World War Two. The problem is, what I'm learning about Hitler is too interesting. Odd that despite growing up in Germany, I didn't know anything about him. Maybe he made sure nobody knew these kinds of things about his background. He just wanted to be seen as the glorious leader who would make Germany the most powerful country in the world.

Anyhow, I should move Hitler's story along until he starts the war. But before I write about that, I have to write that Hitler was part of a attempted coup known as the "Beer Hall Revolt," an armed street protest in which the Nazi Party tried to emulate Mussolini's march on Rome. For his role in the coup attempt, Hitler was sent to prison, and that was where he began to write his book, *Mein Kampf*.

When he was finally released from prison, he set about trying to rebuild the Nazi Party. He tried to gain political power for the party by again trying to get the German people riled up about how unfair the surrender conditions of World War One were. And he continued to blame the Jews. The great worldwide depression of the late 1920s and early 1930s helped his effort by making the German people dissatisfied with their government.

I stop writing again. This essay is getting too long, especially when it's just supposed to be about the war. I decide to skip over all the things Hitler did to consolidate his power, and I just describe how Hitler began saying the presence of an ethnic German population in part of Czechoslovakia meant those "Germans" should have autonomy. Of course, his real intention was to go to war against Czechoslovakia. Britain saw through that, and fearing a greater war, they forced Czechoslovakia to give up that part of their territory. The agreement also required Germany to go no further militarily. Britain also said they would guarantee the future independence of Poland, another of Germany's neighbors.

But compromise was not part of Hitler's approach. He declared Britain to be Germany's greatest enemy, and he said Britain's deal with Poland was an attempt to "surround" Germany.

He was privately telling his cohorts it was almost time to go against Britain. The book's author suggests that Hitler might have been in a hurry to get into a war before he got too old, but I don't add that to my essay.

In 1939, after first securing secret agreements with Italy and Russia, Hitler ordered the Germany Army to attack Poland, and that became the start of World War Two.

I sit back and wonder if that's enough of an essay to prove Hitler was the most important person in the war. Although most of what I've written is about Hitler the person, I think my essay does show how he came to power in Germany, and how that led him to start World War Two.

I quickly add a few more paragraphs about how Britain responded to Hitler's aggression by declaring war on Germany, and how Italy came to align with Germany. Finally, I write a bit more about how the United States resisted getting involved in the "European War," other than supplying England with war materials, but when Japan bombed the US naval base in Hawaii, the US had to declare war on Japan. Germany responded by declaring war on the United States. The US quickly converted their economy into manufacturing weapons to go to war against both Japan and Germany.

The book also says Hitler's grandiosity led him to overreach, eventually spreading the war into such faraway places as Africa, and even made him turn against his largest European ally, Russia. I add a few sentences about that to my essay, adding that it was the combination of the United States, England, and Russia that eventually led to Germany's defeat.

I sit back and look at what I've written. It's a lot more than the one page assignment he gave us in class, but I wanted to be thorough.

Finally, I add some punctuation and spelling errors just in case he likes what I've written.

But will he like it? If he *is* Jewish, he'll probably just flunk me.

Maybe I should put in more about how Hitler used the Jews as scapegoats, and how he set up extermination camps to try to kill them all.

Oh the other hand, it's possible that the teacher doesn't like Jews either. It's hard to tell what the people of the United States think. After all, based on what I've read, they didn't do much to help the European Jews during or after the war, and there's still discrimination against them here.

When I was a child in Germany, I never understood why the German people didn't like Jews. The Jewish people my mother hid in our barn for short periods seemed the same as anyone else.

Oh well, I've spent enough time on that essay. I did learn some new things about Hitler and Germany, so I shouldn't care what the history teacher thinks of it. I'd better get busy doing what Officer Flynn said I'm supposed to be doing here at this library, studying important stuff.

I'm just getting back into the book on philosophy when I'm distracted by the overhead lights flashing on and off. That's odd. What could it mean?

I go back to reading, but soon, I see Julie coming toward me between the rows of bookshelves. She says, "We're closing. Didn't you see the lights flash?"

"Oh, right. I didn't know that's what it meant, and I wanted to keep on reading." I hold up the book. "This book about philosophy is really interesting. It covers all the different areas of philosophy. As soon as I finish it, I'm going to read some other books about philosophy. And then I might start reading books about astrophysics."

She does her usual little chuckle and says, "Well, Curt, I'm glad you found something that got your interest besides playing pool."

"So your dad told you about that. Well, I wasn't really very interested in the game of pool, I was just learning about new things."

She smiles. It's all right, Curt, I understand. And more importantly, my dad also understands. He thinks you've got a restless mind."

"A restless mind? Is that what he said?"

"Yep. He said it just needs to be redirected. That's why he sent you here."

"Oh, I see. Well, I'm glad he did. I'm learning lots of new things. Let me tell you something. This book says there's a branch of philosophy called epistemology. It's the study of knowledge itself, what we know about the world, or maybe more importantly, what we *can* know. It says—"

"That's all very interesting, Curt, but like I said, the library is closing. Why don't you check out that book and take it with you."

"Oh, right. I guess I could do that."

"Just bring it to the front desk, and I'll issue you a library card."

"Okay. Can I do a real quick look for some other books to check out?"

"Tomorrow, Curt. Tomorrow. Then you can look over all the books and check out as many as you want to."

I grab the philosophy book and follow her to the main desk. After she issues me a library card and signs out my philosophy book, she lets me out the front door and locks it behind me.

Out on the street, it's completely dark. I wonder what time it is. It can't be all that late; it's just that the sun just sets early this time of year. I'll go right home and continue reading this great philosophy book. Amazing how interesting a topic can be that I didn't even know existed.

Twelve

Walking home from the library, I have the feeling somebody is back there in the darkness, following me. To find out, at the next intersection, I make a turn and after a short distance, I stop and look back. Sure enough, there is somebody back there. I start walking again, and when I look back, I can tell he's staying about the same distance behind me, keeping mostly in the shadows. I make another turn and duck into the dark doorway of a closed business. Hopefully he'll just go on past.

But he doesn't go past. He stops and looks right at me.

"So, you stopped," he says. "I wondered where you were goin' this time of night."

In the darkness, I can't see his face, but I think I recognize that voice. "Is that you, Pan?"

He steps forward and says "Yeah, it's me. How you been, Curt?" He sticks out has hand, but I don't want to shake it.

"I'm all right, Pan. Why were you following me?"

"Don't get upset, Curt. I just need to talk to you. I uh, kinda need your help."

"You need my help? And why should I help you after what you did to me? You tricked me into getting you into that poker game so you could rob it. And then you left me there to get arrested."

He shakes his head. "Not true, Curt. I thought you'd run out of there with us. I even hung around to make sure you *didn't* get arrested. When I saw that cop bring you out and put you in his car, I followed you in my car. But he didn't take you to the jailhouse. He took you downtown to the library. What was that all about?"

"None of your business, Pan. Now get out of my way. I've got to get home."

I try to step out of the doorway, but he puts his hand against my chest.

He's taller than me, and heavier, and I expect he knows how to fight, so I'd better not try to fight him.

Pan removes his hand from my chest, but he's still blocking my way. He says, "I don't mean you any harm, Curt. Like I said, I need your help. Just give me a few minutes to explain."

"Okay, so explain."

"It's like this, Curt. I'm in trouble. Big trouble. I need to talk to your cop friend. Right away."

He needs to talk to my cop friend? "If you're referring to Officer Flynn, he isn't my friend. He just believed me when I told him I didn't know what you and your friends were up to."

"Well, anyhow, it means now you know him. You gotta tell him I'm ready to make a deal."

"A deal? What are you really up to, Pan?"

"I mean I'm ready to turn myself in, if he's willing to make a deal. I have some information for him, important information."

I should just walk away right now. "No, Pan, I only met that policeman that one time. I don't really know him at all. Now let me go."

"Just hear me out, Curt. The information I have will be important to those cops. Real important."

"Then you should tell him yourself. It's none of my business."

"Hell, Curt, I can't go see him myself. He'd just throw me in jail."

"Well, why shouldn't he?"

Pan looks down at the ground for a long moment, then he backs up a step and looks up and down the street.

What is he looking for? In the darkness, I can't see much of his face, but I'm pretty sure he's scared. Something's got him really spooked.

"Listen, Curt, I know you don't owe me a damn thing, but just do me this one favor and I promise I'll never bother you again. Please."

I shouldn't have anything to do with him, and I'm for sure not going to go to the city police station to see Officer Flynn, no matter what Pan says.

But maybe I could get word to him through his daughter. I could just tell Julie that the guy who robbed that poker game came to see me and is ready to turn himself in. "Okay, Pan. I'll get word to him. But that's it."

"That's all I want. Just tell him I'm ready to make a deal."

"Then you'll go to the police station to meet with him?"

"Maybe, but first he has to agree to the deal."

'I'm not going to be your go-between. I'll just let him know you're ready to make a deal, and that's it. Now let me go."

He steps back. "Fine. That's all I want. I'll meet you right here tomorrow night to find out what he said."

"No, I don't want to meet with you. Anyhow, he'll probably want to talk to you himself."

"*¡De ninguna manera!* He can't even find out I'm still in town. I know that sooner or later, I'll have to go in and meet with him, but first, I have to know if he's willing to make me a deal."

It doesn't seem likely that Officer Flynn would go along with something like that, but I'm not about to say that to Pan. I just want to get away from him, so I say, "I'll let him know. Then, I'm out of it, right?"

"Sure, sure. Not your problem. But make sure you tell him this information I got for him is real important. It's about drugs. Tell him that."

Drugs? Is that what Pan is into now? "Fine, I'll tell him." I quickly push past him and hurry on down the street.

When I finally slow down enough to look back, he's gone. Good. Tomorrow at the library, I'll tell Julie what he said. She can tell her father or not. That's as far as I'm willing to go with it.

Thirteen

Walking to school in the cool early morning, I can't stop thinking about my meeting with Pan last night. Why did he think I'd help him? Does he think we're pals? We are not pals. He got me involved in his crime and all but got me thrown into jail.

Actually, I'm surprised Pan is still in town. Officer Flynn will probably also be surprised. I'll just tell Julie what Pan said and ask her to pass the message on to her father, but that's absolutely as far as I want to go with it. I need to make it clear to her that I want nothing more to do with Pan or his friends.

My first class, English, is as boring as usual. The teacher is always trying to drill into us what she calls "the prescriptive rules of writing," punctuation and grammar rules she says we must know if we are to be successful in what she calls "the real world." I already know those rules—this is the third time she's gone over them.

I manage to get through the hour by sitting at the back of the room, pretending to take notes. I'm actually writing out a summary of the propositions Wittgenstein listed in his *Tractatus Logico-Philosophicus* that I read about last night in the library. For example, his belief that everything that can be thought can be thought clearly, and everything that can be said can be said clearly. What a great concept: that in an age of scientific advancements, why should ultimate truth be thought of as something mystical?

My next class, Science, is sometimes interesting, but today it's frustrating because the teacher is once again going over the general rules of science. His lectures usually boil down to telling us that knowledge of how things work will always come from scientific experimentation. Today, he tells us it was scientific inquiry that led to the inventions of our modern appliances such as the telephone and radio.

But he doesn't explain how that happened. It would be a lot more interesting if he'd talk about the things I've been reading in the school library, how credit for the invention of the telephone is usually attributed to Alexander Graham Bell, but such inventions are more often the product of the labors of many inventors and investigators. He could tell us that radio came about after an Italian inventor, Guglielmo Marconi, developed radio telegraphy when he was trying to figure out a way to use the telegraph without the need for wires. He used the ideas of several other inventors who were working with electricity, and the ideas of physicists who were studying electromagnetic waves.

And I wonder why the teacher doesn't talk about all the inventions that came out of the war, especially the atom bomb. But then, the war ended only six years ago and this country was very involved in it, so maybe high school science teachers are not supposed to go into such things. On the other hand, maybe it's simply that the science textbook the teacher uses for this class isn't up to date, and he wants to just stick with what's in it.

O course, I don't have that textbook. At the start of the term, we were supposed to go in and rent the textbooks for each class. I specifically wanted to look over the science textbook. In it, there was a lot about science that I already knew from my own reading, and what I didn't know was so basic, I was pretty sure I could find in books from the school library. I didn't want to waste Mom's money renting a book that couldn't teach me anything new, so I didn't rent that book. The other textbooks also seemed pretty basic, so I ended up not renting any of them.

I wish the science teacher would at least talk about scientific things that are currently in the news, like Einstein and his theories. From my reading, I've learned that Einstein has been publishing science-changing theories since the turn of the century, so that seems like something that by now should be taught in every high school science class. Maybe this teacher doesn't understand Einstein enough to talk about his theories, but the information must be out there somewhere.

This afternoon, I'll have to search the downtown library to see if there are any books that talk about Einstein's groundbreaking work.

In study hall, I'm glad to see that nobody is looking at me. Except for Haru, of course. That must mean the usual school rumor mill hasn't heard that I nearly got arrested last night.

At history class, as soon as I enter the room, I try to hand my new essay to the teacher, but he just says, "Put it on the desk."

I do that and go to my usual place in the back row.

Today, his lecture is about how heroic our soldiers were in the Pacific theater. He says MacArthur's island-hopping strategy was what won the war against Japan. He goes into great detail about how the brave American soldiers had to kill every single fanatical Jap that was hiding in their underground lairs, even if they had to burn them to death with flame throwers.

The teacher doesn't look in my direction, but I have the uncomfortable feeling he might be talking to me because in my essay about Truman I implied that maybe the US shouldn't have dropped the atomic bomb on innocent Japanese civilians. I now know he was in the US Navy and was involved in a support role of that "island hopping" strategy, so that must be why he has such strong personal feelings about it. For some reason, the personal way he's talking about the war makes me pretty sure he won't like my essay on Hitler either. He'll think I should have written an essay about MacArthur, and how the United States Navy and the Marines bravely ended the war in the Pacific. After class, I should try to get my Hitler essay back before he can read it.

But wouldn't that just make him want to read it more? No, he probably wouldn't allow me to take it back anyhow. I'll just have to let it be. I hope he'll just give me a bad grade on it and forget about me from now on.

When the bell rings, I hurry out of the room before he can say anything to me. I head for the school's side exit door, doing my usual staying to the side of the hallway, well away from the other students.

Nobody seems to be paying any attention to me. Good.

Outside, I immediately head downtown for the library. Now, I don't care what the history teacher thinks of my Hitler essay. He'll either think it's all right or he won't. If he gives me a bad grade on it, that's okay with me.

"Hey, Curt, what's the hurry?"

I turn. "Oh, it's you, Haru. Are you following me?"

He grins. "I just happen to be going this way. Headin' home. You live this way too?"

I don't especially want to let him know where I'm going, but I sure don't want to tell him where I live either. Better try to throw him off the track.

I shake my head. "No. I'm heading downtown."

"Okay, well, I see you're not carrying your science book this time, so I guess you can't use it to ward me off. We can walk together, right?"

I almost say it's a free country, an Americanism I've learned, but that might insult him by reminding him of how this country wasn't exactly free for him and his family. I just shrug.

Apparently, he's going to take my shrug as approval. He falls into step next to me.

"I can't figure you out, Curt. You're a good looking all-American sort of guy, but you don't seem to have any friends."

"So, you've been watching me?"

"Sure, why not. It's a free country, right?"

Kind of weird that he would choose exactly that response right after I almost used it. I again just use the shrug.

"What I've noticed, Curt, is that you don't have any friends at all. In fact, you intentionally avoid everybody. You don't seem to be going out for any sports, which is the best way to make friends in this high school. Not me because I'm obviously too fat. Well, maybe not exactly fat. Pudgy, that's what my mother calls me." He does a sharp laugh. "She says I'm making up for just about starving in that government prison camp. Well, maybe we were not exactly starving, but you have to remember I was just a little kid. Scared of the men with guns up in the towers and scared about the angry talk about America from my Dad. You can't blame me for squirreling away every bit of food I could get my hands on in that terrible place. Before he got killed in the war, my father didn't blame me for hiding food. He said the Americans might try to starve us to death. He even said if anything bad happened to the American Army in the war because of the Japanese, they might just kill us all. My mother didn't believe that, but then she always thinks the best of everyone."

He stops talking, laughs, and slaps the back of my shoulder.

"There, see? I did it again. My mother says I'm a little jabber box . But it's not true. That's only at home. Normally, I don't talk much to the other students. It's only that there's something about you, something that . . . "

He stop without finishing whatever he was going to say, and for a short distance, he just walks next to me in silence.

Then, he stops and says, "Well, this is where I turn off. Sorry to bend your ear off."

"I don't mind."

"You don't? Hey, my home isn't too far from here. You want to come an meet my mother. I'm sure she'd like you."

"I can't tonight, Haru. I've got some things I have to do."

"Okay, well, anytime then. We live over by the golf course. Not that we're rich or anything. My mother works as a cook for a rich family. They let us live for free in a little house behind their big house. It's not bad. You should come over some time. I know you don't have any friends, so don't try to tell me you do. I don't have any friends either because nobody wants to be the friend of the dirty Jap kid. But maybe you don't want to be my friend either."

"It's not that, Haru. I just study a lot."

"And that's why you don't have any friends? I don't believe that. There's something else. Anyhow, like I said, come over anytime. You can't miss it. It's the little house behind the big two-story house near the golf course.

Come for supper. Mom brings home some good eats from the food she cooks for the big house. Hey, after we eat, we can go over to the big house and play pool in their basement rec room. Ever play pool?"

"Once."

"It's a fun game. And they have a pop machine there. But you don't have to put any money in it to get the pop. Just reach in pull out whatever pop you want."

"Sounds good, Haru, but I'd better get moving."

"Okay. See ya."

He hurries off in the direction of the country club golf course. The time I went there to try to make some money caddying for the golfers, I noticed there were some big houses in that neighborhood.

As I walk on to the library, I wonder if Haru was telling the truth about normally not being much of a talker. He sure likes to talk to me. And he did get me curious about where he's living. If as he says, everyone in this country still hates Japanese people, why would a rich family hire a Japanese housekeeper and let them live for free on their property? And why would they let the Japanese kid have free access to their basement recreations room? Curious.

Fourteen

When I arrive at the library, I don't see Julie at the main desk. Maybe this is her day off.

Well, that's okay, I didn't want to get involved in Pan's troubles anyhow.

But I wouldn't mind talking to Julie. She seems like a smart person, and she was very friendly to me. But if she's not here, I'll just do my studying and wait to see if she comes in later.

But before I start today's studying, I remember I wanted to find books about Einstein. I go to the card catalogue, but surprisingly, there are no books about him listed. Tomorrow, I'll have to see if they have any books about him at the downtown bookstore.

While I'm here at the card catalogue, I remember that when I was at the pool hall, I wanted to learn some Spanish so I could find out what Pan and his pals were talking about. Mom says she's picking up quite a few Spanish words just from hanging around with the other workers at the motel. She thinks it's an easier language to learn than English.

The card catalog lists a number of books on learning Spanish. I go to the specified bookshelf and pull out few if them. I take them to my little study table and open the first one. I quickly read the introductory pages about Spanish grammar, and punctuation, and word endings that indicate gender. The first lesson consists of Spanish phrases you might use while traveling, such as *¿Dónde está la estación de ferrocarril?* which means "Where is the railway station?" Another one is *¿Dónde hay una casa de cambio?* which means "Where is the currency exchange?"

Learning specific phrases seems like a very slow way to learn a foreign language. Did the author expect you to just memorize those phrases in case you might ever need them? What about words you might need in unpredictable situations?

I try to think back to how I learned English so quickly, but I can't really remember exactly how I did it—I was young, and I just learned it. When we first came to this country, I started hearing English words, and I quickly memorized what they meant. I also read a lot at bookstores, and the only books that were available were in English. I figured out the rules of the English language by reading. Why not learn Spanish the same way?

I put the Spanish textbooks back on the shelf and go back to the card catalog to find a book that lists the most common words in the English language. After I find one, I also get an English-Spanish dictionary.

I take the books back to my study table, open them side by side, and start memorizing the Spanish equivalents of all the most common English words. No need to learn the exact rules of Spanish grammar and syntax. As I discovered when I was learning English, they are not necessary in order to be understood. After all, if a very young child says, "Want go out," the parent knows the child wants to go outside to play. The child gets rewarded by being taken outside, despite using such an incorrect form of the English language. Likewise, I'm not concerned that native Spanish speakers might think of me as being uneducated; I simply want to understand Spanish words.

That taken care of, I should get back to my main task, learning important things. But what are *important* things? I like learning about philosophy, but I don't want to learn only that. I suppose most people would say science is the most important subject. But my high school science class is so basic, I know if I want to learn anything significant about modern science, I'm going to have to learn from reading. The teacher does talk about some important things, like astronomy, but he only teaches general ideas about stars and planets, not even mentioning the mathematics, physics, and chemistry involved in the creation and function of the universe. What I've learned about that has been through my own reading. Maybe the high school thinks more advanced science should wait until we get to college. But will I ever get to go to collage? Not likely. Colleges cost money.

Also, if I applied to a college, they might find out where I came from. There's no point in even thinking about it.

But why am I thinking about things like that? We might very well get caught and deported at any time, especially if I keep on doing things that draw attention to me. There's still a lot of anti-German feeling in this country because of the war, so I don't suppose they'd be too happy if they found out a couple of German citizens illegally snuck into their country.

"Oh, you are here."

It's Julie. I didn't see her coming down the aisle. That's not like me; I'm usually more aware of anyone being nearby.

I stand up and say, "Oh, hi, Julie. I didn't see you at the main desk, and I wanted to get started reading.

"Okay. I thought maybe today you'd decided to . . . no, I guess I should always assume you'll be here. You really do want to learn."

"I sure do. I actually appreciate your dad putting me on this probation. I'm learning a lot."

"Okay. Well, I'll leave you alone then. I was just making sure you were here." She hesitates and then says, "But listen, Curt, you don't really have to be here every single day. I mean, if you have to be somewhere else . . . sometimes."

"No, I don't have anywhere else to be. My mother doesn't get home from work until late. And besides, this is exactly where I do want to be. I like studying."

"All right, I'll leave you to it, then."

"Wait a minute, Julie. I was going to come see you at the front desk anyhow. I need to talk to you about something."

"Oh, what's that?"

"Actually, it has to do with your father. Is there a phone we can use to call him?"

"Call him? Well, yes, I guess so. We can use the phone in the office."

"Is it private? I mean will anybody else overhear?"

"No one is usually in the office but me. What's this all about, Curt?"

"Well, like I said, it's kind of private. Can we talk about it in the office?"

She seems curious, and maybe a little irritated, but she does lead the way to the office without asking any more questions.

When we get there, she has me sit down in a chair and asks again why I need to use the phone.

"Well, it's a little hard to explain, Julie. Did your father tell you why I'm here on this sort of studying probation?"

"Well, he doesn't like to talk much about his police work. He just said you'd gotten yourself involved with some bad apples at the pool hall, and they'd gotten you involved in some kind of robbery."

"What happened was I ran into a guy named Pan, from Puerto Rico, and I lost some money to him playing pool. He said I could pay him back by doing him a little favor. Helping him get into a motel room."

She raises her eyebrows. "And you went along with that?"

"I know. Not smart. It seemed innocent enough at first, but actually he and his friends were planing to rob the illegal card game that was going on in that room. I had nothing to do with it, but the men that got robbed thought I was with them. They called the police, and that's how I met your father."

"I see. And what does that have to do with needing to use the phone?"

"Well, now that Pan guy thinks I know your father. He thinks I can help him give up to your father. He wants to make a deal."

She shakes her head. "No way. My father is a real straight arrow. By the book. Sometimes he and I butt heads over that. He won't bend the rules, even a little bit."

"I don't mind that, Julie. I *want* to follow the rules. And I don't want to deal with Pan in any way. You can't trust anything he says."

"Okay. So why do you want to call my father?"

"Well, I never thought I'd see that Pan guy again. Like I said, he's from Puerto Rico, so I assumed he'd go back there right after the robbery. And maybe he did, but he's back now, and he stopped me in the dark last night after I left here. He said he wanted to turn himself in, but only if he could make a deal with your father. He says he has some important information to trade."

"So you want to call my father and help this Pan guy make a deal."

"No way. I don't want to have anything to do with it. But I know your father is looking for him, so I thought I should tell him Pan is still in town, and he's willing to turn himself in."

"Okay, my advice is to just call him and tell him that. It's best to be straightforward with my father."

"Uh, can't you do it?"

"No, you should call him, and like I said, just be very straight with him."

"Okay, if you think so."

She dials a number from memory and asks for Lieutenant Flynn. He apparently answers because she just says hi to him and says Curt wants to talk. She hands the phone to me.

I take it and hesitate. Maybe I shouldn't have even gotten this much involved with Pan again. But now I guess I'm committed. "I'm sorry to bother you, Mr. Flynn, but that Pan guy, you know, the guy from the pool hall that tricked me into helping him and his friends? Well, he's still in town. He contacted me and says he wants to turn himself in."

"That's surprising."

"Yes. He followed me after I left the library last night. He wants to make some kind of deal."

"A deal? What kind of deal?"

"He wouldn't say. He just said he has some important information for you. About drugs. That's what he wants to trade."

"You tell him to come to the police station and ask for me."

"That's what I told him to do, but he said he was afraid you'd just arrest him."

"Well, of course I'll arrest him. If he has some extenuating evidence that might help lessen his penalty, he can explain it to me, after he's arrested. You tell him that."

"Uh, actually, I hope I never see him again, sir. But if I do, I'll tell him."

"See that you do. Now, how are your studies going? Is Julie helping you out?"

"Yes, sir, she is. And my studies are going very well. I'm enjoying being here in the library."

"Glad to hear it, son, glad to hear it. Now put Julie back on."

I hand the phone back to Julie, and it sounds like they're talking about some kind of family event they're planning. I try not to listen.

After Julie hangs up the phone, she says, "What did he say?"

"He said Pan should just come down there and turn himself in."

"Didn't I tell you? My father goes by the rules. Straightforward. That's him all over."

"Yes, I can see that. Well, I'd better get back to my studying."

I start to get up, but she holds up her hand to stop me. "Wait a minute. Tell me more about what you're going to do next. What if this Pan guy shows up again on you way home tonight?"

"I sure hope he doesn't. Now that your father knows he back in town, he'd be pretty stupid to approach me again."

"That's true. But if he does, tell my father right away."

"I will. For sure."

"Listen, Curt, you don't owe that guy anything."

"I know that. Actually, I think he'd be smart to just turn himself in, serve his time, and be done with it. I don't think he's that bad a person, just a bit of a conniver. It's his pals that are the hard types. But I think Pan wants to be the leader. I think he wants to show them he can be as tough as they are. But he isn't, not really."

She nods, but she doesn't look happy. Maybe I said too much. I wonder what she'll tell her father when she gets home tonight.

"Well," she says, "I'd better get back out to the desk. Let me know if I can help you with your studying."

"Thank you for that, Julie. I really appreciate the help you've already given me.

She leads me out of the office and doesn't say anything more to me, so I just head back to my study table. I sure hope she doesn't think less of me because of what I told her about how I got into trouble.

Fifteen

On the way home from the library, I keep thinking about my phone conversation with Officer Flynn. I'd better not tell Mom. She worries so much about us getting caught and deported, I'm sure she wouldn't like the idea of me talking to a policeman. She was really scared of the police back in Germany. She told me that all it would take was saying the wrong thing to them and you could get "disappeared." She's sure if we ever get sent back to Germany, bad things will happen to us.

Walking quickly, I again have the feeling somebody is back there in the darkness. Pan must be following me again. I stop and turn around.

But it's not Pan. It's two tough-looking guys, a little guy and a really big guy.

I hurry away, but in moments, they've caught up to me.

The little guy gets his face very close to my face and says, "Where ya goin' this timea night, kid?"

His breath smells like liquor, and the big guy is so close behind me, I can feel his breath on the back of my neck

I point. "I'm just going home."

Maybe I can outrun them, but what if they follow me home? I sure don't want that.

"Ya know, kid, we sure could use a few bucks? How about you help us out?"

They're not really asking. They plan to take my money. "Oh, sure. I'd be glad to help you out. But I don't have any money."

The little guy scoffs, and now his breath not only smells like liquor, it smells kind of rotten. What has this guy been eating?

"Don't give us that crap. Search him, Bear."

I turn to face the big guy. "No need to search me, Mister Bear. I don't have a dime."

I start to empty my pockets, but the little guy grabs my arm and spins me back around. "Who you callin' names, asshole? Nobody calls him Bear but me. How about we take your money and your jacket too. Take it off."

"How about you takin' your hands off him, *cabron*."

The two robbers turn to see who spoke. It's Pan.

The little guy moves toward Pan, waving his finger in Pan's face. "How 'bout you buttin' out, greaser?"

Faster than I would have expected possible, Pan gets ahold of the guy's finger and bends it backwards.

The little guy screams in pain, so the big guy moves to help him.

Pan holds up his other hand and says, "Back off, ¡*estúpido!* You want me to break his damn finger?"

But the big guy does not stop moving toward Pan, and I hear a snap. I think Pan broke the little guy's finger.

Then, without letting go of the little guy's finger, he uses the stiffened fingers of his other hand to stab the big guy in the throat.

That stops the big guy instantly. He's holding his throat and coughing. Pan kicks him in the knee, which takes him down.

The little guy is finally able to pull his hand free. He goes running off down the dark street, leaving his big friend lying here on the ground.

Pan leans down to the guy and says, "We're leaving now, and you're not going to follow us, right?"

The big guy nods his head repeatedly. He's holding his knee and his throat at the same time. He looks so scared I think he might start crying.

"And you're never again going to bother my friend here, right?"

The big guy continues nodding. He gets up on all fours, but Pan kicks him in the butt, knocking him down again.

"Crawl," says Pan. "Crawl the hell out of here before you really get hurt. ¡*Sal de aquí!*"

The guy crawls away quickly until he can finally scramble to his feet. He goes limping off down the street after his little friend.

Pan turns to me. He's grinning. "Lucky I happened to come along, eh?"

"You just happened to come along? Maybe you were watching, waiting for the right moment to come in and be the hero."

Pan laughs. "Now, would I do something like that?"

"Probably."

"Naw. Fact is, Curt, you're the only friend I've got in this damn town, and I really need a friend right now."

I'm not so sure Pan is the kind of friend I need, but I guess he did help me out this time. But of course, he wants something from me. Is it just to be a go-between with Office Flynn, or is it something more?

I ask him, *¿Qué quieres,* Pan?

He chuckles. "You're asking me what I want? You know what I want. And now you're talkin' in Spanish? *¿Ahora estás aprendiendo español?*"

"I'm starting to learn Spanish. I figured if I was going to talk to a foreigner, I might as well learn your language."

He points his finger at my face and says, "Hey, watch who you're calling a foreigner, *amigo.* I'm as much a US citizen as you are. I'm from Puerto Rico. It's a US territory. I can come and go in this country anytime, just like you can."

As much a citizen of this country as I am? If he only knew. I'd better not react to that in any way. He's a smart guy. He might get suspicious.

"That may be true, Pan, but that's not why we're here talking. I told you how Officer Flynn would react, and he did. I talked to him on the phone, and he said if you want to make a deal, first you have to come to his office and turn yourself in."

Pan shakes his head. "No can do, Curt. Not without protection."

"Protection?"

"That's right. *Proteccion.* The information I have would be important to him, but really dangerous for me. If I tell him my information, he has to agree to protect me."

"You'll have to tell him that yourself, Pan. I did what you asked. I told him you had information about drugs, and you wanted to make a deal. He said no deal unless you come in and tell him yourself."

Pan looks around, and then he pulls me into a dark doorway, just like he did last night. What is he so scared of?

"Listen, Curt, you gotta help me. If they knew I was even talking to you about this, they'd kill me."

Kill him? Is he trying to make his information deal sound more important? "Come on, Pan, kill you? Who's going to kill you?"

Pan again looks around as if he's afraid someone might hear what he's saying, but now that the two hoodlums have run off, there's no one at all on the nighttime street.

"Okay, I'll tell you what it is. Then, you can tell your cop buddy."

"I don't even want to hear it, Pan. I told Officer Flynn you were willing to make and deal, and that's it. I did what you asked, but now I'm out of it."

"*Escúchame, amigo.* This is some serious shit. It's the Colombians, and they don't mess around, *¿Comprendes?*"

"Colombians? What Colombians?"

"Colombian drug runners. First, they came across and started landing their boats onto one of our outer Puerto Rican islands. They off-loaded their dope there, and later they hid it inside of some big ships that were coming to this country. Puerto Rican ships get into this country easier. At first, all they brought in was marijuana. But that was just to get their *pies* into the US drug market. Cocaine is their real business, what they really wanna get goin' here. They found me and my pals 'cause we had a small-time pot business goin'. They showed up with guns sayin' we had to go to work for them. Sellin' their dope."

I'm not sure where he's going with this. Is he trying to get me involved in another one of his criminal activities? I should just tell him I'm not interested and hurry on home. The problem is, I *am* interested. Is this drug business something important that I should learn about? Are drugs a big deal in this country? I've never heard anybody at school talk about drugs, and when I read the local newspaper at the school library, I never see any mention of an illegal drug problem here. Are the Colombians just getting started in this city?

"Are you listening to me, Curt? This is important stuff. And it'll be *importante* to your cop friend too. Once the Colombians get it goin' it's gonna be big."

"So you think you can make a deal with Officer Flynn by telling him about these Colombians?"

"*Correcto*. I bet he'll want to stop them before they really get goin' here."

"Listen, Pan, he may want to know about what you're saying, but I don't think he's going to change his mind about you needing to go in and give yourself up before he's willing to talk about a deal."

"No way I'm goin' in, not unless he promises to give me some protection."

Now I know for sure I should just walk away. But I'm sure Officer Flynn *will* want to know about some drug criminals from South America trying to set up the cocaine business here.

"Pan. why don't you just go to a pay phone and call him yourself?"

"Aw, he wouldn't believe me. He knows you. You gotta convince him I'm a good guy. Tell him I can be trusted."

"Trust you? That's a laugh, Pan. Why would anybody trust you? I trusted you, and look what happened to me."

"Hey, it's not my fault that you didn't follow us out of that motel room. I even wanted to give you some of the money." He reaches into his pocked and pulls out a handful of bills. "Here, take it. Take as much as you need."

"I don't want your stolen money, Pan. Are you trying to make me an accomplice?"

"Hey, Curt, I told you I took a chance just hanging around and following you when that cop put you in his car and drove you downtown. I wanted to help you. I still do. I like you, Curt. Liked you ever since you took me on at pool when you didn't even know the game. Listen, Curt, just call that cop and tell him what the Colombians are up to. That's all I'm asking. I'm doin' him a big favor. I could just take off for home, back to Puerto Rico, but I don't like what the Colombians are up to. If we don't stop 'em now, they'll get all the kids in this country hooked on their shit drugs."

Looking at Pan's face, I can't be sure if he's telling me anything close to the truth. Pan, the good citizen trying to help out US society? That doesn't fit the picture I have of him. More likely, he's just afraid of the Colombians and wants them gone so he can have his marijuana business back. Still, I'm sure Officer Flynn would like to know about this.

"Okay, Pan, I'll call him and tell him what you've told me. But that's it. One more phone call, and I'm out of it."

"*Acuerdo*. Just tell him what the Colombians are up to. Tell him I can lead him to 'em, but I'll need protection. These guys aren't messin' around. Word gets out I'm talkin' to the cops, they'll kill me for sure."

"Fine, I'll tell him. But from now on you have to stay away from me. I just want to do my studying and be left alone."

"Just tell him. That's all I want from you. I'll come here again tomorrow night, and you can tell me what he said."

"No! Don't come back here. Didn't I just say I want to be out of this? Don't you have a phone? He can call you himself if he wants to talk to you."

"No, Curt, damn it, I don't have a phone. Like I told you before, I live with my mother, and she can't afford no damn phone."

"So, that's where you're hiding out now? With your mother?"

"None of your business where I am these days. You talk to the cop, and I'll call you to find out what he said."

"My mother doesn't have a phone either, Pan."

"Okay, then I'll call you tomorrow night at the library. You seem to be gettin' along just fine with that pretty girl behind the desk there."

I start to protest, but he's already walking away.

As I hurry home through the darkness, I think about what Pan said. So, he has been watching me. Why didn't I ever see him? Am I getting too comfortable playing the role of a normal young American boy?

And what about the Colombians he seems so afraid of. Can they really be that dangerous? Pan didn't seem worried about telling me that he and his pals were also in the illegal drug business. If I tell Officer Flynn about that, it'll be another thing he could charge Pan with. I guess all I can do is tell Officer Flynn what Pan told me and let him do whatever he wants to do with the information. And should I reveal to Officer Flynn that Pan is still in town, living with his mother? If so, the police should be able to find him.

One thing's for sure, tomorrow, after I pass his message along to Officer Flynn, I need to get myself completely out of this.

Sixteen

Walking to school in the windy early morning, I keep thinking about what Pan told me last night. He said Puerto Ricans are US citizens that can come into this country at any time with no questions asked. Therefore, it makes sense that Colombian criminals would go through Puerto Rico to get their drugs into this country.

Pan said he was as much of an American citizen as I am. If he only knew how untrue that statement is. My status as an illegal immigrant makes it even more urgent that I get myself out of the middle of this situation. If only I would have never met Pan.

No, that's not the real problem; the real problem is that I was stupid enough to get involved with him. But he is a likable guy, so how could I have known he was going to go into that motel room and rob that illegal card game?

No, that's not right either; If I'm so smart, why didn't I see through what he was up to? I guess all my reading hasn't helped me in that regard. In fact, it's the opposite: I prefer reading and I avoid people, so how can I expect to understand people? It's something I need to think more about.

When I get to school, I head upstairs to the library, as usual. I should stop thinking about Pan and get my mind into something else. And I should stop complaining about how boring my Science class is and read all the science books they have in this library. I stand next to the science bookshelf and leaf through the books. There's not much here that I haven't already read, but I take some of them to a table and go through them anyhow, reviewing, until the clock on the library wall shows it's time for me to head for my first class.

This time, the English teacher surprises us by saying that today, for a change, our assignment is to take out a piece of paper and write a story. She says we have the rest of the hour to do it.

She makes a strong point that it shouldn't be autobiographical, nothing personal. It should be an entirely made-up story.

It sounds a lot more fun than the punctuation assignments she usually gives us, but there are audible groans from the other students. Apparently, they see it as a hard assignment.

What should I write about? Despite her instructions that it should be entirely made up, a fiction, I know the other students will probably try to turn something they already know about into a story, and they'll write it in first-person, as if they were the person in the story..

I don't want to do that. So, what kind of story should I write that's not about me in any way. If it's to mean anything, it should be something that represents a basic human issue.

Thinking about basic human issues, when I first started studying at the downtown library, I read philosophy books. In one of them, it said one of the most discussed questions in philosophy is whether humans are innately good or evil. There must be a story in that.

I know, I'll make up a character and have him think about that.

Okay, here goes.

When George Everyman woke up, he was puzzled about why it was still dark. He turned over to look at the clock. Four AM. Why did he wake up so early? He didn't have to be to work until eight, and he usually didn't wake up until the alarm went off at six. Was there something on his mind?

Lying there, staring up into the darkness, the only unusual thing he could remember doing before he went to bed was that he read that letter he got from his brother off there in Montana. He had only scanned the letter because he was watching TV, just as the home team got a lucky win over the in-state rivals by kicking a long last-minute field goal. He couldn't remember much of the letter, but there was one line he did remember: *Are humans innately good or evil?*

Such a thought was probably not all that unusual from his brother now that he's gotten so deep into religion, but usually, he didn't write such things to George, knowing that he hadn't been to church since he was a child. Usually, his brother's letters were about cattle breeding and the tough Montana winters. So why had he included such a line in his letter this time? Was it something his religious brother wanted him to think about? Was he going back to playing the role of the big brother?

George shook off the thought and turned over. If he got right back to sleep, he could still get in two more hours before he had to get up and go to work.

But he couldn't sleep. He couldn't stop thinking about the good versus evil question. Were bad people good by nature but somehow they've been changed by their life experiences to become evil?

He thought about the people at work. He normally only thought of them as his coworkers, but now, as he lay there in the darkness wide awake, he tried to decide what kind of people they were.

What about that guy who was always trying to help everybody? Was that in his nature, or was he just trying to get in good with the rest of us? And what about the woman who was always acting tough? Was that her nature, or was she just trying to make the point that nobody should take her for granted just because she's a woman? In other words, were the people at work acting the way they acted because of their nature, or was it done for a specific purpose? Maybe all behavior was done for a purpose.

And what about him? What kind of person was he? Odd that he'd never thought about that before. Now that he did think about it, he realized he didn't really know.

He wondered how his coworkers would answer that question. What kind of person did they think he was? Did he do everything he did because he wanted his coworkers to think of him in a certain way? Or was he how he was because of something in his nature? That just didn't seem likely. When he was only a newborn baby in his mother's arms, there is no way his future adult behavior could already be determined. No, things must have happened to him along the way to make him the way he is now.

It must be the same for everybody.

At work today, he would pay attention to not only to his own behaviors, but also to how his coworkers were responding to him.

Darn, the bell is ringing, and I haven't finished my story, but the teacher says we have to stop writing and turn in our stories. To make sure I don't get too good a grade on it, I quickly misspell a few words. I wish I would have added "ly" to a few adjectives to turn them into adverbs. I know she pays a lot of attention to little mistakes like that.

After I turn in my story and leave the classroom, I realize I'm not exactly sure where my story was going, but writing it was the most interesting school thing I've done in quite a while. Maybe I should become a fiction writer. Can you be a scientist, a philosopher, and a fiction writer all at the same time?

For the rest of the school day, it feels like things are moving even slower than usual. It all seems incredibly boring as compared to the exciting things I'm learning at the library. I sit at the back of each classroom as usual, and it's good that the teachers aren't paying any attention to me.

In my last class of the day, History, as I walk in, the teacher waves me over and hands me back my Hitler essay about who was the most important person in World War Two. He doesn't say a word to me, but there's a large red F at the top of the page. I try to catch his eye, but he won't look at me. So, he hadn't liked my essay about President Truman, and now he obviously didn't like my essay about Hitler either. Is he mad at me for writing so much about Hitler's life and not enough about the war, or is he just unhappy that I thought Hitler was the most important person in the war? Well, he was, wasn't he? He started the war, and he was the one who carried the war all over the globe. Maybe the teacher didn't like my essay because I didn't put in anything about Hitler killing the Jews and the "undesirables." More likely, he just didn't like me refusing to follow his advice to write about an American war hero.

As he starts the class, he seems to be in a bad mood. We soon find out why: he says the only reason the basketball team lost yesterday was because of a bad call by the ref. After complaining a little more about how unfair it is that refs can change the outcome of the whole game. And then, without any lead-in, he asks when the Cold War with Russia began.

Nobody volunteers an answer.

He looks right at me and says, "How about you, Mister Smith? You're supposed to be the genius. How about you give us the answer."

Oh no. He called me a genius. Has he been talking to the counselor?

He's still glaring at me. "Well, Mr. Smith? We're waiting."

All the other students are looking at me. I should just answer the question quickly and try to get out of the spotlight.

"Well, maybe when President Truman announced the Truman Doctrine in 1947."

"That's one answer. Now, how about you tell us what the Truman Doctrine was."

Uh oh. This is drawing way too much attention to me. Maybe I should just say I don't know. "Uh, I'm not sure how to answer that."

"Can't answer that? But aren't you supposed to be the smartest student in this entire school? Come on now, Mr. Smith. Surely someone as smart as you could at least make an educated guess."

He's baiting me. Trying to show me up. Well, it's too late to back out now.

"The Truman Doctrine pledged support for democracies against authoritarian threats."

That stopped him. He doesn't seem at all happy that I came up with the right answer. Have I gone too far?

"Obviously, you read a book, and not the textbook for this course. In fact, it sounds like an exact quote from a book. Isn't that right?"

"Yes, sir."

"Okay, since you read a book about it, how about you tell us what happened thereafter. Let's say two years ago, in 1949."

Just keep answering. Keep it simple. Don't challenge him.

"In 1949, NATO was formed."

"It seems Mr. Smith has all the answers. And now he will tell us what NATO is."

"NATO is the North Atlantic Treaty Organization."

"Which is?"

"An alliance between member states to enforce the North Atlantic Treaty."

"My, my, you have been reading. How about you tell us how many members there are in NATO."

"Twelve."

"Name them."

"Well, the United States, of course, and—"

"In alphabetical order."

"Belgium, Canada, Denmark, France, Iceland, Italy, Luxembourg, the Netherlands, Norway, Portugal, United Kingdom, United States."

His face changes from irritation to anger. Obviously, he didn't want me to be able to answer his questions.

I'd better just look down at my desk and keep my mouth shut.

Why did I let myself get caught up in his challenge? What's the matter with me? Is it pride? Was I showing off? I can't let that part of me take over.

The teacher doesn't seem to know how to go on. He looks at his notes. Finally, he looks up, and thankfully, he's not looking at me anymore. He says, "All right, now that Mr. Smith has shown us he can remember things he read in a book, it doesn't matter who's in NATO anyhow because Taft will get us out of it as soon as he's elected president. Now, let's talk about the Allies. Who can tell me which side Russia was on in the war?"

Luckily, one of the other students, a skinny red-headed boy raises his hand.

When the teacher calls on him, he says, "Russia was on German's side until Hitler invaded them."

The teacher says, "Correct. Very good. Yes, Russia did join the Allies. They were an important ally that helped the United States defeat Germany."

I know that boy's answer was not quite correct, but I'm not about to say anything. There was never a formal alliance between Germany and the Soviet Union, just a non-aggression pact. And the Soviet Union was watching when Germany invaded Poland, which meant they could use the moment to grab some of Poland for themselves. Of course, that non-aggression pact fell by the wayside when Germany made the mistake of opening up an Eastern front against Russia.

I also know the teacher's comment about Russia helping the United States with the war is not correct; the Soviet Union has their own ambitions in that part of Europe.

He goes on talking about the cold War, describing, at length, how only two years ago the United States stupidly let Russia get ahold of the secret of how build an atomic bomb. I've read that's not true, that Russia had been working on their own atomic bomb for years, but happily, he doesn't call on me anymore.

When the bell rings, I hurry out of the room.

Unfortunately, the red-headed kid catches up with me in the hallway. Even though I'm walking fast, heading for the school's side exit, he's keeping pace with me.

He says, "You sure know your World War Two history. Do you like to study history?"

"Oh, I just happened to read a book about it recently. In the school library. But I have to hurry. Somebody is waiting for me."

He says, "But what was that stuff about you being a genius?"

"Beats me. Maybe he was being sarcastic."

"He didn't sound sarcastic to me. It sounded like he was mad at you."

"Aw, who knows? But like I said, I have to go."

"Oh, okay. See ya."

Sticking to the side of the hall, as usual, to avoid the clusters of students standing and talking, I finally make it to the exit and hurry off the school grounds. As I walk, I keep thinking about that teacher calling me a genius, the smartest student in the school. He must have talked to the counselor. That means he was checking up on me. If the counselor is telling the teachers about my test score, it means my trying to avoid attention is not going to work. So, what am I going to do now?

Seventeen

At the library, I see Julie behind the main desk, so I go right up to her. "I'm sorry, Julie, but I have to call your father again."

She doesn't seem happy that I said that. She says, "Is this more to do with that Pan guy?"

"I'm afraid it is."

"I thought you said you weren't going to have any more to do with him."

"I sure don't want to, but this time, he caught me walking home last night and told me exactly what his important information was. I think it's something your father will want to know about."

"Okay, come back to the office. We'll call him right now."

She leads me into the office and calls her father.

When she hands the phone to me, I quickly tell Officer Flynn what Pan told me about the Colombians trying to get the cocaine business started in this town.

He seems interested, but again, he says Pan will have to come in to his office and turn himself in.

I hand the phone back to Julie. For a few moments, she listens to whatever her father is saying and then hangs up.

She says, "He's not happy that you're involved with that Pan guy again."

"Listen, Julie, I really don't want to have anything to do with Pan. This time, now that I've passed his information on to your father, I'm done with it. I told Pan that."

"Okay. I hope you'll stick to that promise."

I'm not sure I can say anything more to convince her, so I just nod and get up to leave the office.

She touches my arm. "Wait a minute, Curt. Are you interested in physics?"

"I'm very interested in physics, Julie. What I'm getting at

school doesn't get into physics at all. It's just science basics."

"I hoped you'd say that. When I was at that high school, I had the same feeling. All too basic. And now, there's a lot of talk that maybe our students are falling behind the students of other countries. I heard that Germany especially was ahead of us in science. During the war, they invented those V2 rockets, and near the end of the war, they also developed a jet plane. Even Oppenheimer, our so-called 'father of the atom bomb,' had to go to Germany to get his physics PhD at the University of Göttingen. "

When Mom and I were still living in Germany, we never heard anything about the war weapons the German government was developing. We for sure never heard anything about Germany developing an atomic bomb. The only thing we ever heard about the war was propaganda about our great victories. Because of that, when the end came and Germany lost, nobody expected it. We were lucky there was talk in our little town about the Russians coming, and my mother was smart enough to get us out of there before they invaded.

"Well, Curt, that sure got you to thinking."

"Oh, right. Sorry, Julie. I was just thinking about what makes countries put lots of money into science and technology. Wars, mostly, I guess. But yes, I do want to learn more about physics. A lot more. What kinds of books would you recommend?"

"That's what I'm trying to figure out myself, Curt. I'm taking classes at the local college, but as a college freshman they'll only let me take the basic General Ed requirements. I'm hoping I can eventually transfer up to the state university and become a physics major. We do have some science books here in this library, but I've read them all and they're also mostly about the basics. Still, you have to start with them before you can get into the really heavy stuff. That's what I've been doing, learning the basics. Hey, maybe we can study together. I mean if you're interested."

Is she asking me to study with her here at the library? But what about her job at the main desk? Maybe she's suggesting I could go to her home and study with her. I wonder what her father would think about that. Whatever, you'd better grab this opportunity. "That sound great, Julie. When do we start?"

"Well, we're both busy here in the evenings, so why don't you come over to my house on Sunday. After church."

So, she *does* mean we should meet at her house. Does that mean she wants us to be friends? Whatever she means, just say yes. "Sure, Julie. That sounds good."

She smiles. "So, you wouldn't mind studying with a normal person? I'm no genius you know."

You've got to get her to stop thinking of you as some kind of genius freak. "Listen, Julie, all I did was score high on a test the school gives all the students."

She's staring at me. What is she thinking?

She does her funny little chuckle again. "To tell you the truth, Curt. I'm actually taking advantage of you. Of your smarts. I've been learning the basics of physics as best I can, but I want to take the next step, and I think I need help. I've been trying to learn more about theoretical physics, things like quantum mechanics and quantum electrodynamics. It's hard to even figure out exactly what they are."

"I've run across those terms in my reading, but all I know is what you said, that they're aspects of the newest thought in theoretical physics."

"Yeah. It's about physics at the very smallest level, at the level of atoms. Or even smaller. And it's not just Einstein stuff. It's new ways of looking at the smallest forms of matter."

"Uh, tell me, Julie, do you understand Einstein's theories?"

She shakes her head and frowns. "Not at all. I've read a little bit about his theories, but all I know he was a Jew who escaped from Germany and came here to the United States while Hitler was still coming to power. He's still living here in this country, at Princeton University."

"I've read that too. In my reading, I've come across references to his theories, related to gravity and space, and even those related to the basic theory behind the atomic bomb, but that's all I can find out about him. I really would like to learn more about the new physics, but the truth is, Julie, my reading hasn't been very well directed. While I'm here at the library, I'd like to get my studying more organized."

"Good. Well, let's start organizing it. Here's what I've done. I used the library's account to subscribe to a couple of advanced physics journals, but I can't make heads or tails of them. Would you like to see them?"

"I'm not sure I can determine any more from them than you can, but yes, sure, I'd like very much to see them."

"Okay, I'll take them home with me, and this weekend, when you come over, we'll study them together."

"I'd like that, Julie. Uh, as long as it is okay with your father."

"My father? You don't have to worry about him. He may be the head cop is this town, but he's really a nice person. He helps a lot of people that get into trouble."

"Okay. Just write down your address and what time. I'll be there."

Eighteen

Walking to school, head down against a really cold early morning wind, my mind is full of last night's happenings. The phone call to Julie's father, followed by Julie inviting me to study with her at her home—which of course, is also her father's home. What will he think of me being there, perhaps alone, with his daughter? But then, she is, after all, about four years older than me, and I'm only a high school student, so maybe he won't be worried about us being together.

Once I'm in the school library, it's good to be out of the cold. In the science section, looking for any books that even discuss modern physics, I find that they do mention Einstein, but they don't really get much into the significant contributions he made to modern theoretic physics. Hopefully, I'll find more up-to-date information about modern physics tonight at the downtown library. I should ask Julie which books I should start with.

I pull a few of the science books off of the bookshelf anyway and take them to a reading table. I make it through a few of them before I see Haru coming through the door. He comes right over and sits down next to me,

"Hi, Curt. Hey, do you know everybody in this whole school is talkin' about you?"

"Me? Why?"

"They're sayin' you had a run-in with your history teacher. That right?"

"I wouldn't call it a run-in. I just answered his questions."

"That's not what I heard. I heard you showed him up. Real bad. Everybody's laughin' about it."

So, the students in my history class did talk about what happened. I was afraid of this. "I don't know why anybody would say that. He just asked me some questions, and I answered them."

"Yeah, but I heard he was calling you a genius. What was all that about?"

I glance at the clock on the library wall. "Oh, I think he was just being sarcastic, Haru. But I've got to get to class."

"Okay. Just wanted to let you know what everybody is sayin' about you. Hey, I knew there was something special about you right away. I bet it has somethin' to do with why the counselor called you into his office the other day."

I stand up. "That was just about a test I took, Haru. But like I said, I've got to get to class. See you later."

I hurry out of the library and go straight to my first class of the day, English. When the teacher arrives, she says we didn't do a very good job on yesterday's assignment of writing a fictional story She says everybody wrote mostly what she calls "silly stuff," either youthful adventures that sounded very autobiographical or action adventures that sound like what they see in comic books. However, she says wants to read one story that is quite different, the only story written in the third person. She reads my whole story, but she's reading it in a way that sounds derogatory instead of the introspective way I intended it.

When she finishes reading it, she holds up the paper and point at it. "This story was turned in by Mr. Smith. That's him at the back of the room." She points at me, which of course causes all of the other students to turn to look at me.

Uh oh, I've done it again, drawn attention to myself.

"Now, Mr. Smith," she says, "how about you tell us where you got this story."

I don't know what to say. Doesn't she believe I just made it up?

"Well, I was thinking about good and evil, so I wrote a story about that."

She's still holding up my paper and scowling at me, as if my story made her angry at me.

"Now, Mr. Smith, we all know you didn't make up this story. Where did you read it? I can't quite place the style, but it seems familiar. I looked for it in some popular magazines, but I can't find it. So, why don't you just tell us where you got it, and I'll at least give you credit for having a good memory."

Now I've done it. I've not only drawn her attention, but I've made her think I cheated on an assignment. She's still scowling at me. I have to say something. "Well, I don't know what to say, ma'am. I just had a thought, so I wrote a brief story about it."

That seems to make her even more irritated. She throws my paper down on her desk and says, "All right, if you won't confess, I'll just have to give you an F on the assignment. Now, let's move on from this unfortunate situation and talk about the assignment itself. The reason I asked you to write a completely fictional story was to show you how different fiction writing is, structurally, and in function, from writing non-fiction. Now, let's look at some published examples."

Thankfully, most of the students have stopped staring at me and have turned to listen to her lecture. I have no idea why she thought I copied my story from somewhere; I guess she just didn't think a high school freshman could write such a story. I guess I should take it as a compliment, but it tells me I'd better be careful in the future. Apparently, I not only have to look and act like a fourteen-year-old high school freshman, I'd better also try to understand how they think.

For the rest of the day, walking between classes, I notice some of the other students are staring at me. I just stick to the edge of the hallway and keep my eyes down.

When the school day is finally over, to avoid running into Haru, I go out the front door instead of the usual side door and take a different route to the downtown library.

Nineteen

As I enter the library, I see Julie is at the front desk, but she's busy helping an older woman who seems to be asking her a lot of questions.

I head straight back to the book stacks and gather up every science book that seems likely to include anything about modern physics. I take them to my little hidden-away study table and open the first one. It starts out describing the nucleus. It says early physicists assumed the nucleus was made up of protons, but atomic mass numbers indicated there must also be other particles, perhaps electrons. I stop reading. Protons? Electrons? Atomic mass numbers? I've heard of those things, but what are they? I'm only getting into the first chapter, and I can already tell I'm going to need more background to even be able to read this kind of material. I need to first memorize physics terminology.

I can also see that studying physics is going to be hard for me because of my impatience. I always want to know it all right now! But now that I'm committed to study advanced physics with Julie, I've got to buckle down—as Americans like to say—and get more deeply into it. I go back to the science shelf and find another book that says it's for beginners. I bring it back to my study table. Because of my usual impatience, I skip over the introduction which describes what physics is and why someone would want to learn about it. When I get to the part where it starts defining terms, I make sure I have clear definitions in my head. This weekend, when I get together with Julie to study, at least I'll know what she's talking about.

The book defines a proton as a stable subatomic particle with a positive electrical charge. It defines an electron as a subatomic particle with a negative electrical charge. It defines atomic number as the nuclear charge number of a chemical element: for ordinary nuclei, it would be equal to the number of protons found in the nucleus of every atom of that element.

I continue memorizing terms until I hear Julie's voice saying, "There he is. He always hides out back here to do his studying."

Uh oh, she's with her father, and he doesn't look very happy.

I quickly stand up and say, "Hello, Mr. Flynn. Uh, am I in trouble?"

He's still frowning, but he says, "No trouble, son. But I need you to come with me."

He says I'm not in any trouble, but then why would he want me to go with him? I say, "Oh, sure. Just let me put these book away."

Julie says, "I'll hold onto the books for you. Just go with him. I already asked him if you're in trouble, and he said no. He just wants you to see something."

Officer Flynn gestures for me to follow him. He seems in a hurry.

I look at Julie. She gives me a stern look and whispers, "Just go. He promised me he'd bring you right back here."

I nod to Julie and follow her father as he hurries between the rows of book shelves.

He leads me out of the library and has me sit in the front seat of his police car.

It reminds me of the last time I sat in this seat, but hopefully, this is something different. But I am wondering why he isn't saying anything. He's looking straight ahead as he drives, and he still has that grim look on his face.

Finally, without looking at me, he says, "Have you heard from your Puerto Rican friend again?"

It that what this is about? I'd better make it clear to him that Pan is not my friend, even though he did save me from those two hoodlum types. "No, sir. And he is not my friend. I think the only reason he contacted me was because he thought I knew you. I made it clear to him that I didn't want him contacting me anymore."

Officer Flynn doesn't immediately respond to that, but finally he says, "Maybe I'm going to need you to stay in touch with him." He pauses, but before I can complain that I don't want to be involved, he adds, "Something's happened. It may have to do with what you told me."

He doesn't say anything more. He just drives on with that same grim look on his face.

I assume he's taking me to the police station, but when he finally stops the car in front of a large brick building, there are no police cars around. However, there is a parking place marked for "POLICE ONLY." He parks there.

He leads me up the concrete steps and into the building. There's still no indication of what kind of building it is. He leads me through a set of swinging double doors marked "RESTRICTED AREA."

Inside, a man wearing a light blue smock-type uniform leads us to another, smaller room. A metal table is in the middle of the room, and something is on the table, covered by a sheet. It must be a body. Did Officer Flynn bring me here to identify a dead body? Is that dead body Pan? I guess that wouldn't be too surprising, but then, why would Officer Flynn have asked me if I'd heard from him?

After the man in the blue smock pulls back the sheet to uncover the man's face, Officer Flynn asks me, "Do you know this man?"

I do know him. It's Esteban, one of Pan's pals. The tough one who didn't seem to like me. I say, "Yes, it's one of the men who helped Pan rob that card game. I only know his first name, Esteban."

Officer Flynn nods. "Somehow, I thought he maybe be one of those robbers. And what do you think of this?" He gestures to the man in the blue smock, who pulls the sheet down farther.

Officer Flynn points. Esteban's hands are missing.

I say, "His hands are gone. Why?"

Officer Flynn says, "I haven't seen this kind of thing before, but I've heard of it. In Chicago, gangsters cut their victims hands off so they can't be identified by fingerprints."

I try to imagine anybody doing such a thing. It's a gruesome thought, but back in Germany, I heard whispers about the Nazis doing even worse things to a body when they wanted to send a warning message. Was this done to Esteban to send a message? Or only to keep him from being identified as Officer Flynn said? It could be both.

Officer Flynn leads me back out into the deserted main hallway. "You called me to tell me your Pan friend said some South American drug dealers were moving into this town. Do you think this could have something to do with that?"

I resist the urge to again protest that Pan is not my friend. Better to just answer the question. "It might. Pan seemed very afraid of the Colombians. He said they'd kill him if they knew he was talking to the police."

"But it wasn't this Esteban guy that was trying to make a deal with us, it was Pan. So why would they kill him?"

"I don't know, but I think Esteban was tougher than Pan. He may have been wanting Pan to resist dealing with the Colombians, so they might have killed Esteban to put pressure on Pan."

"That makes sense. Okay, you have to get back in touch with Pan and tell him about this. Tell him I want to talk to him."

"To make a deal?"

"I don't make deals with criminals. But now that this is a murder case that may involve international movement of drugs, I had to contact the FBI. I'm sure they will want to talk to Pan."

"The FBI?"

"Yes. They said they'd send us a man right away. Listen, son, you are our only contact with Pan, and he's been telling you that he's willing to provide us with information. All I'm saying is if he contacts you again, find out as much as you can about these so-called Colombian drug dealers. Tell him I want to talk to him. Here, I'll write down my private number so you can give it to him."

"Pan said he was afraid to contact you directly. He thinks you'd track him down."

"I'll tell my men to back off looking for him. We need him to come in willingly. Robbing an illegal card game is small time compared to murder and possible international drug trafficking. The FBI may want to use him. That's how they work."

I put the note with Officer Flynn's phone number into my pocket and say, "All right. If he contacts me again, I will tell him to call you. But I really don't want to get involved with it."

"Julie says you're a good kid. We both just want you to focus on your studying, so I'll try to make sure your name doesn't come up. Now, I'll take you back to the library so you can get back to your studying.

Twenty

After Officer Flynn drops me off back at the library, I go to the front desk. Julie is still there, and she returns my physics books, but oddly, doesn't ask me anything about why her father took me away for a while. Maybe she's learned not to ask about her father's business. Or maybe she already knows what it was about.

I go back to my little study table and finish reading the physics books. Then, knowing the library is about to close, I grab three more physics books off the shelf and take them to the front desk to check them out.

The elderly lady checks out my books. Julie is nowhere to be seen. Maybe she's back in the office. Could she be talking to her father on the phone?

On my way home from the library, I keep expecting Pan to appear out of the darkness. Maybe he knows what happened to his buddy Esteban and has gone into hiding. That might mean I'll never hear from him again, which would be all right with me. I don't owe Pan anything, but I'd hate to see him end up dead with his hands cut off like his friend Esteban.

All the way home, I keep looking back. I'm not only looking for Pan, I'm lookin for whoever cut Esteban's hands off. It doesn't seem like they could know about me. Or could they? Maybe they tortured Esteban for names before they killed him. But I can't think of any reason why he would have mentioned me. But what if they've been watching Pan? Could they have seen him talking to me? They might have even seen me talking to Officer Flynn.

I make it home safely, and I don't think Mom is not home yet. Or else she was so tired she just went straight to bed. I sure don't want her to know anything about what I've got myself into. She might want us to immediately pack up and hear for another town.

I don't want to leave this city; it's the first place we've stayed in long enough to make it feel like home. Or at least as close to a home as anyplace since out little house in Germany. And then there's Julie. Lying on my couch/bed, staring up into the darkness, I can't stop thinking about her. I'm looking forward to studying with her at her house. To be honest with myself, I might as well admit I'm also looking forward to being with her. Could Julie be becoming so important to me that I won't leave this city, even if I'm in danger?

But then, she's probably not interested in me for anything more than being her study partner. Like she said, she's just taking advantage of what she calls "my smarts."

Julie's father wants me to make contact with Pan again. Wants me to convince him to turn himself in. But Pan said the Colombians would kill him if he talked to the police. And now they've shown that they will kill.

Oh well, there's no use thinking about that all night. I should just turn on the light and read the books I brought home. I should keep my mind on physics. It's going to take a lot of focused studying to catch up with all I need to know before I can get deep into modern theoretical physics.

Twenty-One

On my way to school, I'm resisting even going. The days at school are so boring, they're starting to seem longer and longer. I'd rather just go to the downtown library and do my own studying. And meet with Julie, of course.

Thankfully, I haven't heard from Pan for days. Maybe they killed him too. Although I'd be glad not to have to deal with him anymore, I hope he's not dead. I hope he just went back to Puerto Rico.

I can't stop thinking about the image of Esteban lying naked on that metal table with his hands cut off. If Pan is right, it must mean the Colombians are doing whatever it takes to get established here. Could they be doing the same kinds of ruthless things in other cities? Officer Flynn said the FBI was coming here to get involved in the case. Is that because illegal drugs are becoming a nationwide problem?

As soon as I round the last corner before the high school, I see Haru waiting for me. He's still been staring at me in study hall, but he hasn't tried to talk to me in while. I thought maybe he'd finally realized I'm serious about not wanting any friends. But here he is again. How could he know my route to get to school? Maybe I need to vary my route and come in from another direction.

When I get to him, he's grinning. "Hi Curt. I've been waitin' for you. I got up early just to see you. I know you like to go to the school library before classes start."

So, he has been watching me.

He reaches out to touch my jacket. "Geez, Curt, it's getting too damn cold for you to be out here with only that light jacket on."

Just ignore that. Better not to let him get too close, no matter hard he tries. "Oh hi, Haru. Yeah, like you said, I've got to get to the library. Class assignment."

"Okay, I'll just walk with you. But I wanted to ask you if anybody has been bothering you at school."

"No, why?"

"Well, I'll guarantee you that everybody is gonna to be starin' at you today. Some of the mean ones might even make fun of you. If you really did want to be left alone, you sure shouldn't have done so well on that test we all took when we started at this school."

How could he know about that? Has the counselor been talking?

"And you shouldn't have created a scene with your history teacher. And now I hear you created a scene with your English teacher too."

"Scenes? I didn't create any scenes."

"Well, that's what I heard. They're sayin' you showed the history teacher up real bad, and now the word is he's out to get you. He's been investigating you. Lookin' up your school records."

Really? Can that one encounter with the history teacher really have done the one thing I wanted to avoid? "Now, what a minute, Haru. Where are you hearing this?"

"All over. Yesterday afternoon, after school let out, kids were whispering in groups in the hallways, and it was all about you. You didn't notice any of that?"

"Are you saying you just happened to hear all this? I thought you said the other students didn't like you."

"Oh, I'm pretty good at getting close enough to listen. A few even wanted to talk to me cause somebody said I'm your friend. They'd seen me talking to you."

"Well then, stop talking to me."

Haru lets out a short laugh. "Too late now, old buddy. In fact, I think you could use a friend right now. If you really are a genius, some of 'em will admire you, but others will go after you. How about it? Can you fight?"

"Fight? You're saying some of the students will want to fight me because they think I'm a genius?"

"Sure. They're threatened by anything they don't understand. Some will want to up their tough reputation. Draw attention to themselves. Like how they went after me when they found out I'd been in a Japanese concentration camp. I just let em hit on me. Laughed at 'em til they got tired of it. Don't worry. Even if they do beat you up for a while, before long, they'll move on to somebody else. That type has brains the size of a pea."

I don't know what to say. First, I get myself involved with Pan and his problems with the Colombians, and now this. It's exactly the thing that could get my mother want to leave this town.

When we arrive in school, I see Haru was right: there are some students gathered in the hallways, and they're staring at me as I pass. One girl points at me and says, "There he is." Her friends all turn to stare at me.

I say goodbye to Haru and hurry upstairs toward the library. But Haru sticks right with me.

Am I never going to get rid of this guy? I need to be alone to think about what this means.

Apparently, the librarian hasn't heard anything about me, because she hardly looks up as we enter.

I get a few physics books and take them to a reading table. Haru sits down across from me.

He says, "Why didn't you tell me you're a genius, Curt? "You could have helped me with my homework."

"Was that your first thought, Haru? That I could help you?"

"Easy there, Curt old boy. I was just making a joke. Maybe wherever you're from, you never heard jokes like that."

Why did he says that? "Wherever I'm from? "What do you mean, Haru, wherever I'm from?"

"Yeah, like that. You just now said, 'What do you mean?' Anybody else would've said, 'Whata ya talkin' about?' You always talk real formal like that. Is that the way they speak where you come from? You said you came from down South. Where exactly?"

He's been listening to the way you talk. Whether we have to leave this town or not, I'm going to have to learn to speak more like they do. A few, like Haru, might be paying attention. "Aw, listen, Haru, it doesn't matter where my mother and I lived before we came here. It's just the way I am. I try to be exact."

"So, you're saying it's just the way you geniuses talk? Maybe I can buy that. Tell me more about being a genius, Curt? How long have you known?"

"Aw, Haru, don't get hung up on the word genius. I'm not really one of them. Not like Einstein or something. I just scored high on that one test I took when I first came to this school. I think I'm just good at taking that kind of test."

The way he's looking at me, I can tell he doesn't believe me. Or else he doesn't want to believe me.

He says, "Oh, yeah, I remember that test. Hard as hell. But I bet you aced it. Just good at tests, eh? What about showing up your teachers? The other kids a saying you've been showing the teachers you're smarter than they are."

"If you're talking about history class, Haru, the teacher just happened to ask me some questions on a subject I knew about. From a book I'd just read."

I don't think I'm convincing him. I think he really wants to believe his new friend is a genius. Maybe I should let him believe whatever he wants. And maybe he's right. If things are going to get complicated in this school, maybe I will need a friend. "Listen, Haru, I'll tell you the truth. I don't know if it qualifies as a genius or not, but I do have a very good memory. I can read something in a book and then days later, I can tell you exactly what it said."

Haru lets out a low whistle. "So that's it. Perfect memorization. That probably is what makes a kind of genius."

The librarian comes and stands next to us. She got her hands on her hips. She says, "If you boys want to talk, go somewhere else. This library is not for talking."

I thought we were talking very quietly back here, but with nobody else in the library, but she's probably very sensitive to the sound of talking.

I stand up. "Sorry, ma'am." I glance at the clock on the wall. "I guess we'd better get going to class anyhow."

We hurry out of the room, and sure enough, as we head down the hallway, groups of students are turning to stare at us.

I hurry toward my English class, but Haru continues to tag along. I think he now likes being seen with me. But what do the other students think about me being seen with him? So soon after the war, they may still think of him as the "dirty Jap. But why would these young people feel like that? Do they get it from their parents? Most of their fathers could have been in the war. In fact, some of their fathers might have served in the Pacific theater, and that could mean some of their fathers could have died over there. It's no wonder Haru got picked on when he first came to this school. Maybe he's lucky it didn't get worse. Did he tell them his father had died in the war too? If that word got around the school, they might have left him alone. But I can't tell them that my father died in the war. They'd want to know more about that, and sure can't tell them he was in the German army.

When we arrive at the door to my English class, I turn to Haru. "Thanks for all you told me, Haru. I'm sorry I wasn't nicer to you before."

"It's all right, Curt. I get it. I was that way too when I came to this school. But let it lie, and you'll eventually fit in. I did. Hey, I still want you meet my mother. Come with me after school today. We can have some good eats. And I'll show you the pool room in the main house, with that free pop machine."

I hesitate for a moment, but then say, "Well, I've got to get to the downtown library after school. To study. But maybe I could stop by for a few minutes."

"Cool. I'll meet you outside after school."

Twenty -Two

Going into the English classroom, I see that I'm the first student there. The teacher is sitting at her desk going through some papers.

I avoid making eye contact with her and quickly go sit in a desk at the back of the room. I open my physics book.

But I've hardly gotten into the book when the teacher comes to stand over me.

She says, "I've been hearing things about you, young man."

I look up at her. Does she want me to say something in response to that?

She sits down in the student desk next to me and says, "They're saying you're some kind of genius. Is that true?"

So, now is it going to be not only the other students talking about me, but even the teachers? "No, ma'am, I just took a test and scored high on it."

"Very high. I looked it up. That test was the standard test taken by every student entering this school. You scored higher than any other student. Were you a standout in elementary school?

"No, ma'am."

"Well, seeing that test score, I'm not sure I believe that. And then there is the matter of that story you wrote for me. I'm having second doubts about it. Now tell me, young man, once and for all, did you make up that story?"

This may be a situation you're going to face repeatedly in this school. How to respond? If you say you did made it up, you will stand out even more. If you lie and say you copied it, you will be marked as a cheater.

"Well, are you going to answer my question or not?"

"I'm sorry, ma'am. It's just that I'm not sure how to answer your question."

"Avoiding the question is not the right answer. Okay, then let me ask it in a more direct way. Did you read the story somewhere?"

"No, ma'am."

"So, you did make it up."

She's waiting for an answer. You have to say something. Maybe a philosophical answer will work. "Well, ma'am, do we actually make up anything? Elements of all our thoughts must be somewhere in the collective consciousness of our society, aren't they?"

She seems unsure how to respond, but now other students are entering the classroom, so she quickly gets up and goes to the front of the room.

I can tell by her reaction, that answer was definitely not the right answer to get her to pay less attention to me. Perhaps, just the opposite. I need to think through how people are going to take the words I say before I speak them.

Even as the rest of the students are getting settled, the teacher announces that today she's going to read from a book. She says the task is copy down what she reads and properly punctuate it.

Another punctuation assignment. Does it mean she's more comfortable with that kind of assignment? The assignment for us to make up a story was a rarity for her. Is it my fault she's no longer comfortable with that, or was she just disappointed with the results in general?

For the rest of the class, as she dictates, she keeps glancing at in my direction. For that reason, I put in a few more punctuation mistakes than usual.

As soon as he bell rings, I hand my paper forward and hurry out of the room, ignoring the curious stares of the other students.

I keep my head down as I hurry to my next class, but I can tell many of the other students are looking at me. Even though I'm sticking to the side of the hallway, an older boy bumps into me and says, "Oh, 'scuze me Mister Brainy. Musta not seen ya there."

I don't respond and hurry on. It looks like what Haru warned me about might be going to happen, no matter what I do. I'd better be on my guard and be sure not to make eye contact with anybody. Some of the boys might take it as a challenge.

I manage to get through the rest of the day without being bumped into anymore, but there are a few sarcastic calls at me as I try to make my way between classes.

Thankfully, I don't have anymore confrontations with teachers, not even with the history teacher.

Twenty-Three

As soon as the final bell rings, I hurry out the school's side door and walk fast to try to avoid any contact with the other students.

"Hey, wait for me, Curt!"

It's Haru. With all the nonsense going on at school today, I forgot I told him I'd drop by his house for a brief visit. I stop and wait for him.

"Well, Curt, didn't I tell you? I said everybody'd be talkin' about you. And they were, all day long."

"Yes, you were right. it's surprising how fast a rumor can get around a school."

"It's the hallways, Curt. Between classes, there are those who wanna be the ones with the latest gossip. I went thought it too when they were all takin' about me. But don't worry, it'll calm down soon as they have somethin' else to talk about."

"I hope so."

"So, did any of the teachers give you any trouble today?"

Should I try to explain to him about the English teacher? He expects me to be his friend, so I should be as honest as possible. "One thing, Haru, but it's kind of hard to explain. The teacher in my English class thought a story I wrote was unlikely to have been written by somebody my age."

"Ha! That's funny. I bet the teachers do get used to the kind responses they get on assignments. If they get somebody as smart as you, they can't quite believe it. Hey, this is where we turn. I live down this lane."

He leads me down a long shady lane that ends at a tall black-metal fence. Behind the fence is a handsome two-story house surrounded by a large well-kept lawn. Sculptured shrubs line the stone walkway. The house looks like one of the magnificent British homes I've seen pictures of in books.

"Quite a house," I say."

"Yeah, but that's not my house. It belongs to Mr. Hansen. Like I told you before, he lets my mom and me live in the little house out back. She works for the Hansens. As a cook. She's a real good cook."

"What does this Mr. Hansen do?"

"Owns some kind of big company. Not sure what they do. Construction, I think. He's out of town a lot. They used to have servants, but Mom says his wife didn't like having them around. Mom offered to be their full time housekeeper, but Mrs. Hansen wouldn't hear of it. She said when she can't clean her own house, it's time to put her in the rocking chair. She's kind of a funny lady. At least that's what Mom says. I've never met her. Met Mr. Hansen once. He came down to the pool room. A tall man. Real nice. Said he saw me come into the pool room and wanted to meet me. He asked me if it's true that Mom and me were locked up in a government concentration camp. That's what he called it. A concentration camp. I told him yes, and he just said 'Hmm.'"

Haru laughs and slaps his forehead. "There I go again. Talkin' your ear off. Don't get much of a chance to talk to anybody. Well, com'on, we gotta go to the side gate. I got a key."

He leads me along the fence until we get to a small gate.

I notice what looks like a large camera on top of the fence. I point. "Is that some kind of camera?"

Haru glances up at it. "Yeah. Don't know why."

I follow Haru through the gate, and I notice he's very careful to make sure it locks tightly behind us. I wonder what the tall fence and camera is all about. Is Mr. Hansen the kind of person who worries about burglars, or is it something else?

Haru leads me along a curving sidewalk to a small house behind the big house. He opens the front door and tells me to wipe my feet on the mat. "Mom's a stickler."

A woman appears holding a wooden spoon. She's a short Japanese woman, dressed in an apron over a plain off-white dress. The only thing even slightly self-embellishing about her is that she's wearing fuzzy red slippers.

She says, "Oh, you brought home a friend. That's nice. Bring him into the kitchen. I've got cookies. Made them this afternoon, and they didn't eat them all. Mrs. Hansen told me to bring the leftover cookies home for you. They're on the table."

Haru pushes me forward. "Mom, this is Curt. He's the genius at school I've been telling you about."

"That's nice. Now both of you sit down at the table and have some cookies. I'll bring you some milk."

We sit at the table, and Haru winks at me. I'm not sure what that wink is supposed to mean. Maybe he thinks his mother is kind of funny or something.

While we eat, Haru's mother busies herself at the large stove.

Haru leans closer to me and whispers, "She's making supper for them up at the main house. She does all the cooking here and carries the food up there. Keeps her busy, but they pay her a good salary. And no rent or nothin'. A darn good deal. Not sure how we fell into it. Kind of a miracle, I guess. Came along when we really needed it."

As soon as we finish eating the cookies, Haru says, "Come on. Let's go up to the main house. I'll show you the pool room."

He leads me up the sidewalk to the big house, and then down some stairs to a basement door. Inside is a wood-paneled room with a pool table in the middle. And just as Haru promised, there really is a pop machine. It has a coin slot, but I assume he was telling me the truth when he said you don't have to put any money in it.

As if to prove that point, he opens the pop machine's glass door and pulls out an orange soda. He holds it up. "Want one?"

"No thanks."

"Well, come on then, let's play some pool."

There's a rack on the wall with several pool sticks. Haru grabs one, probably his favorite. I pick another stick while Haru arranges the colorful pool balls into a triangle shape. He's about to hit the white ball into them when a door at the far end of the room opens, and a tall man with dark hair walks in. He has a serious, but kindly-looking face, and he's dressed in a very clean-looking dark suit, with a white shirt and a blue tie. Is he the type of man who wears a suit and tie all the time?

Haru says, "Oh, hi, Mr. Hansen."

Mr. Hansen says, 'Good afternoon, Haru. I saw you were bringing in a friend."

Haru seems nervous. "Oh, right. This is Curt, a friend from school. I hope it's all right."

Mr. Hansen smiles. "Of course, Haru. You can bring a friend in, as long as it's only one at a time."

Haru grins. "Well, it'll only be one at a time because Curt's my only friend."

Mr. Hansen nods. "So, Haru, are you still having trouble at your school? Because of your heritage?"

"Not really, sir. It's just that nobody really wants to be friends with . . . uh, a person like me. But Curt here's different. He's my friend. And he's a genius, a real genius."

Mr. Hansen looks me over. "A genius? Is that right?"

His dark eyes seem to be trying to penetrate my head.

"Yes, sir. Everybody at school's talkin' about him. But he doesn't want to have any friends. Except for me, that is. I'm his only friend."

Mr. Hansen is still looking at me. He again says, "Is that right?"

"Yes, sir. At first, he didn't even want to be my friend. But not because he's like the other kids. He doesn't care that I'm Japanese. He agreed to come home with me so he could meet Mom."

Mr. Hansen nods again. He's still staring at me, but he doesn't say anything.

Haru holds out his pool stick and says, "If you want to play, sir, we can leave."

Mr. Hansen smiles. "No, no, I just came down to meet your new friend. I was just leaving to go to a meeting. You boys stay as long as you want. Have fun."

He leaves the room, and Haru seems relieved.

"Geez, that's the only the second time he ever came down here to see what I was up to. I'm sure glad he's not mad at me for bringin' you."

"Why would he be mad at you about that?"

"Oh, I don't know. It's just that last year something changed. He had that tall fence built. He gave me a key to the small gate and made me promise never to lose it."

We play several games of pool, but while we play, my mind is elsewhere. I can't stop wondering why a businessman like Mr. Hansen would invite Haru and his mother to live on his property for free, and then pay her a salary to cook for him and his wife. If Haru is to be believed, most people around here still don't like anybody of Japanese heritage. Mr. Hansen even mentioned Haru's Japanese heritage, so he does think about it. It makes me wonder if the fact they are of Japanese heritage is actually why he might have selected them in the first place. And then there's the newly-installed tall metal fence, and the camera at the gate. I wonder if that could have something to do with Mr. Hansen's business, whatever it is.

Twenty-Four

After a couple of games of pool, I tell Haru I have to get going to the library. He lets me out the gate, and I head straight downtown. If I'm going to go to Julie's house this weekend to study advanced physics, I've got to do a lot more reading to get ready.

At the library, I see Julie is busy at the front desk dealing with patrons. I don't bother her. Instead, I go to the science shelf and take grab the two science books that have the most recent publishing dates.

Back at my little study table, I open the first book. I'm not expecting to find much in it about modern physics, but there is a brief discussion of quantization, which it defines as the systematic transition procedure from a classical understanding of physical phenomena to a newer understanding known as quantum mechanics.

Finally, something in a published book that at least mentions the area of modern physics I'm most interested in.

The book describes quantum mechanics as a theory that provides a description of the physical properties of nature at the scale of atoms and subatomic particles.

This is exciting reading. Up to now, I've been reading about physics as concerning the physical properties of nature—such things as Newtonian principles, thermodynamics, and electromagnetism. But this book says quantum mechanics is an evolving science, and it is often theoretical. The book goes on to mention Paul Dirac, an early pioneer that made significant contributions to the development of quantum mechanics.

I immediately stop reading and go back to the science shelf try to find something about him. Of course, there are no books by him, but I do find another book that has a brief section on him. It says Dirac was born in 1902 and is a Professor of Mathematics at the University of Cambridge.

It says Einstein wrote about Dirac, describing him as 'balanced on the dizzying path between genius and madness.'

That's an interesting thought. I wonder if other early pioneers of quantum physic were considered to be a little crazy. Maybe you have to be a bit crazy to imagine what's going on at such a tiny, unobservable level.

The fact that Dirac was a professor of mathematics shows me a problem: it's clear physics theories generally arise out of these professors' understanding of mathematics. Right now, that's one of my weaknesses. I'm going to have to get more serious about studying math. It's one more thing that tells me my study of modern physics is going to be a long-term study. I wonder if it can even be done by just reading, without going to a college. If so, my quest might be hopeless.

No, I can't let those kinds of thoughts deter me. Reading is all I've got right now, so I've got to keep on reading. More modern books are bound to be published soon that will cover the new, emerging theories. And then, there are physics journals, like the ones Julie ordered. I hope they really do get into new developments in quantum mechanics.

I take the book back to my study table, and it says that even if Dirac was considered to be an odd character, the book says he shared the 1933 Nobel Prize in Physics with Erwin Schrödinger. It says Dirac made early theoretical descriptions of fermions, elementary, very light particles. I've previously read that fermions, the basic building blocks of atoms are composite particles made of an odd number of protons, neutrons and electrons, while those made up of an even number of such particles are bosons.

I feel lucky to have found even this brief mention of modern physics, but it's frustrating to not be able to find out more.

I look up to see Julie coming down the aisle. Once again, I didn't notice her coming, Am I getting so involved in this new area of physics I'm forgetting to pay attention to my surroundings? That's not like me at all.

"Sorry to bother you, Curt, but my father called."

"Oh, hi, Julie. I'm learning as much as I can about physics so I'll know what you're talking about when we meet at your house."

"Ha! With your big brain, you'll probably have already caught up and passed me by then."

I almost blurt out that I don't want her thinking about me like that, but actually, maybe I do; otherwise, she probably wouldn't have invited me to her house in the first place.

She says, "Anyhow, the reason he called was to find out if you've been able to find your friend Pan."

Find him? Does he think you're going to go looking for Pan? "Uh, no. Actually, the only time I've seen him is when he finds me. And he's not my friend in any way."

She frowns. "I still don't think it's fair of my father to get you involved."

"Well, I think he's under pressure. Did he tell you that one of Pan's pals got murdered."

"No, really?"

"Yes. Your father thinks it might have been a warning to Pan."

"Do you think so?"

"It probably was."

"Even more of a reason my father shouldn't be getting you involved in something like that, and I'm going to tell him so."

"You don't need to do that, Julie. He's just doing his job."

"Well, you're job is to study, and that's what you're doing. When we meet at my house, I'll be curious to see what you've learned. Well, I've got to get back to the desk. See you Sunday." She gives me a little wave over her shoulder as she hurries away.

I'm ready to do as she said and just focus on my studying, but I can't help but wonder if Pan will show up to talk to me on my way home tonight. If so, what should I say to him? Does Officer Flynn want me to tell him that the FBI is getting involved?

He said he wanted me to convince Pan to come in and give himself up, but I don't know how I'm supposed to do that.

And besides, like Julie said, that shouldn't be my job. Pan would be better off just going right back to Puerto Rico. He should just let the police and the FBI take care of the drug dealers. But something tells me he's not going to do that. I suspect I'll be seeing him again, soon.

Twenty-Five

Walking home from the library in the dark, I keep looking back to see if Pan is following me. But by the time I'm halfway home and there's no sign of him, I'm pretty sure he's not going to show up tonight. I hope he's not dead. Maybe he really did go back to Puerto Rico. If he's smart, that's exactly where he'll go and never come back here.

I stop walking. It's not all that late. Maybe I should I go to the pool hall and ask if anybody has seen him. Or should I do what Julie said and stay out of it?

I turn back and head for the pool hall.

When I get there, I find it's the same old smoky place. It's full of pool players, but I don't see Pan or his pal Diego.

I approach the first pool table, and as before, two guys are playing for the money stacked on end of the table.

I say, "Hi, guys. Anybody seen Pan around?"

The two players both stop and stare at me. Then, they go back to playing and ignore me.

I say, "I used to play pool here against him. I just wondered if he was still playing here."

One of the two players looks Hispanic. He might know where Pan is. I say to him, "How about you? Do you know where Pan is?"

He takes his shot and misses. He says, "*¡Mierda!*" and turns to me, looking angry.

Is he blaming me for the missed shot?

He says, "Get lost, kid. Your *policía amigos* have already been here."

Of course, the police will have been here looking for Pan. If these guys didn't tell the police anything, there's no reason why they would talk to me. But this pool hall is the only lead I've got, so I should keep trying. "My cop friends? I can guarantee you the cops are not my friends. In fact, I helped Pan and Diego and Esteban do something illegal, and now the cops are after me too. I came here to warn Pan."

The Hispanic pool player stares at me for a few moments, and then says, "Listen kid, we don't know where Pan is. Didn't you know Esteban got killed? "

I nod. "Yeah. Somebody killed him and cut his hands off."

Now, some of the other pool players have stopped playing and are coming closer to listen.

I say, loud enough for them all to hear, "I heard that's what they do in Chicago. Cut off their hands so the cops can't get fingerprints. It's also a kind of warning."

The Hispanic pool player says, "Yeah, that's what I heard too."

I again say loud enough for everybody to hear, "So, nobody knows where Pan is? Did he go back to Puerto Rico?"

The Hispanic pool player says, "I got a pool game to play here, kid. Time for you to get lost."

I say, "Well, he told me he was staying with his mother. But I expect the cops that been there already."

The other player says, "I heard his mom has disappeared."

The Hispanic pool player holds up his hand. "Just shut up, everybody. We don't know who this kid is."

I say, "I'm a friend of Pan's. That's all you need to know. But if you won't tell me anything, maybe I will have to go to the cops."

He shakes his head. "I wouldn't do that if I was you, kid. We don't know where Pan is, and my advice is don't get yourself involved. If somebody was willing to kill Esteban and cut off his hands, you'd be smart to stay away from it. Pan can take care of himself. He doesn't need help from a kid."

I nod. "You're right. Better to just let him take care of it. I just wanted to warn him."

He hesitates, and then says, "Well, if I hear from him, the next time you come in here, I'll let you know. Now, do ya wanta play or not?"

I shrug. "I sure would like to, but I'm flat broke. Next time."

Everybody goes back to playing pool, ignoring me as if I'm not even here.

I leave, and as I walk home, I think about what I learned from them. They seem to know what Pan has been up to, but I don't think they know where he is. I should go back to the pool hall later, like he said. Maybe they'll have heard something more by then.

On the other hand, maybe I should just do what Julie said and stay or of it, no matter what her father wants me to do. From how those pool players reacted, I'm now pretty sure Pan is still around here somewhere, and I would like to know what he's up to. But I've heard an American saying, that curiosity killed the cat, and I know I have too much curiosity for my own good.

Twenty-Six

When I arrive at school, as I head for the library, many of the other students are still staring at me. I ignore them.

In the library, I go straight to the science shelf, but I can't find anything I'm interested in, or that I haven't read already.

I wander back to the philosophy section, which I haven't explored for a while. I discover they've recently received a copy of Sartre's *Being and Nothingness*, which I once looked through at the downtown library. But I haven't actually gotten very deeply into it. I've got some time before my first class, so why not see if Sartre has anything to say about the kind of reality modern physicists are exploring.

Sitting down to read the book, I leaf past the translator's notes, and go to the first chapter, "The Origin of Negation." Saying it is an essay on phenomenological ontology, Sartre begins by analyzing what others have said about being. Before going into his own thoughts about existentialism, he discusses Descartes's ideas, analyzing his dualistic theory of mind and matter.

I know Descartes was both a philosopher and a physicist. Interesting that I would, almost randomly, pick up a book that would start with Descartes, who uses the scientific method to look at philosophical questions. I'm not sure others would agree, but to me, philosophy and a physics are a perfect study combination.

Sartre then discusses Laporte's idea that an abstraction is made when something not capable of existing in isolation is thought of as an isolated state and contrasts that with the concrete, which can exist by itself. Sartre mentions that Husserl is of the same opinion.

I've read quite a bit about Husserl, a philosopher with a mathematical background, and I like his idea that every science can be looked upon as a system of propositions interconnected by inferential grounded relationships.

I don't think *Being and Nothingness* attracted much attention when the book was first published in France, which makes sense because it was published in 1943, right in the middle of the war. At that time, France was occupied by the German Army. But thinking about it now, it's too bad nobody noticed what Sartre was saying, because it might have helped them better understand the war and why the Nazis wanted to conquer the world. I recently read that Sartre himself fought for France in the war, but was soon captured and spent some time in a German prisoner of war camp. He was either released or escaped—the truth of which is hard to find now that he has gone back to teaching. Reading this book now, a book he wrote after leaving the prisoner of war camp, I think I can see how the war did, not surprisingly, influence his thinking.

I continue to read Sartre's book until the clock on the wall tells me I have to hurry in I'm going to make it to my first class on time.

But I don't make it. Two older boys have decided to block my way and make fun of me.

I go around them and walk on. They yell insults after me, and that makes some of the other students laugh.

Why do boys do such things? Are their lives so limited, this is how they want to spend their time? And why do the other students laugh? That just encourages them.

In my first class, some of the students stare at me, but nobody says anything to me, and the teacher doesn't either. She does keep on glancing at me, but she doesn't call on me. It gives me the oddest feeling of being all alone in the middle of a crowd.

Later, on my way to the cafeteria to get my free lunch, I'm wondering if the confrontations with older boys will be even more problematic in the lunch room when there will be no teachers around to rein them in. I wish I didn't have to go to there, but I know it's the only food I'm going to get all day.

I manage to get my tray full of food without any problem, so I go to my usual place in a far corner, as far away as I can get from all of the other students.

It's a place I found where I can get some reading done while I eat, nowhere near the jabbering of the little cliques of students whose voices fill the cafeteria.

But I've hardly started eating when a couple of older boys come to confront me. One of them says, "So, here you are, mister genius. Too good to eat with the rest of us?"

I ignore him and go back to my reading. I don't care what they think, and I'm pretty sure they won't try to beat me up here in front of everybody.

After a few more unintelligent wisecracks, they give up and leave.

I quickly finish eating and head back to the school library, the only other place in this building where those types won't come to bother me.

I wonder what they get out of giving me trouble. Are they jealous, or do they just think there's something so unusual about me it makes them unsure of themselves? Maybe I should read a few psychology books to see if they have anything to say about that.

But not just yet. Tonight at the library, I'd better read as much about physics as I can in order to be ready to read those physics journals at Julie's house on Sunday.

Twenty-Seven

Sunday morning, even though I'm awake early, I'm pretty sure Mom has already left in order to catch the bus that takes her to work at the motel. She never comes into the living room to wake me this early in the morning. I wish she would sometimes. I'd like to spend more time talking to her. I told her she could wake me anytime she wants to talk, but she just said her growing boy needs his sleep.

But what about her? Doesn't she need her sleep? She works late at her janitor job, and she has to get up before dawn every day to get to work at the motel. Every time I think about how hard she works, it make me want to redouble my studying. Not only do I love studying, I hope it will eventually give me a way to make enough money to take care of her.

Not quite ready to get up, and feeling how cold it is in the room, I stay covered up in my living room couch/bed staring up at the familiar water-marked ceiling. At least the ceiling of this dreadful little apartment doesn't leak now.

I turn my head to look into the little kitchen alcove, the only other room in this tiny apartment other than her bedroom. I can see that she left the box of corn flakes and a banana on the kitchen table. She's always thinking of me. I often wonder if I'm the main reason she got us out of Germany. There wasn't much schooling going on in Germany near the end of the war, but she was always telling me I was smarter than anybody because I taught myself to read. Seeing the impending disastrous outcome of the war, she probably thought I could get a better education in the land of the enemy, the United States.

I get up and get dressed. I sit at the kitchen table and read while I eat the banana and handfuls of corn flakes.

After reading for quite a while, I decide to go to the downtown bookstore to see if they've received any new books.

I hurry downtown, and luckily, the bookstore is open. Turns out, they do have a newly-published, somewhat thin, book about Einstein. Standing by the book table, I read it.

It starts with Einstein's well-known, world-shaking theories about light, special relativity, and mass–energy equivalence. He published those theories way back in 1905, but despite their significance, the content is not well known.

I've been wondering what Einstein thinks of quantum mechanics, and although few associate Einstein with it, the book says his 1905 paper on light is considered by some to have been the birth of quantum theory. The book also included Einstein's more recent thoughts about quantum mechanics. It said that despite recent research findings, Einstein still has doubts about how observation can affect research outcomes in the subatomic realm. In fairness to Einstein, those results have also baffled many other physicists, but Niels Bohr, the Danish physicist and philosopher, has been challenging Einstein and the others to accept the research findings, whether they make sense or not. The book's author suggests that Bohr will eventually be proven right, and it also describes Bohr's assertion that the only way to make predictions about reality at the subatomic level is through statements of probability.

Not really taking a position one way or the other, the book's author does point out that like Max Planck, Niels Bohr received the Nobel Prize in Physics for research on quanta. But I've read elsewhere that Einstein 's 1921 Nobel Prize for his work on the Photoelectric Effect also contributed to quantum theory.

I manage to finish reading that book and a few more by the time the clock on the wall says it's past noon. By now, Julie and her parents should be coming home from church. She didn't say what time to come over, other than after they got back from church. I figure that by the time I walk all the way over there, they should have finished eating their lunch. That seems like the right time to get there.

I go out and start walking, and despite the cold and the snow that's starting to fall, I'm happy to finally be heading for Julie's house. Just thinking about studying with her makes me feel like it will be productive, and even fun. I'm ready to get the nonsense at school and the trouble with Colombian drug dealers out of my head and get deep into some advanced physics. And of course, if will be great to finally spend some time alone with Julie.

As I walk, a nagging worry again creeps into my head. Julie has been critical of her father for getting me involved in what she thinks of police business. She thinks it could be dangerous for me, and of course, it could. And it might also be making it more likely that Mom and me could get deported and sent back to Germany. If we get sent back to Germany, I may not get blamed for escaping to the United States—after all, I was only a child— but what will the current government think of her arranging our escape? I read about the Potsdam Agreement that was made between the United States, England, and Russia that divided Germany, and I've looked at the resulting maps. They indicate the little town we lived in is now in the Russia sector. There is no way to tell what sort of government is in place there now that the Russians have taken over. The reports only say the Russians are being very secretive about what life is like there now.

By the time I get to Julie's house, I'm really feeling the cold, probably because my hair is getting soaked from the snowfall. I wish I could find a better coat, maybe one with a hood.

I ring the doorbell, and Julie answers the door.

I'm glad it isn't her father who answered the door, but that makes me wonder if he is intentionally leaving us alone. Maybe Julie insisted on that.

She leads me upstairs and gets me a towel to dry my wet hair.

That's really nice of her, and very perceptive: she could tell I was cold, even though I didn't say anything about it. She also offers to get me a blanket to put around my shoulders while we study, but I tell her I'm fine, and I know I will be because her whole house is nice and warm. In fact, it's the warmest place I've been in for a long time. I can't imagine how they are heating the house since I can't smell the coal fumes I can always smell at our apartment. Our little apartment is always so cold, I spend most of my time on my couch/bed under a blanket. The school building is hit or miss, with some classrooms very chilly while others are so overheated everybody gets sleepy.

Julie leads me into her room. It's very neat and tidy with plain white walls, and surprisingly, no personal pictures or any other decorations.

It's not at all what I would have thought a girl's room would look like. But then, what did I expect; she's a smart librarian college student.

Books are stacked on a small table next to the narrow bed, which I also should have expected. She has two chairs set up in front of a small desk, close together.

She notices me looking at the chairs and says, "Yes, I put them right next to each other, instead of us sitting across from each other. I hope you don't mind. Ever heard the expression getting your heads together? Well, that's what I want to do. Like I said before, I need to pick your big brain."

Once again, I think about asking her not to think about me that way, but on the other hand, I guess I do want her to think I'm smart; otherwise, why would she invite me to her house to study with her?"

Without waiting for me to answer, she gestures for me to sit down.

Once I'm seated, she sits right next to me and shows me two thin journals.

She says, "This is them, Curt, the most recent physics journals. I looked through them, and I recognize some of it, but I'm not at all sure where the reported research is going. I guess I don't have enough background."

"I probably don't either, Julie, but let's take a look."

I open one of the journals, and the first article is about linear accelerators as part of a cathode ray tube, the type of vacuum-filled tube used in TVs to emit the electron beams that display images on the TV screen. I'm not all that interested in that, and I don't think Julie is either.

We turn to the next article which is about the acceleration of electrons by magnetic induction. Also, probably not what Julie invited me here to learn about.

I say, "This journal seems to be mostly about applied physics. Is that what you were looking for?"

She seems frustrated. "I told you I didn't know what I was doing. I don't even know enough to know what I'm interested in."

"I think we should look at the other journal."

She doesn't reply, but pushes the second journal toward me.

The first article in the second journal is about least action in quantum mechanics.

Julie says, "What the heck is least action?"

I quickly read the start of the article. "It seems to be referring to a previously described principle regarding how a physical system changes over time. This article takes it down to how a single particle moves, related mathematically to the particle's kinetic energy."

Julie frowns. "This is exactly what I was worried about. That you'd explain it to me, and I wouldn't even get your explanation."

"It's not that hard, Julie. Let's go through it together."

It doesn't take me long to realize that this physics studying is going to be harder than we thought because the authors of the articles are assuming the readers have extensive backgrounds in physics.

"Tell you what, Julie. Let's break down the sentences into their main elements, and then we can refer to your physics books to get definitions."

She agrees, and using that method, we start breaking down the article enough to understand what it's about. We then read another article that's about the analysis of standard equations used to detect positrons. It soon becomes clear that we don't need to understand the equations themselves; all we need to know is that since Dirac predicted positrons as a form of antimatter, they've been discovered experimentally. This article is just suggesting ways to predict them.

We use the same approach to understand an article on quantum electrodynamics, and then an article that's a discussion of field theory. The field theory article takes it all the way back to Maxwell.

We're just getting into a very interesting article on the evolution of quantum theories when Julie's father comes into the room.

I look up, not sure if he will be happy to see me there. He isn't smiling, but then I've never seen him smile.

"Hello, Curt. Julie told me you'd be coming over to study. How's it going?"

Julie says, "It's going great, Dad. I already knew Curt was a genius, but I never suspected he'd be go good at explaining things. He could be a teacher."

He looks at me and says, "Is that right?"

Maybe she shouldn't have said that. Her father will probably think she's exaggerating and wonder why she's being so nice to me. I quickly say, "Well, I don't know about that. Julie is just good at picking this stuff up."

He says, "Sorry to interrupt your studies, Julie, but your mother says it's time for supper."

Julie says, "Oh. is it that late already? Uh, can Curt stay and have supper with us? Then we can study some more afterwards."

Officer Flynn hesitates, so I quickly say, "I'd better be getting home. I had no idea it was getting so late. My mother will also be holding supper for me."

I know that's not the truth, but I sure don't want to mess up this studying relationship by interfering in their family life.

He says, "Okay. Well, Julie, why don't you go on down. I've got to talk to Curt for a minute."

I can tell she's not happy about him wanting to talk to me, but she does leave.

However, she's barely out the bedroom door when she comes back and hands the two physics journals to me. "Take these with you, Curt. If you don't mind, that is. You can study them and bring them back to the library tomorrow."

"Sure. Okay."

As she hands me the journals, she gives my arm a quick squeeze.

I try not to register any surprise.

As she goes out the door, I glance at her father to see if he noticed what she did, but if he noticed, he's not reacting.

When she's gone, he moves closer to me and whispers, "Were you able to find out where your pal Pan is?"

"I'm sorry, sir. He hasn't contacted me again. I even went back to that pool hall, but the guys there said they didn't have any idea where he is."

"Did you believe them?"

"They seemed a bit protective of him. I'm not sure why."

"My men have been there a couple of times questioning them. Maybe that's why they're getting cautious about what they say. From what my men tell, me I doubt if those guys down there are directly involved, but I suspect they know more than they're saying. Another thing. The representative from the FBI has arrived in town, and he seems in a hurry to get to the bottom of this. They don't seem quite sure the South American drug connection is real, but if it is, they say it could turn out to be a big deal. I can tell they want to get a handle on it right away."

He stops talking and seems to be thinking about something. Maybe he's not sure how much he should be telling me.

"Anyhow, son, all I want you to do is keep your eyes and ears open."

"I will, sir."

"One more thing, Curt, have you heard any talk at school about drug usage?"

"Well, I don't really interact much with the kids at school, but like you said, I'll keep my eyes and ears open."

"Good. You've still got my phone number, right?"

"Yes, sir. We don't have a phone at home, but if I hear anything, I'll call you from the library."

"Good."

He starts to open the bedroom door to leave, but then he stops and gives me a sharp look. "There's no way Julie could get mixed up in any of this is there?"

His question catches me off guard. Get Julie involved? I don't see why he'd think anything like that. But maybe it's just a father being overly protective. I quickly say, "No, of course not."

"Good. Well, I won't hold you up any longer. Have a good evening."

After I leave the house, I walk fast into the cold wind. At least the snow has stopped.

But as I walk, I'm hardly noticing the cold. My mind is full of thoughts about the afternoon I spent with Julie. I'm not only satisfied with all I learned, I'm also happy that she enjoyed it.

The streets are completely deserted, probably because of the cold, and it feels like it might start snowing again any minute.

I look back to see if Pan might be following me, but there's no sign of him, or anybody else. I sure wish I didn't have to always be watching for him. I wish I'd never gotten myself involved with Pan in the first place. I wish I didn't even know about that drug nonsense. I just want to stay focused on learning.

Twenty-Eight

Today at school, not as many students are paying attention to me. The few who do just stare at me as if they're curious about what kind of person I am. Thankfully, none of them try to talk to me. I hope it means I was last week's interest, as Haru predicted..

In my first class, English, the teacher won't look at me at all as she does her usual dictating of lengthy paragraphs for us to punctuate.

As the day goes on, I'm as bored as usual and having trouble focusing on what the teachers are lecturing about. I keep thinking about studying physics with Julie yesterday. I wish I could read my physics books during my classes, but of course that would again draw attention to me.

In my last class of the day, the history teacher is totally involved in telling us, detail by detail, how it was pure bad luck and referee bias that made his basketball team lose this week's game. The other students seem quite interested in what he's saying. I have no idea why.

After the final bell, I go to my locker to get the two physics journals, and then I hurry out the side door.

I'm about to head downtown to the library, when I see the same three boys that I saw go behind the band building head in that direction again. Are they going back there again to smoke and do their silly betting?

I should probably ignore them and hurry to the downtown library, but Julie's father wanted me to keep my eyes and ears open around school to see if any of the students were getting into drugs. If so, these three boys seem like the type that would probably be in on it.

I follow them. Sure enough, they're smoking. But I can tell right away they're not smoking commercial cigarettes; they're smoking small poorly-rolled cigarettes. From a story I read in a newspaper, I suspect it might be marijuana.

The last time I was here, the tallest guy was their leader, so I walk right up to him and say, "Hi guys. What are you up to back here today? Smoking again?"

He says, "Just a quick smoke. Want some?"

Surprisingly, he's a lot friendlier than the last time. His two friends don't seem as friendly. They seem kind of nervous and are hanging back.

I smile and say, "No, thanks. I'm tryin' to give it up."

He takes one of the crooked little cigarettes out of his pocket and says, "You might wanna try this stuff. Different. I think you'd like it. Got any money?"

"No. Sorry. Flat broke."

He takes a big inhale off of his little cigarette, and while still holding is breath, says, "Take it anyway. No charge." He forces the little cigarette into my hand, and says, "Share that with your friends, and tell 'em where they can get some for themselves."

So, these guys are now in the business of selling this stuff. Officer Flynn will definitely want to hear about this.

I look over the little cigarette, and smell it. It doesn't smell anything like tobacco. I dump a little of the cigarette's contents into my hand and eat it. It tastes like weeds.

"Hey, man, you're supposed to smoke it, not eat it."

"Just checking the quality. How about if I want a large quantity? How much can you get me?"

He laughs. "I thought you didn't have any money."

"I don't, but I have friends with money. So, how much can you get?"

"Any amount."

"Okay, let's say I want to buy a kilo."

He glances at his two friends, but they both look baffled. He turns back to me and says, "I don't know how much a kilo is, kid, but I can get you a big bag for a hundred bucks." He holds his hands out about a foot apart.

I say, "Okay. I'll get back to you."

I walk away quickly and head for the downtown library.

When I get there, I see Julie is behind the front desk, but she's dealing with other people. I wait until she's finished with them, and then I go to her and hand her the physics journals.

"So, how much of it were you able to read last night?"

"All of it. We need to get more."

She does her usual odd little chuckle.

I'm learning what her chuckle means: she thinks my perseveration is excessive. But I can tell she likes it.

"We should talk about what I learned. Some really interesting stuff. But unfortunately. first, I've got to call your father again."

"So, that Pan guy contacted you?"

"No, I need to talk to him about something else."

She seems unsure, but she leads me back into the office.

"Well, what it is?

I show her the little cigarette.

"What is it?"

"Marijuana, I think."

"Really? Where did you get it?"

"Your dad asked me to keep my eyes and ears open around school to see if there was any drug use. Turns out, I didn't have to ask. This was given to me, just a little while ago, from a student trying to sell large quantities of the stuff."

She frowns. "My father shouldn't have asked you to do that. I thought you wanted to keep your focus on your studies."

"I do. But I should at least tell him what I found out."

I can tell she's not happy about it, but she goes to the phone and dials his number. She's short with him, saying only "Curt needs to talk to you." She hands me the phone.

I don't even say hello. I just say, "I did what you asked. I mean about looking for drug usage at school. Turns out, you were right. Some boys were smoking little hand-rolled cigarettes on school grounds. Probably marijuana. I have one if you want to check it out."

He says, "You have one? How did you get it? You didn't buy it, did you?"

"No, that's the important part. They wanted me to show it my friends to get them to buy some. They said they could get large quantities."

"Sounds like somebody's setting those kids up in the drug business."

"That's what I thought."

"Do you think your pal, Pan, is involved?"

"He's not my—"

"I know, I know, he's not your friend. But you said he had been selling marijuana."

"I'm not sure he's even in town anymore After the Colombians killed his friend, it seems likely he would go back to Puerto Rico. At least nobody's seen him since then."

"All right. I'll come by the library right now. I need to see that little cigarette of yours."

I hand the phone back to Julie, but all she says is, "Goodbye," and hangs up.

I say, "He's coming by to look at it."

"All right. Maybe after that, he'll just leave you alone. Now, you said you were going to tell me what you found out from reading that journal last night."

"Oh, right." I pick up the journal. "There are some important articles in here."

"Really?"

"Important to the field of science in general, I mean. From what I read in this journal, it seems like the current world of science is focusing on new directions, most of them related to quantum mechanics. A lot of the articles in this journal are related to new theories having to do with the realities of matter at the subatomic level. It seems to be completely rewriting basic physics."

"It's that important?"

"I think so, Julie. It seems like progress in the rest of physics, in areas like astrophysics, biophysics, and optics have always moved forward slowly, based on careful research.

On the other hand, quantum mechanics is moving forward in huge bounds based on surprising new theories that are stimulating new research. It's forcing Newtonian physics theories to undergo significant rethinking. One article in this journal implies that even Einstein could be wrong about some things."

She smiles and says, "I've never seen you so excited, Curt"

"Well, this is exciting stuff, Julie."

"I can tell you think so. Well, I've got to get back out to the desk. I'll take this journal home with me tonight and try to get through some of the articles by myself. But I feel like you're picking it up much faster than me. I wish we didn't have to wait until Sunday to go over it together."

"I can come over any time."

She hesitates. "Yeah, but I've got classes at the college almost every day, and then my parents want me to spend time with them." She shrugs. "The one disadvantage of living at home."

I sure would like to spend more time with her, but I'd better not push her on this. She may be hinting that her father doesn't want me coming over there too often.

"Okay, Julie, but can you order us some more of these physics journals?"

"You bet. This journal only comes out once a month, but there are others. I'll order them for the library. Now, I really do need to get back out to the desk."

Once we are outside of the office, I see that some library customers are at the desk waiting for someone to help them. Julie hurries to her station, and I head back to my little study desk to get more reading done.

On the way, I pull a few more science books off the shelf. I'm not holding out much hope that these books have anything to offer me other than the basics, but then, I shouldn't be resisting learning more about the basics of physics. I need to get better grounded in classical physics before I can fully comprehend how the new research is changing it.

I've hardly started reading when I see Officer Flynn coming down the aisle. He has a grim look on his face.

Before I can say anything, he says, "We can't talk here. Come out to my car with me.

I leave my books on the table and follow him out to his car. He surprises me by opening the car's back door. Is he going to take me somewhere? Before, he always let me ride in the front seat with him.

As soon as I get in, I see what's going on: there's another man, already in the back seat. He's a stern-looking man wearing a well-worn dark suit. He's not a big man, but he has a big chest and very wide shoulders. He's staring at me as if he's suspicious about something.

I'm not sure how to react to his stern look, so I just try not to show anything.

Officer Flynn gets into the front seat and turns back to face us. He gestures toward the man and says, "This is Mr. Carter. He's with the FBI."

I'm not sure I whether I should shake hands with the man or not, so I wait to see what he does.

He just stares at me, and says, "Lieutenant Flynn here tells me you got your hands on some marijuana."

"Yes, sir. At least that's what I think it is."

"Well, let's see it."

I take the little cigarette out of my shirt pocket and hand it to him.

He looks it over, and then he smells it.

He says, "I'm no expert, but this probably *is* marijuana. I'll have to send it back to the lab to be sure."

He continues to look the little cigarette over.

I wonder if that's all he wants of me. I look toward Officer Flynn, but all I can read on his face is concern. I'd better just wait.

Finally, Mr. Carter says, "All right, son. How about you tell me where you got it."

I glance toward Officer Flynn, but I still can't tell what he wants me to say.

I say, "As I told Officer Flynn, some boys at school tried to sell it to me. When I told them I didn't have any money, they gave it to me. They said they could get a lot more if I told my friends about it."

Mr. Carter is still looking over the little cigarette. But finally, he looks at me and says, "Now, Smith, you know that story doesn't make sense. They wouldn't just give it to you. Now, how about you tell me how you really got it. From your Puerto Rican friend, maybe?"

"Pan is not my friend. He's just a guy I met playing pool."

Mr. Carter shakes his head. "Maybe, maybe not. Anyhow, we're not interested in him if he's only a small-time drug dealer locally. But if he's bringing in this stuff from Puerto Rico . . . well, that's another matter."

"I haven't seen him in quite a while. He said some criminals from South America— Columbia, he thought—were trying to take over all the drug sales in this city."

"So Officer Flynn told me. That's the only reason I came to this city. But this Pan guy could have been just making that up."

It feels like he's trying to get me to say something in particular, but I don't know what. Better to just keep quiet.

He leans closer to me, still looking very stern. He holds up the little cigarette. "Under the 1937 Marijuana Tax Act, simple possession of this class one drug is a serious crime. You could go to prison. And I have now witnessed you having possession of it. Therefore, you'd better start telling me the truth, or I'm going to have Officer Flynn here arrest you."

Officer Flynn says, "Now wait a minute."

Carter waves his complain away. "Just making it clear where we stand. Officer Flynn here says you've been willing to help him track down this Pan guy, but so far, he's still out there doing who knows what. You've been associating with a known criminal, and now you're in possession of an illegal drug. Therefore, I'd suggest you start cooperating and tell me everything you know. Right now!"

"Sir, I have been telling you what I know, which is very little. I'm a high school student, and I just want to focus on my studying. But I've been trying to be a good citizen and let Officer Flynn know whatever I hear."

"And how did you happen to know Officer Flynn?"

I don't know how much Officer Flynn has told him. Better just stick to the one fact he may already know.

"I study with his daughter, Julie. She's the librarian here." I point in the direction of the library. "Now, if you wouldn't mind, sir, I'd like to go back into the library to study physics books."

He's still staring at me, but then unexpectedly, he smiles. "Physics, eh? A young boy like you interested in physics?" He glances at Officer Flynn. "Flynn here did tell me you're supposed to be some kind of kid genius. But you should know that doesn't carry any weight with me."

Then, he seems about the say something else, but he just goes back to examining the little cigarette. He says, "Maybe the boys in the lab can tell me where this was grown. Backyard stuff or professional imported stuff like you claim. We'll see. Okay, young man, go back in there and study your physics. But be aware, I'll be watching you." He waves me away.

Officer Flynn, with a nod of his head, is telling me to get out of the car.

I get out quickly and hurry back inside the library.

Back at my little study desk, my physics books are still there. I want to get right into them. but first, I need to think through what just happened. I did what Officer Flynn wanted me to do, and found out there was some drug usage going on at school. I even managed to bring him proof. But now, that seems to have gotten me in trouble with the FBI. And Julie's father didn't say much to defend me. Does Carter have some kind of authority over him just because he's from the FBI? More importantly, will Carter use FBI resources to look into me?

What if he finds out where my mother and I came from? We can't leave town now; that would make us look suspicious. But how could he find out we came from Germany? He must be with some kind of drug enforcement branch of the FBI, not someone looking for illegal immigrants. I try to shake off such worrisome thoughts and get my mind back into reading the physics books.

I open one of the books, but it's hard to keep my mind on it. Did Carter really mean what he said? That he'd be keeping his eye on me? Why would he do that? And how would he do that? Does he have other FBI men in this town that could be assigned to watch me? I just keep getting in deeper, and now it seems like there's no way out.

Twenty-Nine

I feel like I should go up to the main desk and tell Julie what happened, but I'm not sure I want to talk to her right now. She's already unhappy her father got me involved in his police business. No, I'll just stay here and get my mind back into physics.

I start looking through the books I grabbed off the shelf and find one with a newer publishing date. It does at least mention the kinds of things I read in that physics journal. It says physics has long theorized about matter, and now there are some new theories about the nature of matter and energy at the subatomic level. It says classical physics does a good job of describing nature at the ordinary scale, but it cannot explain what scientists studying quantum physics are finding at the subatomic level. It mentions a German physicist named Werner Heisenberg and describes how he interpreted the physical properties of particles as matrices that evolve in time. It says Heisenberg came up with the idea that an electron's position has to take into account momentum, implying that the electron's position cannot be said it ever be in one place. That means we can only state an electron's position as a probability. Since Heisenberg was a famous, Noble Prize winning German scientist, I wonder if Hitler ever tried to use him to develop new weapons.

The book also mentions another German physicist, Erwin Schrodinger, who also won a Nobel Prize. It says he provided a way to calculate the wave function of a system and showed how it changes dynamically over time. The books says he fled Germany due to his opposition to the Nazis. It also mentions that when the Nazis invaded Denmark, Niels Bohr fled to England, and then to the United States, where he ended up helping Oppenheimer develop the atomic bomb. However, he had some disagreements about how to use it—probably because of his background in philosophy.

I read a derogatory article in a newspaper saying Bohr had sent a letter to the United Nations suggesting international cooperation on the use of nuclear energy. He was also sympathetic to Oppenheimer, even though he has now been disgraced for being a communist—at least as alleged by Senator Joe McCarthy.

I wonder how many other scientists fled Europe during the war because of Nazi policies. One more reason why Germany lost the war.

Another one of the books I grabbed does mention quantum mechanics, but only as a fundamental theory in physics that provides a description of the physical properties of nature at the scale of subatomic particles. It also mentions quantum chemistry and quantum field theory, but it doesn't go into them. I guess I'm going to have to find newer books to get information about that.

By the time the lights flash to tell me the library is closing, I've got a huge stack of books on the desk, and I'm so deep into them, I really don't want to stop reading. But for now, I'd better just focus on which of the books I want to check out. I especially want to see if any of these books have anything at all about quantum mechanics, but now I see Julie coming down to aisle between the bookshelves.

She says, 'Didn't you see the lights flash?"

She seems perturbed with me, but she almost always has to come get me to stop reading at the end of the day. I wonder if she is actually upset that I keep going along with her father's needs instead of keeping my focus on my studying. "I know, I know, Julie. It's time to close the library. Sorry. I've been trying to decide which of these physics books to check out, and I let the time get away from me again. Listen, Julie, there's big stuff going on with quantum physics. New discoveries being made every day in quantum mechanics, but it's hard to find out anything about them. One of these books says the mere fact of gathering data when doing research at the subatomic level can affect outcomes. Do you realize what that means? It means—"

She frowns and holds up her hand. "It means I'm going to get in trouble if I don't get you out of here so we can close this library. I know if you could, you'd just stay here reading all night. You wouldn't sleep. You wouldn't eat. You'd just spend your life right back here reading. It's like you're becoming some kind of monster that ingests information instead of food."

I smile at the image of me she's creating. I know she's got a point; I've had the same thought about ingesting information. But I do need to go home and get some rest. After all, these books will be here tomorrow. I stand up and grab the four books that I've already noticed have the newest publication dates.

She shakes her head at my stalling, but I'm glad to see she's still smiling.

She leads me toward the front desk so she can check out the books. Once that is done, she reaches out to lightly touch my wrist. "It's all right, Curt. I want you to be excited about learning. I want you to learn as much as you can so you can teach it to me when we get together on Sunday."

I'm tempted to take her hand in mine and keep hold of it, but I resist. When she touched me like that, she was probably just being sympathetic.

"I'm really looking forward to Sunday, Julie."

She glances toward the front door, so I know that means I should just go. "Yes, right, I'm going. Sorry, Julie. By the way, you didn't ask me why you father took me outside."

"I assume he wanted to see that little cigarette."

"Yes, that was it. Well, uh, see you tomorrow."

"Yes, tomorrow. Maybe tomorrow I can get away from the desk a little more so you can tell me about what you're learning."

I resist trying to summarize for her a little of what I'm learning. I know she has to close the library, so I just nod and head for the front door.

Once I'm outside, the stark reality of the cold reminds me I've got to focus on getting all the way home as fast as I can. I can get back into these physics books when I get there.

As I hurry away from the library, I notice a large black car that's parked by the curb. It has darkened windows, but I'm sure I saw some movement inside. Now who would be parked here in front of the library on this cold night? Could somebody be watching me? Could Pan be in that car?

I shake off that thought. There's no way Pan could afford such a car.

I walk fast, often looking back to see if that car might be following me. But there's no sign of it. I must be imaging things.

The important thing is to get home fast, so I can get right back into reading the physics books I checked out. From what I've read tonight, it feels like the whole world of science, is changing. Things like black cars with darkened windows, and even things like the new illegal drugs coming into this country, suddenly don't seem all that important.

Thirty

Despite staying awake reading most of the night, I wake up early, and the first thing I think about is quantum physics. I may have finally found something big enough to hold my interest for a while.

Keeping the blanket up under my chin against the cold in the room, I turn my head to look toward the kitchen to see if my mother is up yet. The box of cereal she always leaves for me is on the kitchen table. It means she is not only up, but gone. With her working such long hours, that box of cereal she leaves out for me is the only indication she was ever here. I sure wish we could spend more time together. When we were escaping Germany and making our way through this country, we were as close as two people could be. .

But I can't just lie here thinking about the past. Last night, I read all of the physics books I checked out from the library, so now I need more. I should hurry to school to see if the school library has anything about quantum physics. Probably not, but I know they do have books on basic science. Maybe if I read them, I'll get some insight into how quantum physics is going to change all that.

I get dressed quickly, and grab a handful of cereal before I hurry out the door.

As I near the school, I see Haru waiting ahead. Is he going to make this walking to school with me a regular thing?

When I get to him, the first thing he says is, "Hey, Curt. Check out this warm coat." He holds out his arm. "Feel it. It stays puffed up to keep out the cold. Mr. Hansen gave it to me."

I touch the fabric. It does look warm.

"First thing I thought was, I should give my old coat to my friend Curt. I won't be needing it now that I've got this neat new one."

I say, "Okay." I'm not sure what else I can say about such a generous gesture. He really is a nice fellow, and a warmer coat in this weather sure wouldn't be bad at all. But maybe his mother might not like the idea of him giving away a perfectly good coat. I'd better not count on it.

We hurry on toward the school with Haru rambling on about what a cool guy Mr. Hansen is, how he's always help him and his mother.

We haven't quite made it to the school grounds when a car pulls up next to us. I recognize it right away; it's Officer Flynn's police car.

But Pan is in the passenger seat. He looks worried. Did he finally decide to turn himself in? He rolls down the window and says, "Get in the back seat, Curt. *¡Apresúrate!*"

Officer Flynn gestures for me to get in the car. He also looks worried.

I ask, "What's going on?"

Officer Flynn says, "It's your mother, Curt. You've got to come right now."

My mother? Is she hurt or something? And why would it have anything to do with Pan?

I turn back to Haru and say, "I've got to go with them, Haru. I'll see you later."

He looks shocked. I guess he also heard Officer Flynn say something about my mother.

He says, "Okay. Well, if anybody at school asks where you are, I'll tell 'em you'll be there soon."

At this point, I don't care what anybody at school thinks. I just want to get into the car and find out if something bad has happened to my mother.

As soon as I'm in the back seat, Officer Flynn turns on his siren and speeds down the street.

A siren? If he's in that big a hurry, it must mean she's hurt bad. But how could that have happened? All she does every morning is get on the bus that takes her out to the motel. I sit forward and ask, "Is she hurt bad?"

Officer Flynn shakes his head. "I'm afraid we don't know, son. You friend Pan here came to the station this morning to turn himself in. He said—"

Pan says, "It's the damn Colombians, Curt. They caught me this morning. Caught me comin' out of the place I was stayin' and said I'd better stay away from the cops. They said that goes for your smart-ass friend, Curt too. They said if we don't do what they say our mamas will end up like Esteban."

"My mother? How could they even know about me and my mother? What have you got me into, Pan?"

He shakes his head. "It's not me, Curt. The only other time they talked to me was to try to get me to sell their dope. I never once mentioned your name."

"Well, then it means they were following you. To see who you contacted."

"You can't blame me, kid. you're the one who's been hangin' around a cop's daughter."

Officer Flynn says, "Hey, knock that off, Pan! You're in enough trouble already, so shut up about my daughter. She's just a librarian where Curt goes to study."

Pan says, "Well, they must think she's more than that if he goes to your house on the weekend to see her."

How could Pan know about that? He must have been following me.

Officer Flynn hits the steering wheel hard with his hand. "Just shut up, Pan. You don't know what you're talking about. Just sit there and keep your damn mouth shut."

Pan shrugs and says, "Whatever you say, officer. But if this kid's mama is in trouble, it's not my fault."

Officer Flynn says, "And what about your mother? Aren't you worried about her?"

"Damn right I am. That's why I'm sending her back to Puerto Rico. I got friends there that can keep her safe. Your problem is keeping Curt's mama safe here. Those damn Colombians don't mess around. If they say they'll get her, they will."

Officer Flynn looks at me in the rear-view mirror. "Don't worry, son. I'm going straight to the motel where Pan told me she works at. We'll make sure she's safe."

Pan knows where she works? Obviously, he's been doing more than following me. Why?

When we get to the motel, Officer Flynn says he'll go in and talk to the manager.

I want to get out and go with him, but Pan holds me back and whispers, "Let him go alone."

As soon as Officer Flynn is out of sight, Pan tells me we should go talk to the people she works with. We get out of the car, and he leads me to a side door of the motel. He seems to know where he's going.

He leads me to a small room with shelves stacked with towels and bedding. A couple of maids are sitting in there, smoking cigarettes.

Pan says, "*Estamos buscando a la madre de este niño. Su nombre es—*"

One of the maids interrupts him. "I speak English. And you don't have to tell us who she is. You must be talkin' about the German. This must be the kid she's always bragging about. *El niño genio.*"

Pan says, "*Así es*. The genius kid. You called his mama the German?"

"Ya. She speaks German. Not too much English. Everybody abound here calls her "*La dama Alemana.*"

Pan looks at me and says, "A German lady?"

I shrug and say, "She came here from Germany. When she was a child."

I'm not sure he believes me, but it was all I could think of in the moment.

He says, "This country just fought a war against Germany. I don't think they would like Germans being in their country."

I ignore him and go closer to the woman who spoke English. "Yes, I'm her son. I need to talk to her right away."

The woman says, "The boss, *el jefe*, would like to talk to her too. She didn't show up this morning, and he's not happy about it. I told him to give the woman a break. It's the first time she's ever missed. Don't worry, kid. We'll make sure he don't fire her."

I grab Pan's arm. "We've got to get back to Officer Flynn. He'll get his men out looking for her."

Pan follows me out of the room, but he looks doubtful.

As soon as we're outside the motel, he stops and says, "You don't know those Colombians, Curt. If they've got her, they'll hang onto her until they get what they want."

"Well then, that's why we need Officer Flynn to get all his men looking for her."

"Okay, but not me, kid. I went to that cop, Flynn, 'cause he knows you. I thought maybe he could help. But they said to stay away from the cops, and that's exactly what I'm gonna do from now on."

"But how else can we hope to find my mother?"

"You get the cops to help. Me, I have my own methods. If I find out where they've got her, I'll contact you."

"How?"

"I'll find you. I know you won't be far from your girl-friend at the library."

"She's not my girlfriend, Pan. Not really."

But he's already moving away from me, running.

Well, he may not think he needs Officer Flynn's help find her, but I do. I go back out front and get into Officer Flynn's car.

As I sit there, waiting for him, I try to keep calm and think through this. I know this is all my fault. The things I've done, getting involved with Pan, cooperating with Officer Flynn, have now put my mother in danger. How am I going to fix this?

Thirty-One

Officer Flynn soon arrives, and he's not happy that Pan took off

I tell him Pan is going use his contacts to try to find my mother.

He says that's a job for the police.

He drives me to school and tells not to worry. He says they *will* find her.

As I watch him drive away, I wonder if that can be true. How will they even begin to look for her? It seems more likely that Pan, with his knowledge of the criminal underworld, is more likely to find her, or at least hear something about where she is.

I start toward the school entrance, but stop. Will I attract too much attention arriving this late? Or does any of that matter now? Standing outside, looking at the school building, I realize that none of what goes on inside that building is of any interest to me now. Instead of sitting in classrooms learning nothing, I should be out trying to find my mother.

But how do I do that? I only know one place to look: Despite everybody's advice, I have to go back to that pool hall. That's where all this started, and hopefully, by now, somebody there will have heard something. This time, I won't let them put me off.

I start walking toward downtown, and as I walk, for some reason, the cold wind makes me wonder if it ever got this cold back in Germany. I was just a child then, and when I wanted to go out and explore the woods near our house, I don't remember even noticing how cold or hot it was. And what about when we escaped from there? I've read that the Russians invaded Germany in the summer of 1945, so it must have been that time of year when we left. I don't remember what the weather was like, but I do remember how harrowing that trip out of Germany was.

In the back of that smelly truck, we kept on passing German soldiers that were marching along both sides of the road. It seemed like they were marching away from the fighting. Several times, they stopped our truck at military check points, and each time, I could hear our driver use the German word, *Flüchtling*. Refugees. Finally, Mom whispered to me that the soldiers we were seeing now were not German, and that meant we were safely out of Germany.

Eventually, the truck dropped us off at a big Catholic Church, and I guess it must have been the priest of that church that helped us get onto that ship that brought us to Cuba.

Maybe Mom wanted to get me out of Germany because there were rumors that the Nazis were grabbing young boys and forcing them to be youth soldiers to make a last-minute defense of the homeland. Now I wonder if getting us here to the United States was her plan all along. She must have been thinking I could get a better education here, and she gave up everything to get us here. Once we arrived here, she didn't much like to talk about Germany, but she once said she didn't want me growing up in a country run by a madman.

But now it appears that she's been caught up in another kind of war, a drug war. And even though it really is my fault, knowing her, she wouldn't blame me; in her eyes, I could never do anything wrong. But I did do things wrong. I should have just stuck to my studies and not let my damn curiosity keep getting me into trouble. Why do I let that part of me chose my path? Why did I ever walk into that pool hall? What's the matter with me?

By the time I get to the pool hall, it's starting to snow again, but very lightly. I hurry inside and see that there are not as many players as usual. Maybe the cold weather is keeping them away.

The tall pool player I talked to the last time I was here doesn't seem to be in the place, so I go up to the first table where four players seem to be playing a team game.

A short guy with big muscles under his tight T-shirt is taking aim at the eight ball.

I wait until he misses the shot and say, "Excuse me, but have you seen Pan around lately?"

He says, "*No sé,*" and turns away from me.

I turn to the others in the pool hall and say loudly, "Well, maybe you don't know where Pan is, but have any of you heard anything? I'm a friend of his, and he said he'd help me find my mother. Somebody kidnapped her."

That stops all play, and the place suddenly becomes very quiet.

I again say very loudly, "I'm afraid it might be the same ones who kidnapped Esteban and cut his hands off."

One big guy steps closer to me. He's holding his pool cue in a way that might be taken as threatening. He says, "*Nosotros no sabemos nada. Irse.*"

He's saying they don't know anything and that I should go away. He turns back to his pool game.

I can't let that stop me. I turn to the others. "Won't anybody help me find my mother? What if it was your mother?"

I gangly young guy with what they call a flattop haircut steps forward.

He says, "Those Spics won't help ya. Tell us what happened."

"I think some drug dealers took my mother. As a warning to Pan. It could be the same ones that killed Esteban and cut his hands off."

"Oh yeah, we heard about that, but why would they take your mother?"

"A while back, I played pool with Pan here, and then I did some illegal things with him. He was selling drugs, and some other big-time drug dealers wanted to stop him. They must think taking my mother would work as a warning to Pan."

"It ain't right they'd take a guy's mother. Me and my buddies will help you find her."

The first pool player has been listening, so I turn back to him. "This guy is willing to help me. Why aren't you?"

He turns away and goes back to his pool game.

I have the strong feeling he knows a lot more about the situation than the flattop guy. I call after him, *"Espera, por favor ayúdame."*

He turns back and says, *"¿Por qué debería?"*

"Why should you help me? Well, what it if was your *madre*? Or don't you have a *madre*?"

That obviously made him angry. He comes at me, holding up his pool cue like a club.

But I don't back down. "Of course, *tienes una madre*. I was just trying to get you to imagine what you'd do if it was your mother. *Si fuera tu madre.*"

He says, *"¿Mi madre? Mi madre está muerta."*

"She's dead? Oh, I'm sorry, but please help me make sure my mother doesn't end up dead too."

He says, *"Quizás,"* and walks away.

Maybe? That's all he has to say?

But if maybe is all he'll give me, I guess I'll have to settle for that. I hope it means he has some ideas.

The flattop guy was listening, but he doesn't say anything. He probably doesn't understand Spanish.

I turn back to him. "I was asking him to help find her. He said maybe. If you find out anything, come tell me. I'm usually at the public library.

He says he'll ask around.

I hope that means he knows some guys involved with drugs, and he'll do what he says, ask around.

This is turning out to be just like the last time I was here. Nobody will admit they know anything, and only a few gringos seem at all interested in helping me. I might as well leave.

As soon as I step out of the pool room, the cold wind hits me and wind-driven flakes of snow pepper my face. It feels like little stings. I'd like to keep looking for her, but it's going to get dark soon, and I can't think of anywhere else to go, so I might was well go to the library and study. I doubt if I'll be able to con-centrate on anything, but at least it'll be warm in the library, and it's a good place to think.

Thirty-Two

At the library, I don't see Julie at the desk. But then, I shouldn't have expected her to be here this early in the day. Her shift is in the late afternoon and evening.

I head for my little hidden-away study desk, and on the way, I pull a random book off the philosophy shelf. But once I'm seated, I just stare at the book. It feels like I shouldn't be sitting here reading when my mother is in such danger out there. I keep imaging all the terrible things they might be doing to her at this very moment. I feel like I should go back out and look for her. But where would I look?

All I can do is sit here and worry. How long will they keep her in order to get their warning message across? To make their warning more potent, they'll threaten to kill her. But killing her wouldn't make sense. I can see why they killed Esteban—it was a clear warning to Pan that they meant to take over the local drug business. But how could it possibly help their drug business goals to kill a woman who has nothing to do with any of it? Did they think it would convince Pan to stay away from the police? Is seems like kidnapping an innocent person would do the just opposite, get the police more involved. Could those drug dealers be operating at such a low level that violence is their only mode of operation, the only tactic they understand? That's a very worrisome thought.

But it doesn't do any good to just sit here worrying. My "job" is to study and learn. It's my only recourse and my only hope of getting through this madness.

I push aside the philosophy book and head for the science book section. But before I get there, I stop. No, physics takes a lot of concentration, and right now the only thing I want to concentrate on is where my mother might be. Books won't help me figure that out.

Or could they? My first instinct when I came here to the library today was to grab a philosophy book. Maybe that is the right approach: philosophy books might at least give me a clearer way to think.

I go to the philosophy book section and start looking through the books on the shelf. One that catches my eye is titled *"The Wisdom of life."* That's exactly what I need right now, wisdom. I pull the book off the shelf. It says the author is Arthur Schopenhauer, and on a title pages it says it was first published in 1851. I remember coming across his name: he was mentioned in that book I read some time ago about famous philosophers. He was described as a pessimistic philosopher.

That fits pretty well with how I'm feeling right now. I remain standing next to the bookshelf and start looking through the Schopenhauer book. At least his introduction in the book doesn't sound pessimistic. He writes about ordering our lives so as to obtain the greatest possible amount of pleasure. He seems to think a successful life is one that could be defined as a happy existence. He claims we should cling to that and not get caught up in the fear of death.

I look up from the book. Is that really the best goal of a life, to maintain a happy existence? And what about his warning, to not live a life in fear of death? Is that how some people live? Clearly, Schopenhauer doesn't seem to be talking about young people my age. I'm pretty sure none of my classmates live in fear of death. I doubt if they ever even give it a thought. But now, maybe I should be thinking about that. If they're threatening to kill my mother, wouldn't it make sense that they'd come after me next? Should I be in fear of dying?

No, I don't want to think about that. There's no real reason for them to kill me, and more importantly, no reason for them to kill my mother.

I go back to reading the book. Schopenhauer goes on to say that in exploring the idea of an existence based on happiness, he has had to make a complete surrender of his higher metaphysical and ethical views.

He mentions another book that explores that, a book titled *The World as Will and Idea*. I see that book also on the shelf, so I decide to take both of them back to my study desk.

I open *The World as Will and Idea*. Schopenhauer starts out writing about representation, which he says is the world as we perceive it. He says in human experience, the world is ordered according to what he calls "the principle of sufficient reason." He goes on to say everything that exists must, by necessity, have a cause; the cause can be external: a ball moves because some force was applied to it, or it could be internal: a person make a ball move because they enjoy kicking it. I'm just getting into why he thought that was important when I see Julie coming down the aisle.

What is she doing here at this time of day? Did her father tell her about my mother's disappearance?

The first thing she says is, "I hoped maybe I'd find you here. Have you heard anything from your mother?"

So she does know. "No. And I'm really worried about her, Julie. It could be the same people that killed Pan's friend."

She seems really upset, but she doesn't say anything. She just reaches out and touches my shoulder.

I say, "I skipped school today and went to the pool hall to ask around. They said they hadn't heard anything, but I'm not sure I can believe them."

She shakes her head. "You shouldn't have skipped school, Curt. You don't want the truant officer coming after you. Besides, you'd be safer there. You'd better just go to school as usual and let my father take care of what is police business. He has all his men out looking. And the FBI is also looking. They're doing all they can."

"I know your father will try to find her, Julie, but I feel like I have to do something."

"You are doing something. You're studying. Are you going to be ready for our physics study meeting on Sunday?"

"Right now, I'm having trouble focusing on physics. That's why I'm reading philosophy." I hold up the book.

"Schopenhauer. Of course I've heard of him, but I've never read him. Is he helping you?"

I try to think how to respond to her question. The truth is nothing is helping me right now, but I don't want to tell her that.

She leans down and puts her arm around my back. My first reaction is to lean my head against her chest. But then, she might not want that, so I hold back.

She keeps her arm around me and pulls me even closer.

She's knows what I'm feeling, and she's trying to help me in the only way she knows. But even her closeness and the warmth of her body doesn't seem able to take away the deep feeling of dread I'm having. But I don't want to tell her that, so instead, I say, "The truth is, Julie, I'm at a complete loss of what to do, and I don't know how to deal with not knowing. I've always just . . . I don't know, gone forward, trusting my mind to solve all problems. But now, I know I can't fix this just by thinking and reading. So what should I do?"

She take my hands in hers and says, "Listen, Curt. In this case, it's not up to you to solve this. That's the job of my father and his men."

"I understand that, Julie, but it's always just been her and me since we . . . I mean since my father died. I was only a child then, and it's only been the two of us. She works so hard to take care of me."

She squeezes my hands, and then she surprises me by putting them to her lips. I can feel wetness on the back of my hands. She must have been crying.

I sure don't want to start crying too, especially not in front of her. I need to stay strong and keep hoping they'll eventually let my mother go. After all, there's no real reason to hold her for long, and definitely no reason to kill her.

Julie stands up and wipes her eyes with the back of her hands. "Well, I'd better go. I've got classes at the college today. I just came here to find out if you were all right. For now, you should just stay here and keep reading. But soon, you should go back to school."

I want to say something more to her, but I can't think what. I should at least tell her how much I appreciate her sympathy.

But I'm too late. She's already hurrying away.

As I watch her go, I realize nobody else, besides my mother, has ever been so nice to me.

But what do I do with such closeness? Despite the fact that I'm around other people every day, the teachers and the students at school, I haven't let any of them get close to me. I have sort of become friends with Haru, but being close to Julie feels different. I guess I do want to get even closer to her, but right now I can't think what that would mean. I don't have any experience with girls. Growing up in war-torn Germany, I never went to a school there, and I never spent any time with the neighborhood girls of my own age. In fact, I didn't get to know any kids very well. Back there in Germany, Mom always said it was not safe to let anyone get to know us too well. She said neighbors were turning in neighbors to the authorities if they weren't showing the proper nationalistic spirit.

But the people in the United States supposedly don't have to deal with anything like that, so what would be the problem of letting somebody here get to know me well? The answer is obvious: they might find out I shouldn't be in this country. I'm still, officially at least, a citizen of an enemy country.

That brings up another dreadful thought: will whoever kidnapped my mother figure out she's German? After all, she still mostly speaks German. And if they do figure that out, what will they do about it? Notify the authorities?

Hopefully not. I bet they shouldn't be in this country either. But they might try to use it in some way against Pan, and me.

I've got to stop worrying about such things. I need to think logically. The worst thing that could happen is that we'd get sent back to Germany, and I suppose we'd find a way to survive there, even if the Russians are now in charge of our part of Germany.

I should just focus on reading these philosophy books and do what Julie suggested, let her father and his men find my mother. I can only hope they will.

I finish reading both of the Schopenhauer books and go back to the philosophy shelf. One of the first books I read in this library on philosophy was a book that described all the famous philosophers. I remember it talked a lot about something called phenomenology and a man named Edmund Husserl. It described him as arguing that human consciousness sets the limits of our knowledge.

There are no books on the shelf by him, but there is a book about phenomenology and related philosophies. Surprisingly, it's in German. That's no problem for me, but I wonder why it's in this library. It looks as if nobody has ever opened it. I'd like to read it, but what if anybody catches me reading a book written in German? I guess if anybody comes by, I could quickly hide it under my other books.

I take that book back to my study desk, and the opening chapter describes Husserl as the person who established the school of philosophy now known as phenomenology. It says Husserl mostly studied science and mathematics.

I wonder how that led him to philosophy.

It says he was born in Austria to a Jewish family, but he was never a devout practitioner of any religion. After public school, he went to the University of Leipzig in Germany where he studied mathematics, physics, and astronomy.

By now, I've learned that such a background is not all that unusual for a philosopher, and I've read that some of the most famous scientists studied philosophy. Maybe I'm on the right track, studying both philosophy and physics.

The book says that after earning a PhD in mathematics, Husserl went to Vienna to study philosophy. He ended up teaching philosophy at the University of Halle and then at the University of Göttingen. He published a book, *Logische Untersuchungen,* in which he reflects on pure logic.

Pure logic. That is definitely what I need right now. If there is any hope I can find my mother, I need keep my mind focused on logic and reason. It won't help at all to get caught up in emotion. Getting too emotional about what is happening to my mother right now will not only tear me apart, it will also keep me from thinking clearly.

But what if she never comes back? What would I do without her? It's true that I haven't been seeing her all that much lately, but before we came to this city and were on the move, she was more than my mother, she was my best friend, my only friend.

I have to push those memories out of my head. I can only hope Officer Flynn and his men will find her soon, and she will be all right. I force myself to go back to reading. The book says, Husserl's focus was on how information is presented to us. He said each bit of information is presented to itself, while all others are "presentiated." He used the German word *Vergegenwärtigung,* which refers to pure consciousness. The books says Husserl started to become widely known and gave lectures in Paris and in London, describing phenomenology as reducing personal experience to the sphere of ownness, in which he describes the transcendental ego as paired with another ego, a paired interconnection seen in perception.

However, back in Germany, because his family had been Jewish, the emerging racial laws instituted by the Nazis banned him from using the university library. And they would not let him publish. Eventually, the Nazis forced him out of his university position, and other professors were advised to avoid associating with him. Despite all that, until his untimely death a few years later, Husserl tried to avoid getting involved in politics, preferring to keep his focus on investigating consciousness. After his death, his works were banned in Germany, but luckily someone was eventually able to smuggle them out of the country, and it's the only reason they are known to us today.

There is a lot more information about Husserl's theories, but I have to put the book down to think about my own situation. Thinking about how the Nazis treated Husserl brings back too many troublesome memories. My mother smuggled us out of Germany to escape the national disaster that had been created by the Nazis. It might seem unlikely that such a reactionary group, led by a complete maniac, could come into power, but it did happen, and it could happen again. It could even happen in this country. I'm sure none of my classmates could imagine such a thing, but seeing it happen in such an advanced country as Germany, there's no reason why it couldn't happen here too.

I decide against going to school today. I'll just stay here until the library closes tonight and keep on reading philosophy.

When I'm pretty sure it must be late afternoon, I get up to go check the clock. I know Julie had college classes to go to today, but her shift here at the library should have started by now.

I leave the other philosophy books on the desk, but I put the German book back on the shelf. I go out front, but I don't see Julie at the main desk. I approach the elderly woman at the main desk and ask where Julie is.

She seems irritated as she says, "Her father called and said she won't be coming in today. So guess who had to come in on such a cold snowy night to fill in for her. Right, me. Oh sure, her father wouldn't let her come in. Ha! A father won't let his daughter come in to work when it's her job? A likely excuse."

I don't say a word. I just head back to my study desk.

I think I know what's going on. With the situation my mother is in, Julie's father is afraid to let his daughter go out. Now, he probably won't want her to be anywhere near me.

Back at my study desk, I can't stop thinking about what that woman said. If Julie's father won't let her come in to work, could he have heard something more about the people who took my mother? He's suddenly very worried about his daughter. But he doesn't seem to be so worried about me.

Or is he? Maybe I'm the bait. Maybe they'll be watching me to see if the drug dealers come after me next.

I've got to stop thinking thoughts like that. I should just think about what I'm reading, about how even well-known professors like Husserl had to dealt with the Nazi government. What must it be like there now in the town I was born in? The people there will be living day to day with the war-destruction all around and the Russians in control. It's hard to get any information about what's going on there now.

That brings up the question, what if the police do manage to find my mother, and they then send us sent back to Germany? If so, what would the Russian-backed government do with two German citizens that ran away to the United States, specifically to escape from them?

I have to stop thinking about that and continue thinking logically about what do to about my mother's situation. Logically, if they do release her, where would she go? Would she come here to find me? No, she'd go home. It means that is where I should be right now.

I put the philosophy books back on the shelf and hurry out of the library. I run all the way home, remembering how much I enjoyed running when the PE teacher took us out to the dirt track and told us to chase whoever was ahead of us.

When I make it home, the apartment is not only cold, it feels very empty. I walk into Mom's bedroom, half hoping that, by some miracle, she might be there. But she isn't, and her bed is made as neatly as usual. It means she hasn't been here since she left for work. Staring at her bed, I have the sudden awareness there is no reason to sleep tonight in the uncomfortable couch; I could sleep in here and bury myself in her covers.

But no, I can't do that. It would be almost like admitting she's not coming back. I go out to my couch bed and try to wrap as many covers around myself as possible. I can't turn up the heat because tenants have no control over it. The apartment manager controls it, and he always keeps the furnace turned down low to save money.

Despite how cold it always is in this little apartment, he's always complaining about how much the coal is costing him these days.

Nevertheless, I can tell by the coal gas smell that he does have the furnace going tonight. In the mornings at school, I always wonder if the other students can smell the coal fumes on me. They probably can.

I ignore the smell, and turn over onto my side. I'll try to not think too much about where Mom might be right now and only focus on getting some sleep. I'll go back to looking for her in the morning.

But no, I shouldn't do that. When Officer Flynn took me to school yesterday, he told me to let them find her. Was he implying that if I go out looking, I might make it more dangerous for her? Julie also said I should go to school as usual and let her father and the police do their job.

Maybe I *should* go to school in the morning. At least for a little while. Maybe I can take off at lunch to look for her. I've got to do something. At least I should go back to the pool hall to see if anyone there has heard anything.

Thirty-Three

On my way to school, it's another cold and windy morning. I'm still not used to the winters in this part of the country. I try jogging to try to get warm, but it isn't helping much.

"Hey, wait up, Curt. What's the big hurry?"

I turn back. It's Haru, and he's carrying a brown coat. It's his old coat that he said he wanted to give me. I sure could use it on these really cold mornings.

He holds out the coat. "Here's my old coat. I said you could have it, assuming that is you're not too proud to take it."

"Too proud? In this weather? Hand it over."

He's grinning as he watches me put it on over my thin jacket.

It really is noticeably warmer. I button it up and say, "Thanks, Haru. I'm just not used to this weather."

"Yeah, you told me you came from down south, not that I believe that. But hey, you don't even have a hat. You need a stocking cap, like mine. Maybe Mr. Hansen will buy me a new one, and you can have this one. Assuming that is, that you wouldn't mind wearing one that was on the head of a dirty Jap."

"I thought we were already through talking like that, Haru."

He shrugs and looks down at the ground. "Oh, sorry. It's just that some of the other kids have giving me trouble lately."

"Again? Why would they be back to doing that?"

He looks up at me. "Can't you guess? Because they've seen me talking to you. The smart-ass genius and the dirty Jap. They're saying the two of us belong together."

"I'm sorry to hear that, Haru. I wouldn't want to cause you any trouble."

He waves that idea away. "Naw. Don't worry about it. I'm used to it."

"Well, if I hear anything like that—"

He holds up both of his hands. "No, no, don't do any-thing. Besides it looks like you've got your own troubles. What was that about yesterday when that cop car pulled up beside us? I heard it was something to do with your mother."

"I can't talk about that right now, Haru."

"What? Why not?"

"Just let me work it out. I'll tell you about it later. Okay?"

"Well, if you say so. But if you need anything, you know you can count on me."

"I appreciate that, Haru. I really do."

As we walk on toward school, Haru takes up non-stop chatter about the mean things the other kids have been saying—and the clever things he said back to them.

Oddly, his excited voice calms me down a bit. I've always found a strange kind of calm place inside myself whenever those around me are panicking. Like that time Mother and I went through that hurricane down there in Florida. The hurricane spawned a tornado that tore the cheap motel we were staying in into pieces.

Mother was very frightened, but it only reminded me of the war planes that used to fly low over our house in Germany. I felt sure the tornado would, like those airplanes, just fly right over and leave us alone.

But it didn't, and we got out of that motel just in time. We ran to get inside a big pipe that was under a nearby road, and we were still hiding there when the police and firemen showed up to look for survivors in the ruins of the motel. Mother said we couldn't let them find us, so we took off with only the clothes we were wearing. What little we'd brought from Germany, her ID papers, and even my birth certificate, were gone. But we sur-vived, and we didn't get caught. I assume all of our stuff was just trash to the post-tornado cleanup people.

Mom said that tornado was an omen. She said it was time to get out of Florida, no matter how warm it was. We moved from town to town, her finding odd jobs, as we gradually working our way north, then west, until we got here to the Midwest.

But now, seeing how cold it is here, I wonder if maybe dealing with those hurricanes and tornadoes down there in warm Florida would better than being here; here, it feels like I could freeze to death just walking to school.

Once we reach the school building, I say goodbye to Haru and head straight upstairs to the school library. The few students I meet stare at me, but thankfully none of them bother me. And that's good: the mood I'm in, I might react in a troublesome way.

In the school library, I can't decide what I want to study, so I just gather up a few science books and find a secluded seat near a heat vent. I doubt if staying warm was the main reason Julie so strongly suggested I keep going to school, but it's a good reason.

After reading for a while, the clock on the wall says it's time to go to my first class. I don't feel much like going, but I do it. I sit in the back, as usual, and for a change, instead of lecturing about grammar and punctuation, the English teacher is asking questions. She asks, "What is an allegory?"

I know, but I sure don't want to be the one to answer.

Nobody seems to have the answer, so she looks at me and says, "All right, if nobody knows, we'll have to ask the school genius."

Why is she doing this? She must be angry at me for some reason. Did I embarrass her in that brief conversation we had about writing fiction?

"Well, Mr. Smith, we are waiting."

I should just give her a brief answer, and make sure it's not a direct quote from something I read. Since this is an English class, I guess I should give her a literary example. "A literary work in which the characters stand for abstract qualities."

"Now that wasn't so hard, was it Mr. Smith? But I'm afraid you are incorrect. It's not only the characters in the story, it's everything. The characters and the objects in the story, even the events."

Of course I knew that, but after she chastises me, I make sure I don't change the expression on my face. I have no idea why she's doing this, but it's fine with me if it convinces the rest of the class that I'm not all that smart.

She goes on asking questions, but thankfully, the other students are able to answer them. I just sit quietly until the bell rings, and I can finally get out this class.

As I'm walking down the hall to my next class, ignoring the taunts of older boys, I'm wondering if it's worth spending the rest of the day here. However, as boring as my next classes are bound to be, the rooms are all fairly warm, and for now, I guess that's enough.

Finally, it's time for PE class. I always enjoy running round and round the dirt track because it's the one time I can stop my mind from constantly thinking. The dirt track gets so beat up by the weather, when running fast, you have to watch where your feet are landing, and that requires a relaxing level of concentration. And when the coach starts pushing us to run faster, I like it. I like the feeling of my body being tested and pushing even harder.

Of course, with the cold weather outside today, the coach keeps us inside. He divides us into teams and has us do tag-team races back and forth across the gym.

Oddly, some of the boys, the shy ones, want to be on my team. I don't know why.

After all the running back and forth, we get to go down the circular metal stairs into the basement where we get to take hot showers, for as long as we want to. The longer I stand under the hot water, the more it reminds me of how hard our current life must be for my mother. The water at home is never hot, and for that reason, she told me she takes her showers at work. I don't know if the maids have a shower room or if they take showers in a vacant guest room. She doesn't talk much about her work.

Wherever she is now, I can only hope they're taking good care of her. I turn off the shower and try to push that thought out of my mind.

But it's no use. I keep on imaging where she is and hoping she is enduring her current situation. Actually, she's probably surprising her captors by what a tough person she is. I can only hope they don't hurt her and just let her go.

At lunch, I eat as much as I can, and for the rest of the day, to keep from worrying so much about her, I'll try listen to whatever the teachers are lecturing about. But as the day goes on, I realize that's not going to work: all I can think about is where Mom might be right now and they might be doing to her.

Thankfully, today the teachers are not calling on me. Maybe they've decided I'm a disruptive student and they'd rather not deal with me. That would be all right with me.

But in history class, my last class of the day, the teacher is talking about the ongoing war in Korea, and he asks the class whether Korea it is a flatland or is this a mountain war. When no one seems to know, he says, "Well, let's ask our class genius. Are our brave troops going to be fighting the Communists on level ground, or are they going to have to root them out of mountain caves like we had to do with the Japs in the Pacific?"

I know Korea is largely mountainous, except along its coasts, but I don't want to hook into his little game. I shake my head as if I don't know.

When he realizes I'm not going to answer, he tells the class, "Despite our class genius not knowing the answer, we took back Korea from the Japanese who'd used the war to illegally take it, so the Communists might hide out in the mountains, and we'll have to—"

With what I've been going through the last two days, I've just about had enough of his game-playing. I raise my hand.

He looks startled, but he recovers and says, "Well, it looks like our genius wants to talk after all."

I say, "The Japanese were already in Korea. They annexed it in 1910."

He frowns and says, "Is that right? Well, Mr. Smith, why don't you tell us more."

I try to keep my voice calm as I say, "After Japan surrendered, the Russians were in control of the northern part of the peninsula. The United Nations oversaw what was supposed to be a temporary division of the country at the 38th parallel. The Russians, with Chinese support, gained control over the new government of the northern part, and the United States gained control over the government of the southern part."

"Well, it seems Mr. Smith has been reading again. But he didn't answer the question. Is it going to be a mountainous—"

I say, "Korea is mostly a mountainous country, except along the coastal plains."

The teacher nods. He seems to be thinking about what to say in response to that. Finally, he says, "What Mr. Smith may not know is that after the North Koreans illegally invaded the south last year, goaded on by the Communists, *our* military genius, General MacArthur, took advantage of the coastal plains to launch a seaborne invasion and push them back into the north. Faced with MacArthur's great success, the Chinese Communists illegally invaded Korea to help the weak North Korean Army."

Then, probably to keep me from saying anything more, he quickly switches to an accounting of other past American war successes.

I know that his brief summary didn't really describe the ongoing situation in Korea. From the newspaper stories I've been reading in the school library, I doubt if things are going all that well for us over there. However, from the overly patriotic accounts in the newspapers, it's hard to say what the real situation is.

When the bell finally rings, I make my escape and hurry out of the building. I'm ready to bury myself in reading at the downtown library.

Thirty-Four

Walking to the library, the wind is so cold I'm very grateful for the coat Haru gave me. But my head and the back of my neck are still quite cold. If I only had even only a small amount of money, I could stop by the Salvation Army thrift store and buy a warm stocking hat, like the one Haru wears.

But there's no use thinking about that. I just need to hurry to the library where it's warm.

Finally inside the warm library, I see that Julie is not behind the main desk. Her father must be keeping her home again today. I again have the thought that he, and maybe the FBI, are using me as bait, and that's why he doesn't want her here.

I push that thought out of my mind and go to the philosophy bookshelf. Until they find my mother, I'm just going to keep on reading philosophy.

I look through the philosophy books, not paying much attention to author names; I'm just looking at the titles in hopes of finding something that will be involving enough to stop me thinking about Mom's situation, at least for a little while.

I find a book titled, *Beyond Good and Evil.* It's by Friedrich Nietzsche. That title reminds me of the fiction story about good and evil I wrote in English class. Is that what he's writing about? I take the book back to my little study desk.

The book's first chapter is titled, "Prejudices of Philosophers." An interesting title for something written by a famous philosopher.

As I get into that chapter, I see that he's concerned with the history of philosophy. He begins by examining philosophers' beliefs, and he disputes the idea that there is fundamental truth. He describes it as a philosopher's myth, and asks how we are to break away from that myth. He says, "Given that we want truth: why not prefer untruth?"

I put the book down to think about that. Doesn't every-body prefer truth? Do most people try to always tell the truth? Or does it vary from person to person? That seems more like a psychology question than a philosophy one. I know I don't always tell the truth; for example, I have to lie to protect the secret of where we came from and how we got into this country. So, is that a common reason for lying? Do most people lie to protect them-selves in some way?

But as I read on, I discover that isn't what Nietzsche is writing about; he thinks philosopher lie to themselves because they want to believe in some kind of basic reality. He says there is no proof for such a belief.

Reading on, it's just as I suspected: he's calling on con-cepts more related to psychology than to philosophy. He's also talking about the limitations of language, and he seems to believe we are trapped by such limitations.

I suspect that is true. We can only know what our brains are capable of knowing. Maybe I should also start studying neu-rology, as well as psychology. And I could study linguistics. As Nietzsche is suggesting, we can only express concepts that our human language abilities give us the capability of expressing.

That gets me thinking more broadly about how we think. How do I think? Do I think in words? In pictures? Or a combina-tion of both? Can I form concepts without the use of either? I'll have to think more about that later.

Suddenly, I feel like I shouldn't be wasting my time here thinking about such issues; I should be out there looking for my mother. No matter what Julie and her father advised, I should go back to the pool hall right now to find out if anybody there has heard anything.

I put the book back on the shelf and head for the library's front door. I button up Haru's coat, push open the big front door, and step out into the cold night wind.

Thirty-Five

Less than a block from the library, I start to cross a deserted street when a big black car roars around the corner and screeches to a stop in front of me. Is that the same black car I saw parked outside the library the other day? Should I run?

But before I can do anything, a man jumps out of the car and points a gun at my face. He yells, "*¡Sube al coche, chico!*"

He's saying I have to get in the car. He must be one of the Colombian drug dealers Pan was talking about. No way I'm going to get in that car. If I do, chances are, nobody will ever hear from me again.

I start backing away, but now the driver gets out of the car, and he also has a gun.

Maybe if I run away in a zig-zag path and keep my head bent forward, and they shoot, I'll only get hit in the back. I might be able to keep on running away.

But their pistols look very large. Maybe even getting shot in the back with that large a gun would kill me. Maybe I should just do what they want. Maybe they want to take me to my mother.

No, that's not likely. But what *can* I do? Maybe I should let them put me in their car and watch for opportunities to get away.

I hold up my hands.

They get on both sides of me and grab my arms.

They've almost got me to the car when I hear a gunshot.

One of them falls.

The other man turns and starts shooting into the darkness.

I can't see who is out there shooting at them.

I dive down onto the street.

There's another gunshot and the second man grabs his shoulder. He stumbles into the car and it speeds away.

I'm left sitting on the street, looking at the man who was shot. His eyes are open, and his shocked and disappointed face looks very much like the dead people I saw lying next to the road when we were escaping from Germany.

But who shot him? I stand up, but in the darkness, I can't see anybody. Could it be the police? Were they using me as bait, waiting for the Colombians to come after me?

A voice: "Is he dead?"

I know that voice. It's Pan.

Pan comes out of the darkness from behind the corner of a building. He's holding a pistol. It looks like the same gun he used to rob the poker players.

His hand is shaking, and he's still pointing the shaking gun in my general direction. I say, "Pan, lower that gun before it goes off, and you end up shooting me."

He lowers it, but his hand is still shaking. "Hey, maybe I never did shoot this pistol before, but I got 'em, didn't I?"

I point to the dead man lying on the ground. "Is that one of the Colombians?"

"Sure as hell is. And if they'd got you in that car, you'd of ended up as dead as your mother. Now comon, lets get out of here before somebody comes along."

He puts the gun in his pocket and grabs my arm. He pulls me away, moving fast.

Why did he say my mother is dead? Has he learned something new? "Pan, why did you say that? Why did you say something about my mother being dead."

"Cause she probably is. Diego told me. He found me this morning. The damn *endeble* has gone over to their side. Got real scared after they killed Esteban. He told me your mother was for sure dead and, and mine would soon be too."

"Why would they kill my mother? What good would that do them?"

He pulls me into a darkened doorway. "Listen, Curt, killing is all they know. Diego said they get what they want by killing people. To scare others into cooperating. And he said once they grab somebody, nobody ever finds their body. He said they were for sure gonna kill you too."

Despite his words, I have to try to stay calm and think clearly. No matter what he says, there's no real reason why they would want to kill my mother, or me. "You're saying they kill to try to scare people into doing what they want. But what could they want from me?"

"Diego didn't say, but I think it's because of the girl. I think they learned you were hangin' out with the head cop's daughter at the library. She's a *muy bonita* gal. Anyhow, after Diego told me that, I figured I'd better keep an eye on you."

"So you've been following me."

"Damn right I have. Good thing too."

So Pan thinks the Colombians wanted to kill me because I was friends with Officer Flynn and his daughter? More likely, they're still trying to scare Pan into cooperating with them.

"There you go, Curt, getting silent again. Thinking, right? I can almost see the wheels turning inside your head."

"I have to think this through, Pan. Mostly, I have to figure out where they took my mother."

"Jesus, just look at you, a high school kid. Two men with guns grab you, and you aren't even scared. How the hell does that brain of yours work anyhow?"

It doesn't matter what Pan thinks. I need to think through what happened here tonight, and what it might mean for my mother. "I was on my way to the pool hall, Pan. I've got to find out if anybody knows where they took my mother."

"No! Damn it, Curt. Don't go anywhere near that place. You gotta get out of sight. Don't you get it? Those Colombians are gonna keep right on tryin' to kill you. And besides, nobody at the pool hall knows anything. *Nada.* You gotta go underground, like I'm going to."

"You're going back to Puerto Rico."

"Damn right I am. You think the cops are going to take care of me after I shot a guy and left him lyin' on the street?"

"You were trying to protect me."

"They won't care what the reason was. In your cop friend's mind I'm a wanted criminal, and now a murderer. Well, no thanks. I'm goin'. And if you can figure out any way to get out of this country, you'd better go too."

If he only knew how easy that would be. All I would have to do is tell the authorities who I really am, and they 'd deport me right away. But who knows what would happen to be back there now that the Russians are in charge.

Pan pats me on the back. "Well, so long, my young *amigo*. But before I go, you gotta tell me the truth, how old are you really? Are you really a high school kid or are you an older guy who just happens to look young?"

"I'm fourteen."

He shakes his head. "No shit? Fourteen really? Well, I won't forget you, kid. I hope you make it."

He does a kind of half salute and hurries off into the darkness.

Now that I'm alone, I suddenly feel the cold wind again. Or is it fear?

No, I don't feel afraid. Pan was so frightened he was shaking. So, why didn't I feel afraid? I guess it must be because I know that being afraid won't do me any good. I need to keep my head clear and think. I remember when we were escaping from Germany, with a war going on all around us and dead men lying by the side of the road, my mother was very afraid. But I wasn't. I remember mostly thinking about what it all meant. It's the same now; even if I am in danger, I have to keep focused and use my brain to guide me through it. What is going on in this country right now feels much the same as back then. This is also a kind of war. Or at least an invasion, an invasion of illegal drugs by men with guns.

Thirty-Six

I decide Pan is right; I'd better not go to the pool hall. I should stay our of sight. I should just go home.

I head in that direction, moving as fast as I can, head down into the cold wind.

But wait. If the Colombians knew how to find me when I left the library, won't they also know where I live?

A gust of cold wind tells me I have no choice; I have nowhere else to go. Besides, if Mom does somehow manage to get away, that's where she'll go. I hurry on toward home.

But when I get there, I see clothes and bedding stacked outside the door. A pink piece of paper is tacked onto our front door. It says we've been locked out for "non payment of rent."

I try to use my key to get out of the cold, but it doesn't work. The landlord has obviously changed the lock. In this kind of run-down apartment building, in this run-down part of town, he must do this kind of eviction thing all the time. He probably has a ready supply of pink eviction notices and replacement locks. I suppose there's no use explaining to him that my mother has been kidnapped, and that's why she didn't pay the rent. Actually, I don't even know where he lives. Probably not in this part of town.

I gather up everything and stuff it all inside a pillow case.

But as soon as I turn away from the door, I realize I have no idea where to go.

I guess I could go back to the library. I let there earlier than usual tonight, so hopefully, it's still open.

When I get to the library, I can see that there are still lights on inside. I try the door, and thankfully, it opens.

But as soon as I get inside, I'm met by the sour woman who's been working the front desk. She says, "Sorry, son, we're about to close."

"Uh, I have some things here."

"What things?"

"Just some things . . . for Julie." I force the stuffed pillow case into her hands. "Could you keep it in the office for her until she comes in?"

The woman stares at the stuffed pillow case. "What is this, clothes?"

"Yes. Tell Julie I'll explain when I see her."

"I can't tell her. I won't be here when she comes in. *If* she comes in."

"Oh. Can I leave her a note then?"

"Oh, I suppose. What's your name?"

"It's Curt. Just tell her—"

"I'm not going to be your go-between, young man. I'll leave her a note that says Curt left this for you. That's all I can do."

I thank her and head for the front door.

Outside, I look up and down the street. Where should I go?

Snow is starting to fall, so I know I have to go some-where, somewhere that's under cover. But where?

I know I can't just stand here getting snowed on. I have to go somewhere. I head toward the city's main street. There should be a few stores still open at this time of night where I could get warm, at least for a little while. The pool hall will also still be open, but I suppose Pan is right about staying away from there.

But by the time I make it to the main street, I see that the stores are either already closed or just closing. Are they closing early because of the cold? Or because they heard a major snow-storm is coming? They might as well close a little early; there are no people on the street.

I wrap Haru's coat tighter around me and pull the collar up. I start walking, heading nowhere in particular, just keeping the cold wind at my back. I try walking faster, then jogging.

But the running isn't helping much; it's just way too cold to be out here.

So, where should I go? I could go to Julie's, but I sure don't want to put her in danger. Besides, if her father won't let her work at the library at night anymore because of me, I'm pretty sure he wouldn't want me showing up at their house.

What about Haru? Could I go to his house?

No, I don't want to put him in danger either. Or his mother. Besides, there's that tall metal fence all the way around where he lives. I wouldn't be able to get in.

I come to a narrow alley between buildings and turn into it. In here, at least I'll be out of the wind.

Once I'm between the tall buildings, there *is* less wind, but it's not a bit warmer. Remembering how warm I got running in PE class at school, I try running back and forth in the alley. It does make me a little warmer, but the increasing rate of snowfall is making my hair wet, and that doesn't help.

One of the stores has dumped a couple of cardboard boxes in the alley. I tear one of them apart to use as a sort of wrap-around hood and cape, but it keeps on wanting to blow off as I run.

I know I can't keep running all night. I have to find some-place out of the weather.

I go back out onto the street and try running faster.

I'm getting a bit warmer, but where am I going? I've got to find somewhere indoors to hide out until it's time to go to school in the morning.

I slow to a walk. Think. I have to use my brain. Where is there any kind of building that will be open all night?

The park! Where I went to watch the ducks. There's a boat shed where they keep the kids' paddle boats. It's got a roof, and it's enclosed on the three sides that are not facing the pond.

By the time I get to the park, my cardboard cape is start-ing to get wet from the snow, but I know I should hang onto it; its better than nothing.

The paddle boats are stacked up for the winter in the shed, but I'm able to crawl under the chain and through the boats to the back of the shed.

I huddle down in the back corner and pull the damp cardboard over me like a blanket. Okay, this place is under cover and out of the wind, but it's still really cold. Will they find me frozen to death here in the morning? Actually, it could be months before they start taking these paddle boats out into the pond again. Maybe they won't find me here until next summer, dead.

No, I can't let myself start thinking like that. All I have to do is stay awake. If it gets too cold, I can always go to the police station. If I say I know Officer Flynn, I might be able to convince them to let me stay there for a while.

But I'd never make it. Now that Pan has killed one of the Colombian drug criminals that was trying to capture me, they'll out looking for him, and me. They'll be sure to be watching the police station.

I wish I could just go to sleep and forget about everything that's happened. I can still feel the hard grips those two men had on my arms as they tried to pull me into their car. And then, there's the memory of one of them lying dead on the street, his eyes staring up at nothing. Why did that man have to die? And Esteban. What did they die for? Just for the illegal drugs business? Can they really make that much money selling drugs to the youth of this country?

And why did they capture my mother? How can that help their business? And how would killing her help them? Pan can't be right. She can't be dead. They'll have to let her go sooner or later.

Thirty-Seven

I wake up to see the first glimmers of sunlight reflecting across the pond. On no! I was supposed to stay awake all night to keep from freezing. I stand up, but I'm a bit unsteady. I'm achy all over. But I'm not dead. I guess a person can stay out in the cold all night without freezing to death. That thought makes me wonder exactly how cold the air would have to be to kill a person. I'll have to look that up.

I crawl out of the boat storage shed and do a few warm-up exercises by the water's edge. I look back at the stacked up boats in the shed. I sure don't want to spend another night in that place.

There are a few ducks huddled together, keeping warm at the base of a large tree. They look so peaceful. They have no idea of the violence that's going on in this city. And of course, they have no idea of the horrors this world has just been through in Europe and Africa and Asia. I read that something like eighty million people died in the war, over forty million in Russia alone. And about that same number in China. And it wasn't only soldiers; millions of civilians also died. To what end? What did it accomplish? And now people are dying again, in Korea. Again, what is the purpose? Wars are not logical.

As soon as I start walking, I can feel that my muscles are not working as well as usual, but being logical, at my young age, the cold and stiff feelings should soon pass. All I have to do is keep moving.

Interesting how cold affects the human body. I assume our bodies have special sense capabilities that notify us of when the air around us is colder than our body temperature. But is it equipped to tell us absolute temperature, or is it relative? In other words, does the air around me feel especially cold this morning because I'm already cold? And are there special sense capabilities that warn us not to let that kind of cold go on too long? I should read more about anatomy and physiology.

Well, what's next? Tonight I will again have to find some-where to be, somewhere safe. I might have to go ask Officer Flynn to put me in jail. Would he do that? Would he even be allowed to do that if I haven't committed a crime? I suppose if I told him I was there yesterday when a man was shot on the street, he might be willing to put me in jail while he investigates.

But right now, I do have a warm place to go: I can go to school. It'll be warm there, and I know the doors open early for students doing special projects. If the school is open, I assume the library will also be open. It's always warm in the school library. I can hide out there while I try to figure out what to do next.

I stuff the damp cardboard in one of the park trash barrels and start running toward school.

When I get to the school building, I'm gratified to see that the side door *is* open, despite the early hour. I head straight upstairs to the library, and if the librarian is surprised to see me here so early, she doesn't mention it. When she sees me go straight to the warmest place in the room, maybe she'll figure out I'm just here to get warm.

I grab a random book off a shelf, and once I'm seated, I see that the book I grabbed is on American history. I guess I should read it. It might help me understand Americans.

By the time I've read the early chapters about the Ameri-can revolution and the founding of the democratic political struc-ture, I'm finally starting to feel less chilled.

The book is not very interesting because it's intended for younger students. It glorifies the so-called "founding fathers" and the Revolutionary War, but it fails to mention the persecution and near extermination of the country's native inhabitants, and the bending of the rules of democracy to make sure the institution of slavery was maintained. It does mention that ten of the first twelve presidents were slave holders, but it doesn't comment on how much that fact influenced the making of the country's rules about its leaders get elected.

I finish that book, and grab a few philosophy books off the shelf. With all that's happened, I may not be able to concentrate as much as usual, but to keep from worrying about it all, I'll force myself to think about what the books are telling me, and nothing else.

I didn't even look at the titles of the books I grabbed, but one of them is titled *An Introduction to Existentialist Philosophy.* Interesting that I would happen to have grabbed that book. Right now, I probably *should* be thinking about existentialism.

The book says nineteenth century philosophers, Søren Kierkegaard and Friedrich Nietzsche were among the pioneers of existentialist thought. Kierkegaard was a poet and a theologian, so of course, much of his philosophy has to do with morality. He wrote about personal choice and commitment, oddly often using different pseudonyms to explore complex issues problems from different viewpoints.

Nietzhe, on the other hand, was German philosopher and poet who said "God is Dead." By that, he meant that Christian faith, as practiced, forced people into judgmental roles, what he saw as definitely not the Christian ideal. He saw Christianity as "a religion of pity," and he believed that deprived us of moral strength. But he also rejected nihilism, because some nihilists suggest that life is meaningless and true knowledge is impossible. With the pointless killing in the endless wars, and now that there is even more killings as part of the battles between drug dealers, it would be tempting to adopt that view. But I can't let myself buy into that. I have to believe studying and learning have value, and will always lead to greater understanding, which will lead to us making better decisions. Some nihilists believe that a life of pleasure is the only logical response to the madness of the world. But they are making an overly simple deduction; we have to believe there is value in something, otherwise, what is life about. I believe I can find value in studying and learning, and I enjoy doing it. Rather than rejecting what I do in life, learning, just because I have troubles, I know I can find refuge in it.

When I look up from my reading, the clock on the wall tells me it's almost time to go to my first class, English. I wish my first class was PE. Today, I'd like to run and run until I'm hot and sweaty, and then I could take a really long hot shower.

But I know I need to go through the normal school day routine—I have nowhere else to be that's warm.

I get up and head for the English classroom. By the time I get there, a few students are already in their seats, and as usual, they stare at me as I make my way to the back of the room.

As soon as the teacher arrives, she announces that since we all did such a poor job of writing fiction, we're going to do it again. But this time, she will specify the subject. She says we have to write a fully fictional story about a person who has to solve a problem about money.

The rest of the class groans, but it sounds interesting to me. I wonder if the teacher is having money problems.

I try to think what kind of a story to write. I guess I no longer care if the teacher thinks I copied it from somewhere, so I'll try to write something that interests me. But what kind of story can I write about money? I have no money. I've never had any money.

I look around the class. Most of the others are doing the same thing I am, thinking. Only one girl is writing. I wonder what she's writing about. Something to do with her parents' money problems, maybe?

No, don't starting thinking about parents. Write about something else.

I look up and see that the teacher is staring at me. Is she watching me to make sure I'm not copying anything out of my notebook? I tear a page out of my notebook, and put it on the floor. Then, I just start writing, beginning with a random thought. I'll see where it goes:

George woke up worrying about money. If he pay the rent by the time the landlord came this afternoon, he'd be out on the street.

Interesting. I just started writing random words, and my mind took me into my own situation. That's all right; I'm not going to write anything autobiographical, but I can use that first sentence as a story starter.

George decided he'd just better get out of bed right now and go find a way to get the money. It's the middle of the winter, so there is no way he can let himself get evicted and end up on the streets.

George walked the cold streets, trying to decide what to do. It was windy, and he had the feeling it was the kind of wind that came just before it starts snowing.

After walking aimlessly for quite a while, George realized he was standing in front of his bank. They knew him at this bank. He has an account here, and it wasn't that long ago that the account had some money in it. Sure, he'd lost his job, but so had a lot of other men. Times are hard. Surely this bank would give him a loan until he could find another job.

George walked into the bank and went right up to a man behind a desk. "Good morning," he said. "You know me. I have an account here. I'm in need of a small loan. Just enough to pay my rent today."

The man didn't seem to want to smile, and that worried George a bit. He was a short man, wearing a brown suit, and George was pretty sure the man's unusually black hair had been recently dyed that color.

Finally, the man smiled. A bit. "Yes, sir. And what are you proposing to use as collateral?"

George knew what collateral was. But he also knew he didn't have any. "Well," he said, "since I'm a long-time account holder here, I didn't think I would need any collateral. I'm just looking for a short-term loan."

The man stopped smiling. "I'm sorry, sir. We don't make those kinds of loans here. Maybe another bank."

George tried to think of another argument, but the way the man kept avoiding looking at him, he knew it was hopeless. He silently turned away and left the bank.

The teacher is still watching me write. Why? There is no way I could be copying anything. But there's nothing I can do about what she thinks. There's no way to assure her that what I'm writing really is my story.

Or is there? I wonder what she would think if I throw a surprise into the story, a surprise that's obviously my own addition. Well, why not? It's only a story.

George walked down the street, trying to think what to do. He knew it was a waste of time to go to another bank to try to get a loan.

Or was it? They all have money, plenty of money.

He saw another bank just ahead. Maybe it's the one.

He walked into the bank. It was larger than the other one.

He walked right up to the first teller, a nice-looking blonde girl.

He smiled and said, "I need a hundred dollars to pay my rent."

She smiled back at him. Of course. DO you have your bank book?"

"Oh no, I don't have an account here. I just need a hundred dollars. It's not much. A bank this big must have plenty of money. Surely you can spare me a hundred dollars."

She was still trying to smile, but now she seemed unsure. "Maybe I'd better call my manager," she said, starting to turn away.

George reached out and grabbed her arm. He smiled his best smile. "No need for that. Just give me the hundred dollars."

"But sir, what am I supposed to say when they ask me—"

George continued to smile. "Small bills will be fine."

Now the girl looked a bit scared.

George pointed to her cash drawer. "Just open that drawer and count out one hundred dollars. That's all you have to do."

The girl did as she was told. She was shaking as she did it.

George put the money into his pocket and walked right out the front door.

George had only made it a block before he heard sirens coming, so he put on his invisibility cloak.

The End

When the bell rings, the teacher tells us to bring our papers forward and put them on her desk. Most of others are still grumbling as they do it.

I drop my paper on her desk and try to leave quickly, but she calls out, "Not you, Mr. Smith. You wait here until I've read your paper."

"But I have to get to my next class."

"No, you will wait right here. I can give you a note for your next teacher."

I stand in front of her desk while she reads my story. Why is she making me wait here? Does she again think I somehow cheated? If she thinks I wrote down a story I'd previously read somewhere, she's going to be in for a surprise when she gets to the end.

She's shaking her head as she reads. I wonder why.

But when she comes to the ending, she jumps to her feet and throws my paper down on her desk. "What do you think you're pulling, Smith? Are you trying to make some kind of statement that you're somehow above doing this assignment?"

She's waiting for an answer, getting more and more red in the face.

I don't think there's anything I can say that would assuage her anger.

She shakes her finger at me. "Don't think I don't know what you are doing, young man. You're flaunting my authority, and you're making sure I know it."

She's furious at me. But with what could be happening to my mother right now, what does it matter? In fact, how can anything matter now. How does this compare with the murder of Esteban? And what about what Pan did last night, shooting that man? Or for that matter, with all the trouble in the world? In places like Korea, men are killing each other, and they don't even know why. For some general's glory? Or for some politician's need to get reelected? I shouldn't even bother with her nonsense. I should just walk right out of this room.

As if the teacher read my thought, she says, "Oh, just get out of here. I don't care anymore."

I turn to leave, but when I glance back, I see that she's seated at her desk, leaning forward with her head in her hands.

Oh damn. I didn't mean to do that. Now I guess I have to try to fix it.

I go back in. "I'm sorry, ma'am. I didn't mean to question your authority. Actually, I think you're a pretty good teacher. I was just having fun with the story."

She looks up, surprised. "So, now you're feeling sorry for me? Telling me I'm a *pretty good* teacher." She points toward the door. "Didn't I tell you to get the hell out of my classroom?"

I quickly leave and hurry down the hall to my next class. I feel bad that I upset her. I shouldn't let my troubles affect how I deal with people.

I should just go to my next class, Math, and sit quietly. It's the most boring class of the day because the teacher only lets us study algebra rules, simple rules everybody should have learned the first week of class.

When I walk into the room, the teacher is at the blackboard, as usual. When he notices me come in, without turning away from the blackboard, he says, "Nice of you to show up, Mr. Smith."

It's what he always says when a student arrives late. I could tell him I was held in my prior class, but what would be the use? I just go to my usual seat in the back row, prepared to ignore his boring algebraic rule-making.

On second thought, I should pay close attention to whatever he's saying. I can expand on whatever math he's talking about, and imagine how it could be used to explore theories in physics. After all, Newton invented calculus to help describe motion, and Einstein used tensor calculus to extend the special theory's global Lorentz covariance.

Listening to the teacher's lecture, and then using what he's saying to imagine how it could be expanded to relate to theoretical physics, works well enough to get me thought the hour.

I even take a few notes in my notebook about things to look up at the library. If the teacher notices me taking notes, for the first time, he doesn't mention it.

When it's finally time for PE class, I take my still-sweaty gym clothes out of my locker and hurry up the circular metal stairs to the gym. It's still too cold to go outside, so the coach once again has us choose up sides for relay races.

While we wait to be chosen on a team, one boy who is quite a bit bigger than me, starts pushing me around. When I don't fight back, he says, "What's the matter genius boy, got a big mouth but can't take it?"

The coach comes and pulls the two of us up in front of the whole class. As he always does when two boys get into it, he makes us put on boxing gloves. He tells us to settle our differences right now, in front of the whole class.

As soon as we have the boxing gloves on, the boy starts throwing wild punches at me. I easily avoid them. But when he continues to try to hit me, for some reason, his stupidly wild attacks irritate me. I hit the boy in the face.

I must have punched him harder than I intended, because he goes reeling backward and falls right through the flimsy dividing partition that separates the boys side of the gym from the girls side.Some of the girls scream at the sudden intrusion into their volleyball game, but then they all start laughing.

The boy scrambles to his feet, and I expect him to rush back at me, but he doesn't. Instead, red-faced, he throws down the boxing gloves and rejoins the rest of the students.

I try to go to him to apologize, but he avoids me. He won't even look at me. I'm sorry that I did that to him. Once again, I've let my troubles get the better of me.

The coach patches up the dividing partition, and then, as if nothing at all had happened, tells us to go back to choosing our running teams.

I spend the next hour running as hard as I can, much harder than the rest of the students who are all dogging it, making a joke out of the races.

The coach is watching me. He may be wondering why I hit that boy so hard and why I'm running so hard. But he doesn't say anything.

When the coach tells us that's enough for today and orders us to the showers, I hurry to be the first one into the shower. I turn the water up as hot as I can stand it, and I stay under the water until all the other boys have finished and left the locker room.

Finally, I begin to notice how hungry I am and realize I haven't had anything to eat since school lunch yesterday.

I get out of the shower, get dressed quickly, and hurry to the lunch room.

Knowing this will be my only meal of the day, I fill up my tray with as much food as I think I can eat. Although I know it's against the rules for those of us on the free lunch program to take food out of the cafeteria, I also grab a couple of apples, hoping I can find a way to hold onto them for later.

The cashier lady doesn't seem to notice the extra two apples, but she does notice that my free-lunch ticket expires today, the last day of the month. She tells me to remind my parents to get me the new one for next month.

I take my tray full of food to my usual hidden-away eating place and start stuffing down the food.

"Hey there, Curt. You sure do look hungry today."

It's Haru. I've never seen him in the cafeteria before.

He doesn't have a tray with food. Instead, he has a green tin lunch box with red flowers painted on it. He opens it and takes out a couple of carefully-wrapped sandwiches. I notice he also has an apple.

I say, "Yes, I like to eat as much as I can here on my free ticket so my mother doesn't have to buy as much food."

Haru nods. "I get it. How is your mother? From what I heard that cop say, I had the feeling she was in some kind of trouble. Won't you tell me?"

Should I tell him? After all, he is my only friend.

"She's missing, Haru, and I'm really worried about her."

"Missing? What the hell does that mean? Did she—"

"She was taken, but I'm going to have to wait and tell you about it later, Haru. It's . . . complicated."

"Okay, but what are the police doing about it? Are they looking for her?"

"Like I said, it's better that you don't know. I'll tell you about it when I can."

"Well, okay. But hey, why don't you take one of my sandwiches. I'm not very hungry anyhow."

"No, Haru, I won't do that, but you could help me sneak these two apples out of here in your green box."

"Will do, old buddy."

He looks around and quickly puts the apples into his box.

"Hey," he says, "what you needs to do is come home with me after school today. Get some good eats. Remember, my mom cooks for Mr. Hansen and his wife, and she always makes too much." He leans close to me and whispers, "After all, they're paying for it, so why not?"

He winks at me, but I don't feel like pretending to be in on his little secret, so I just say, "Okay," and keep on eating. But I wouldn't mind going to his house after school, not so much for the food as for the likely warmth.

After we are done eating, out in the hallway, he gives me my two swiped apples. I put them into my pockets for later.

In the rest of my day's classes, I'm finding I can hardly pay any attention at all. I can't even switch my mind into thinking about physics, because I keep on trying to imagine any reason why they would be holding my mother. What do they expect to gain from it?

In my last class of the day, the history teacher is again talking about the Korean war. Unlike his previous patriotic and optimistic mentions of the war, this time he admits that things are not going very well over there now. He says, "Now that the Chinese have illegally entered the war, it seems there 's no stopping them. That is, unless our forces wise up an drop a couple of atom bombs on their heads. That'll teach 'em who's boss."

He's just getting into explaining why people who say using nuclear weapons would be a bad idea are dead wrong when a woman I don't recognize comes into the room and whispers something to him.

She waits by the door while he points at me and says, "Mr. Smith, you are go to the school office immediately."

I get up and follow the woman out of the room. Of course, all of the other students are staring at me as I go. I try not to show any reaction.

As I follow the woman down the hallway, I try to imagine what this could be about. Did they finally find out about my illegal status in this country, or could it be something about my mother?

The woman leads me into the office and then into a small room where I see Officer Flynn waiting.

What would make him come here to pull me out of class? Did he find my mother? Or could he have found out I was there last night when Pan shot those two Colombians?

After the woman leaves us alone in the room, he has me sit down, and then he says, "I'm afraid I have some bad news for you, Curt. We found out what happened to your mother."

I brace myself for what he's about to say

He says, "A young man showed up at the hospital emergency room last night bringing in another man who was suffering from a gunshot wound. Of course, the hospital called me, but the FBI immediately took over the case. After they brought in a Spanish-speaking translator, we learned the young man was Colombian. He was a low-level member of a Colombian drug cartel, and he had been assigned to bring the wounded man to the hospital. He said he didn't even know how the man was shot, but under questioning he admitted he knew quite a bit about what the other members of the cartel were up to. He said he knew that they had once killed a man named Esteban, and he knew they had recently killed another woman. I'm sorry, Curt, but from his description of the woman, I think he was describing your mother."

He stops talking. He seems to be waiting for me to say something, but what is there to say? Maybe he's waiting for me to cry or something, but what good would that do? Because of what Pan told me, I guess part of me was already expecting she could be dead. They'd killed Esteban as a warning, so why wouldn't they kill her too for the same reason?

He reaches out to pat me on my shoulder, and of course that makes me feel even more like crying.

But I won't do that. If she's really dead, I'm all alone in this country now. I have to be strong.

He says, "I'm very sorry, Curt. But the good news is the young man told us where the Colombians were. The FBI swarmed in, and I think they got them all. At least it means you can try to get back to living some sort of normal life. You can go to the library after school without having to always be looking over your shoulder. And I told Julie she can go back to her normal night shift now. And she's been wanting to get back to studying with you. She's been saying it wasn't fair that I'd been keeping her in at night. But you understand why I had to do that, don't you?"

I nod, and that seems to be enough for him.

He says, "She'll be back to her normal hours at the library tonight. He stands up. "Well, again, I'm really sorry, Curt." Then, he surprises me by reaching out to shake my hand. I have the feeling he want to say something more, but after holding onto my hand for a long moment, he turns and leaves the room.

I stay seated there for quite a while. I'm not sure for how long, but when I hear a bell ring, I know it means the school day is over. I should hurry downtown to the library to see if Julie is there yet.

But then I change my mind. No, not yet. First, I need to think about Officer Flynn just told me. I head upstairs to the school library.

Once in the library, I head for the reading table that's at warmest place in the room.

There's a world history book on the table. With what's currently going on in the post-war world, that might be interesting, but I can't read it right now. Right now, I'm overwhelmed with the thought that if my mother is really dead, it means I'm completely alone in this country. Because she worked such long hours, I rarely got to see her, but her presence in our little apartment was always there. It wasn't only that she paid the rent, I know she was always thinking of me. Every morning when I'd wake up, I'd see the box of cereal she always left on the kitchen table for me.

No, I've got to stop thinking about things like that. It's not logical and will only bring pointless tears.

I pick up the world history book. If it's true that she's dead, and now I guess there's no reason to believe she isn't, I should just keep my focus on studying. It's the only thing I'm good at.

I know what I'm going to find in the world history book, stories of wars. World history is mostly about war and changes that were the aftereffects of war. But there is another thing that often results in worldwide change—avarice. Historically, European countries built huge armies and navies to try to control world commerce. So, is this drug business, and the resulting killing of people, a new type of war? Is it going to grow into a new type of worldwide economic war?

Thirty-Eight

I'm almost finished with a fast read of the world history book when I see Haru come in the library door. As he comes down the aisle between the bookshelves, I quickly wipe away the wetness on my cheeks. I don't think he noticed.

I guess now that Haru is done with school for today, I guess he wants me to come to his home with him. I guess I might as well go there for a while before I head for the downtown library. It'll be good to get some hot food and be warm for a while. Now that Officer Flynn says the FBI has captured the drug dealers, my presence shouldn't put him and his mother in danger. Maybe I should ask him if I can stay with him for a while, at least until I can figure out where to go next. I sure don't want to spend another cold night outdoors.

I guess I could go back down to Florida. I don't know anybody there, but at least it would be warm if I have to live outdoors.

Haru is all smiles as he comes to sit down next to me. "I figured I find you here. And look what you're reading now. World history. Every time I see you, you're studying something different. Is that what you geniuses do?"

"Well, with the Korean war maybe about to turn into another world war, I thought I'd better read up on how wars start."

"So, it's a book about wars?"

"Much of any book on world history will be about wars. Wars change history, change borders, and maybe even more importantly, change attitudes."

He grins and says, "Well, what's important to me right now is going home to get some of my mom's good cookin'. Whatta ya say? And then, we could play some pool up at the big house."

"Sounds good, Haru. I really appreciate it."

As we walk to his home, he jabbers on about things he saw or heard at school today. He especially wants to tell me everything he heard about me. He says, "A lot of people are talkin' about how you knocked that bully for a loop."

"I just punched him once, Haru, and he fell backwards. He caught me in a bad mood."

Haru laughs. "You? In a bad mood? I've never seen you in any mood, good or bad. You always seem to be inside your head, thinkin'. So, what happened? Did he attack you?"

"No, he was just pushing me around in gym class. Trying to get me to react."

"I bet I know what happened next. The coach made the two of you put on the boxing gloves, didn't he?"

I nod.

"Yeah, that's what he always does. When I first came to this school, some of the boys would pick on me and call me a dirty Jap. When the coach put the gloves on us, I always got hit a few times. But that was okay. Those gloves are pretty thick, so I didn't get hurt. After a few times, when I didn't fight back, the coach made the bullies fight each other. That pretty much put a stop to it."

I decide not to comment on the subject. Better to just let it drop, so Haru doesn't think of me as a fighter, which I am not.

After only a few moments of silence, Haru starts jabbering about his day at school. He says he heard something about me insulting the English teacher. Apparently, the other students like to talk about me. But then, maybe Haru encourages them.

By the time we get to the tall black iron fence that surrounds the Hansen property, he's pretty much given me the whole accounting of everything he did at school today, and everything he heard.

Thankfully, inside his little house, it's quite warm, probably somewhat because of the huge stove and oven that dominates their kitchen.

Haru's mother seems happy to see me and tells me to sit down at the kitchen table. She says she's heating up the salmon and vegetables and fresh bread she made for them up at the big house today.

As soon as she opens the oven door to take it out, the mixed food odors fills the room. It makes my mouth water, even though I ate quite a bit at school lunch at noon. I wonder if my being so cold last night could be making my body crave nourishment. I'll have to read up on that.

While we eat, Haru's mother insists that he tell her everything that happened at school today, so Haru launches into it. He leaves out the part about me punching the bully in gym class. Maybe he doesn't want his mother to think of me being a fighter.

We've barely finished eating when Haru stands up and says we should go up to the big house for an after-supper game of pool.

I offer to help his mother clean up the dishes, but she says "No way. You boys should just go play and get out of my way."

As Haru leads me up the winding path to the Hansen house, it's starting to snow, and this time, it looks as if it might stick. I again start to think about asking Haru if he has a couch where I could spend the night. I'm not sure I can face the idea of spending another cold night outdoors. But I decide to wait until we've finished playing pool.

After several games of pool, I see through the small window that it's starting to snow harder outside. I guess I'd better ask him about staying at his house tonight. "I have to tell you something, Haru. It's about my mother."

Oh, what?"

But before I can say anything more, Mr. Hansen comes in through the door at back of the room. He says, "Hello, boys. Having a game of pool?"

Haru tries to hide the bottle of orange soda behind his back, but I have the feeling Mr. Hansen doesn't care how much soda he drinks.

Mr. Hansen says, "And I see you brought your genius friend along. Curt wasn't it? Are you a good pool player?"

"No, sir. I'm just learning the game."

He says, "Is that right? Well, how about I show you a few things. In my day, I was a pretty good pool player."

He goes to the rack on the wall, selects a pool cue, and says, "Okay, Haru, rack 'em up."

After Haru arranges the pool balls into the normal triangle shape, Mr. Hansen knocks the white ball into the colorful balls, spreading them all over the table. One of the striped balls goes into a pocket, and he proceeds to knock in two more striped balls before he misses. He really is a good pool player.

We play a few more games, with Mr. Hansen winning them all, before he looks at me and says, "Well, I guess you'd better get going, Curt. With how hard it's snowing outside, your family might be worried about you getting home."

Haru quickly says, "Yes, sir. It is starting to get dark out there. We'll better be going now."

Mr. Hansen says, "Good idea, Haru. But I can't let Curt here walk home in this snowstorm. I'll drive him home before it gets too bad."

Haru quickly leaves, and Mr. Hansen leads me into his house. He stops at the foot of some carpeted stairs and calls up, "Kath, I'm going to drive Haru's friend home. I won't be long."

A very attractive woman with short blond hair appears at the top of the stairs. She's wearing a pretty dress that's very colorful, like crushed blue-green flowers. She seems to be quite a bit younger than Mr. Hansen. She waves to me and says, "Hello, young man. What's your name?"

"It's Curt, ma-am."

"Oh, you're Haru's friend from school. His mother has been telling me you're supposed to be very smart. A genius even."

I don't know what to say to that. And I don't know how to tell Mr. Hansen that I don't need a ride home because I don't have a home to go to.

I guess I'd better just blurt it out and go see if Haru will let me sleep on his couch. "Actually, I appreciate you offering to give me a ride home, sir, but I don't have a home to go to."

Both Mr. and Mrs. Hansen seem startled by my words.

Mr. Hansen is the first to recover. He says, "What do you mean, son? No home?"

"It's complicated, sir. The police say my mother was kidnapped, and now I've been locked out of our apartment because she wasn't there to pay the rent."

Mrs. Hansen comes part way down the stairs and says, "The police are saying your mother was kidnapped?" She looks at her husband. "Edward, find out what this boy is talking about, right now!" She goes back up to the top of the stairs, but once there, she turns back to say, "And do not let this boy go out into this snowstorm. He will stay here tonight."

Mr. Hansen says, "Right, dear. I was just thinking the same thing." He turns to me. "Come with me to my office, Curt."

I'm not sure why he wants me to go to his office with him, but I'm very grateful for their offer of a place to stay tonight.

I follow him down a long hallway and up another flight of carpeted stairs at the back of the house. He leads me into a large office. One whole wall is a bookshelf filled with books. From what I can see, almost all of the books seem to be about engineering.

He has me sit down and sits in a chair opposite me. He says, "All right now, son, tell me what happened."

"All I know, sir, is that some drug dealers, part of what is known as a cartel, came here from South America, and they're trying to establish their illegal drug business in this country."

Mr. Hansen holds up his hand. "Now wait a minute, son, what would your mother have to do with any of that?"

"Nothing at all, sir, but it may have been some kind of warning. They have been killing associates of a local drug dealer. Apparently, they thought I was one of his friends."

"Why would they think that?"

"I met him by chance, and they must have been watching. I guess they thought I was . . . I don't know, allied with him in some way."

"But you weren't?"

"No, absolutely not. In fact, I tried to stay completely away from him, but he kept finding me."

Now Mr. Hansen looks worried. "And are these South American drug dealers after you now?"

"No. The police told me they've captured them all."

"Well, I'm very glad to hear that. But I'm very, very sorry your mother got caught up in all that."

I start to tell him how much I miss her, but I can't seem to get the words out. I don't want to cry in front of this nice man, but I'm having trouble holding it back. I'm sure my eyes are tearing up, but although I'm determined not to cry, holding back the tears is getting very hard. Until this moment, I guess I hadn't fully accepted that she really might be dead, and I'll never see her again.

He reaches out to pat my knee. "I understand, son. I lost my own mother, to cancer, when I was about your age. Maybe a little older. How old are you?"

"I'm fourteen, sir."

He shakes his head. "So young to have to be going through all that. Well, let's get you to your room. It's right next to this office, so I hope my typing in here doesn't keep you awake."

"No, sir, it won't." I stand up, but I know it's too early to be able to get to sleep without anything to read, so I say, "Actually, I usually read myself to sleep, but I don't have anything to read." I point at his wall of books. "Could I borrow . . ."

"Certainly. Take any book want, but I'm afraid they are all pretty much about engineering and such. They might not interest you."

"That's all right. I like reading about new things."

He smiles and says, the top shelf are the newest books. The others are from my college days."

I select two books from the top shelf and one from a middle shelf. I thank him, and he leads me out of the office and into the next room. It contains a large bed with an expensive-looking bedspread on it. It makes me realize I haven't slept in real bed since we stayed in those motels on our way from Florida to this city.

Mr. Hansen tells me he will come and get me in the morning for breakfast. He apologizes that all they will have for breakfast is cereal with fruit.

Not wanting to admit how long it's been since I actually ate a real breakfast, I tell him cereal will be fine.

"All right. And you can watch that TV if you want to. There are no other occupied rooms in this wing of the house, so nobody will bother you."

After he leaves me alone in the large bedroom, and I think about turning on the TV. I haven't seen TV for a long time, but I can't imagine what I would want to watch right now.

As I take off my clothes, I remember the two apples in my pockets. How odd that the one time I decide to get some extra food, I'm not going to need it.

I pull back the bed's covers and start to crawl in, but the bed looks so white and so clean, I'm not sure I should spoil it. But then, I did take a long shower after gym class today at school, so I guess I'm not dirty. I crawl in and pull the covers up to my chin.

What a feeling! I'm lying in a soft bed. My couch at home was lumpy and uncomfortable, but I never thought much about that; it just was what it was.

For some reason, being in a warm house that doesn't smell like coal gas, and being in a very comfortable bed, feels strangely symbolic, as if it's an indication of a significant change happening in my life. But I shouldn't take any of this comfort for granted.

Maybe Mr. Hansen only offered me a place to stay for tonight because it's so cold and snowy outside.

Lying on my back in the comfortable bed, as I stare up into the darkness, I can hardly believe this is the same day. Was it only last night that I almost froze to death hiding out in the park's boat storage place? And was it only yesterday that Pan shot those men that were trying to kidnap me? And that led to one of them being taken to the hospital, which led the FBI to their hideout?

Now I'm here, suddenly warm and comfortable in a big house owned by a nice couple. I wonder why they are being so kind to me. They really don't know anything about me.

One thing is for certain, no matter how nice they are to me, I can never tell them about where I came from. They wouldn't understand the violence and chaos in Germany, and why my mother had to get us out of that, mainly for my benefit. And now if she really is gone, there is no way anybody can ever find out about where I came from. I'll stick to the story that my mother came here from Germany as a child.

So now, that part of my life is over. From this moment on, whatever happens, I will no longer be German. I will be an American. After all, except for the native American Indians, everybody in this country came from somewhere else.

I lie still in the darkness with my eyes closed. I might as well get to sleep and try to think through it all in the morning.

But it doesn't take long before I know the myriad of thoughts in my head are going to keep me from going to sleep. I turn on the bedside light and open the first of Mr. Hansen's books. It's a textbook on mechanical engineering. I guess that must be what Mr. Hansen's college degree was in. The opening paragraph of the books says mechanical engineering is the most diverse and versatile field of engineering, and it plays a critical role in the world's industries, including construction, power generation, and transportation. It says mechanical engineers design and build devices and machines, systems that are the cornerstones of our industrialized society.

Mr. Hansen wasn't sure I'd be interested in his books, but this is interesting reading, and even better, something I don't know about.

The book goes on to explain the various different disciplines within the field of mechanical engineering. I quickly read through each of them.

As soon as I finish that book, I start on the next one. This book is even more interesting because it's a book of readings from within the field.

It doesn't take me long to finish that one, and although I suspect it's getting pretty late, I open the third book. It's titled "The Science of Mechanics." I'm thinking I should just look at the first few pages and go to sleep, but the very first paragraph is enough to draw me in. It says, "The term 'mechanics' applies to a branch of physics regarding the actions of forces, but in this book, we will be dealing with how machinery and mechanical devices are used to apply those forces." The book goes on to remind the reader that it is we humans that created machines for physical purposes, and it is that machinery that led to what we refer to as our modern society. It says the story of mechanics is the story of how we humans developed machines to augment our physical abilities, and it is each new machine era that led to each new era of human progress.

I finish the book and put it down. I look up at the ceiling to think about why I enjoy reading about such things, even if they aren't within my main focus of interest. I guess I just like thinking about concepts. I like grappling with abstract ideas and underlying principles, no matter what field they are from. To me, concepts are the building blocks of all knowledge.

Thirty-Nine

The morning sunlight coming through the big window wakes me up. Not wanting to wake the Hansens, I decide to not leave this room until I hear them up and moving around. I get dressed and turn on the TV, but I keep the volume very low. When it comes on, it's only children's cartoons.

I turn the numbered dial and discover there is another channel, and it's showing local news. After a man finishes showing a weather map to indicate where the most of the snow is falling, another man comes on to describe how the war in Korea is going. He just describes where the fighting is occurring. I get the feeling he's tired of always having to report American losses. The man seems to be middle aged, so he might have previously reported on American successes in the world war. If so, it's easy to understand why he'd be disappointed in how poorly they are doing in Korea. It must be hard for him to report that the Communists captured the capital of Korea, Seoul.

I've read there are peace talks going on, but they don't seem to be going anywhere. Nevertheless, it seems like everybody in this country just wants this pointless war to be over

When I hear Mr. Hansen stirring in his office next door, I quickly turn off the TV and go in there.

He's standing at his desk, looking down at some papers. He seems to be lost in thought, so I'm not sure I should interrupt him.

But then, he notices me and looks up. He smiles. "Good morning, Curt. How did you sleep?"

After he's been so nice, I don't want to tell him I had trouble sleeping in his very comfortable bed, so I stayed awake for a long time reading. I just say, "Fine. Thank you, sir."

"Well then, let's get you downstairs for some breakfast."

He leads me downstairs to small dining room that's off the kitchen.

I see Mrs. Hansen busy in the kitchen, and as soon as we are seated at the table, she brings each of us a large bowl that contains some kind of commercial breakfast flakes, imbedded with raisins and topped with slices of apple and banana.

I take one bite and say, "Thank you. This is very good."

She waves off my compliment. "It's only cereal and some fruit. I'm not much into cooking. Haru's mother is the cook. She's good at it, and she enjoys it."

After a few more bites, I realize how hungry I am. I quickly eat all of it.

I look up to see Mrs. Hansen smiling at me. She says, "Well, I can see you were hungry. Tell me, young man, how long since you had anything to eat?"

"Not that long ago, ma'am. Haru's mother gave me something to eat yesterday afternoon."

"Ah, yes. She's quite a good cook, isn't she? She told me that when they were imprisoned in that awful camp, they never had near enough to eat."

Mr. Hansen says, "That was an atrocious act on the part of our government. It never should have happened. After the Japanese bombed Pearl Harbor, the U.S. government went along with the anti-Japanese feelings in the nation, so they took anybody with a Japanese name out of the West Coast on locked them up in desolate camps. Even long-time U.S. citizens. Believe it or not, they even took Japanese children out of orphanages and sent them to the camps. That proves it was pure racism. By the way, they didn't bother locking up any Germans." He hesitates as if he's waiting for me to respond.

I say, "Yes, Haru told me about being in that camp. A terribly unfair and illegal thing to do." I stop and wait to see if he's going to say anything else. I know I'd better not say any more, especially now that he's mentioned Germans.

He glances at the large watch on his wrist. "But now, you'd better get going. It's time you and Haru were getting on to school. There's a little build up of snow out there. Do you need me to drive you boys?"

I stand up. "No, it's not far. We'll be fine."

Mrs. Hansen shakes her head. "Well, you're not going anywhere dressed like that, young man. Wait right here."

She hurries out of the room.

Mr. Hansen watches her go, then turns back to me. "I see you're wearing that old coat of Haru's. Will that be warm enough?"

"Oh yes, sir. It's quite warm. It was nice of Haru to give it to me. He said you gave him a new one."

"Yes, and I think maybe you'll need a new one too. I'll see what I can do."

Mrs. Hansen is soon back. She hands me a red stocking cap and waits for me to try it on. It seems to fit fine, and it feels quite warm.

"Oh dear," she says. "Maybe young boys your age wouldn't want to be seen wearing a red hat."

"Oh, that's no problem, ma'am. It's fine."

"Well, I hope so. And wear these warm gloves. Red also, I'm afraid."

I try on the gloves. They're a bit tight, but I'm sure they'll be quite warm.

"And this is what will really keep you warm." She wraps a thick red and black scarf around my neck, and then surprises me by giving me quick little hug.

Mr. Hansen smiles and says, "Well, we'd better get a move on."

As I follow him out of the room, his wife call after us, "Now, I'll expect you back here right after school."

I turn back. "All right, but first I have to go to the library. I have some studying to do there."

"Fine," she says, "but try to get here by six-thirty. That's when we eat."

As Mr. Hansen walks me down to the back entrance through the basement pool room, I'm still thinking about why they might be being so nice to me. They hardly know me.

As we get to the back door, Mr. Hansen says, "Now you be careful out there, Curt. And as my wife said, try to be back here by supper time."

I go down the path to Haru's house, and he meets me at his door. He touches my red stocking cap. "Cool outfit, old buddy. And check out that scarf. Mrs. Hansen give that to you?"

"Yes, she did. They're being very nice to me."

Haru nods. "Sure they are. They've always been nice to me too. It's cause they don't have any kids of their own. Mom thinks something's wrong with her that makes it so she can't have kids."

For some reason, talking about that makes Haru go quiet as we walk to the gate in the fence.

Is he thinking about this own family's troubles, the hard life they had in the government camp? I expect he thinks about that a lot. Sometimes I think mother and I had a hard life, but that was only because we had a hard time escaping from Germany when we were constantly on the move and had very little money. Before then, in Germany, despite the war going on, my life wasn't really all that hard. There was a lot of talk about the enemy getting closer, and there were always planes going over and the sound of distant bombs going off, but our little town never got hit. School was on hold, but I always found something to read. In fact, the morning after our neighbor disappeared, I found a stack of books outside our front door. She had been a teacher, and she always liked me, so I knew it must have been her that left the books for me. At the time, I wondered why she went away, but once I got a little older, remembering her contempt for the Nazis, I knew they must have taken her away.

When we get to school, Haru says, "I suppose you're going up to the library, as usual. See ya."

On my way upstairs, several boys point and make fun of my red stocking cap and red gloves. I just ignore them. I'm happy for the increased warmth, and I'm not going to take them off, even indoors. Being warm is what matters, not the color.

By the time I get into the library, I know I won't have much time for reading this morning. Searching random shelves, I run across a book with the strange title, *One, Two, Three...Infinity.* Inside, it says it's about facts and speculations of science. I wonder why it wasn't on the science shelf. This shelf seems to contain a variety of off books. I wonder if it's books that the librarian wasn't exactly sure where they should go.

Standing next to the bookshelf, I open the book to read the title page. It says it was published in 1947. Interesting to find a book in this school library that was published only four years ago, soon after the end of the war.

The book starts out by saying it's an attempt to collect the most interesting facts and theories of modern science. It says it's going to cover atoms, stars, and nebulae, and whether light can be bent by gravity.

The first chapter goes into the history of numbers, which is interesting, but it's not what I'm looking for. He mentions the difficulty of writing very large numbers, such as the number of atoms in the universe. The author says those kinds of very large numbers required the invention of numeric notations like "to the power of." He says a good example is "ten to the power of one hundred," which means the number one followed by one hundred zeros.

The next chapter, "Space, time, and Einstein," sounds more like what I'm looking for. It mentions Euler's polyhedral formula for polyhedrons projected onto a sphere. I've run across mentions of that in my prior reading of physics books, but I don't know why it's important in the history of science. I'll have to look that up later in other books.

The book goes on to talk about space-time intervals being measured with the Pythagorean theorem.

The book gives an example of a bus going down a street, saying it represents a moving point of reference and requires a rotation of the four-dimensional axis-cross. Again, that's going to require more reading, and seems important enough that I'm almost tempted to write it down in my notebook.

But I don't, because I'm sure I'll remember it; I always do, whether I want to or not.

The author then speculates on the future of high-velocity travel. That's also interesting.

He then goes into the famous research that was used to prove one aspect of Einstein's general theory of relativity. The research speculated about the bending of light of stars by gravity. It describes the test of that during the solar eclipse of May 29, 1919. I've read about that before, but the author's take on it is especially interesting. He describes the difficulty to getting all the factors in place at exactly the right time in order to test the theory, and the worldwide fame it brought to Einstein when the eclipse proved he was right.

The next section of the book gets into chemistry and describes some classical experiments of the molecular structure of matter, delving into the possible actual size of atoms. Also interesting reading.

By the time I finish the book, the clock on the library wall tells me it's about time to head for my first class, English.

I start toward the exit door, but then I stop. Do I really need to go to any of my classes now that my mother is gone? After all, now there is no chance anybody can ever find out I'm an illegal immigrant from Germany. The only reason I've been going to classes was to avoid attracting attention to myself, because it might put us in danger of being deported. So why go to class now? I'm not really learning anything at this school anyhow.

On the other hand, I like this school library. And then there is the idea that the truant officer could come looking for me if I didn't show up. And it is relatively warm here in this school, and I'm not sure where I would go when it's so cold outside.

I might as well go to class.

But before I go, I grab another book off of that same shelf. It's titled *The Theory of Relativity and its Influence on Scientific Thought*. I have the librarian check it out for me.

I'm almost to my class when my way is blocked by a very large boy. He says, "Where ya headin' genius?"

He's backed by two other boys, and all three of them are wearing white and red leather jackets with varsity letters on them. The letters have little football emblems sewn onto them. It means they're members of the school football team.

I've been threatened by boys so many times in these hallways, I've lost count, but until now, the boys who do the threatening are always trying to dress and act like hoodlums. This is the first time the implied threats are coming from members of a school sports team. The three boys are all much bigger than I am, but I don't expect they will actually do anything; they won't want to tarnishing their reputations by beating up a smaller kid, let alone beating up a lowly fourteen-year-old freshman. Maybe they're just curious about me and don't know any other way to interact. Still, I'm getting a little tired of these kinds of threats, so this time, I don't even bother to smile. I just say, "Oh, why don't you just go ahead and do your childish threats and get it over with so I can go on to my class."

Their surprised reaction is funny, but I manage to maintain my blank expression as I wait to see what they're going to do.

After a moment's hesitation, they just turn and walk away, laughing and slapping each other on the back as they go.

Thankfully, only a few students are there, and the teacher hasn't arrived yet. I go to my usual seat at the back of the classroom and open my new book.

When the teacher arrives, she doesn't give us any kind of greeting, just launches into her usual lecture about the importance of learning proper grammar and punctuation if you want to appear educated when you go out into adult society.

I decide to ignore her familiar punctuation drills and start reading my new book. I don't bother to hide the fact that I'm reading while she talks.

The title page of the book tells me it's an old book, and that reminds me of how long ago Einstein came up with his theory of relativity. Amazing how something so important to science, presented to the world so long ago, is known by so few people, let alone understood.

The first chapter of the book starts by describing how our knowledge of the universe evolved from the Ptolemaic system to the one described by Copernicus. The author implies science was stuck with the elegant sun-oriented solar system views of Copernicus until Einstein built upon their theories to come up with his theory of relativity. The book says scientists were making the same mistake that science fiction novelists were making, not realizing they had to entirely leave behind the known frames of reference of us earth-bound observers. The author says scientists were using the perceptions and methods of scientific measurement used on this earth, and points out that scientists should not have assumed that the space-time frame elsewhere in the universe would be the same as here on our Earth. He then launches into an examination of current theories of momentum and gravitation that—

"Mister Smith?"

It takes me a moment to drag my mind out of the world of the book I'm reading to realize that in the world of this classroom, I'm being called upon.

I look up from my book and say, "Yes?"

That causes the other students to laugh.

The teacher says, "Well, Mr. Smith, nice of you to join us. Are you reading a book about punctuation and grammar."

"No. Actually, it's an interesting old book about how Einstein's theory of relativity made us rethink our beliefs about the nature of our universe."

My statement results in a few nervous-sounding titters from the other students.

"So, Mr. Smith, you could not find time to do your science reading outside of this class?"

"I just found this book in the school library, and I decided to read it instead of listening to your usual lecture on punctuation and grammar, which I already know about."

She seems taken aback, and then, irritated. "So, you apparently believe it's more important than what I was lecturing about."

"Of course it is. The author was writing in the early part of this century, when scientists were just realizing how significant Einstein's theory of relativity was."

This time, the other students stay quiet. They're waiting to see how the teacher will react.

The teacher too, seems to be waiting for something. Does she want me to go on, or is she just trying to decide how to respond?

I say, "Do you want me to summarize the main points of the book?"

Now, she's trying to hold back her anger, and the effort is causing her face to get red.

"No, Mr. Smith, we do not want a description of your book. What we want, what I want, is for you to put down that book and pay attention. Can you do that?"

"I suppose I can. The clock on the wall indicates it's almost time for this class to be over anyhow." I point.

She seems to be searching for a response to that, but gives up and just stares down at her notes. I think she's waiting for the bell to get her out of this situation.

I wonder if this exchange has effectively ended my peaceful experience at this school. I'm sure the other students in this class are going to quickly tell others about what happened here today. Will it get back to my other teachers?

I raise my hand, but don't wait for her to call on me. "I didn't mean to be disruptive, ma'am. I was just answering your question honestly. Perhaps I was overly excited about this book. I just discovered it in the school library, and I wanted to get right into it. I'm sorry."

Once again, she doesn't seem to know how to respond, and I think she's happy when the bell rings to indicate the end of this class period.

Walking to my next class, I think about what just happened. Has the dire report about my mother, and the experiences of the past few days, changed me so much I'm not going to be able to maintain the pretext of being a quiet fourteen-year-old freshman student anymore? But isn't that what I still am? Isn't there some value in sticking with that role rather than calling attention to myself as something the other students will think of as being unlike them. Maybe the solution is what the counselor suggested, go to a different school. But now with my mother gone, because of the cost it would entail, that seems more unlikely than ever. I'd better just rethink how I'm going to get something of value out of this school experience.

For the rest of the day, I pay close attention to whatever the teacher is lecturing about, but in every case, I already know it, or it's so trivial it doesn't seem worth learning.

When the school day is over, I'm glad to finally be released from what is feeling more and more like a prison. As I walk to the downtown library, I'm feeling like the situation I'm now in at school is my own fault. To protect myself and my mother, I intentionally tried to act like an ordinary student, a student of average ability. As a result, if I'm in an intellectual prison, I have to admit, it's one of my own making. I didn't try to foster relationships with my teachers; instead, I did things, that to them, seemed like a challenge. I tried to play along, but in doing so, I limited what I could get out of the experience. I wasn't willing put my mind into that sort of intellectual prison, attempting to force myself to concentrate on things I didn't want to concentrate on. The problem is, it all seems so slow, even when I listen, I end up feeling like I'm wasting my time, time I could spend doing something more intellectually profitable.

And now, if there is no chance of anybody meeting my German-speaking mother, the danger of being discovered as an illegal immigrant is very unlikely. So, should even bother going to school anymore.

But if I don't go to school, what would I do all day? It's too cold to be outside. I could spend all day at the downtown library, but I've learned there is such a thing as a truant officer, a sort of school policeman who is paid by the school district to track down young people of school age who are not attending. During the daylight hours, I'd be seen as the only school-age student in the library.

Also, school has long been the only place I could get anything to eat. Counting on supper tonight at the Hansens', I slipped lunch today, but I think I could still eat at school by modifying the date on my expired free lunch ticket. The cashier at the lunchroom knows me and never looks very closely at my meal ticket.

But the meals at the Hansens may not continue. If they don't, I guess I'll have to continue to go to the school building every day, if for no other reason than to get something to eat. That would make school even more of a boring trap that I would have to voluntarily put myself into, day after day.

As I get closer to the downtown library, I cheer up, realizing I'm heading for a place I really *do* want to be. I'm already thinking about what I should read today, but I'm not really all that particular about the subject matter. I prefer reading about physics, but actually, anything that will challenge my brain will do.

And of course, I'm hoping Julie will be back at the library. I don't like to admit that I need anybody, but I really have been missing her.

As soon as I walk in the door, I see her. She's back in her usual place, behind the front desk, answering people's questions.

I hesitate near the door, hoping she will see me.

And she does!

She smiles and nods, but then she gets a worried look on her face. Has she been worrying about me? Was she here yesterday, wondering where I was?

As I go through for the book stacks, trying to decide what to study today, I wonder if she'll come back here to find me. Or should I go back out front to talk to her?

No, if she wants to talk to me, she knows where I always study. After my mother was kidnapped, I know her father didn't want her to have anything to do with me because it might put her in danger. The fact that she's back here at the library must mean her father thinks the danger has passed, and she can be with me again.

I go to the science section and grab a few books off the shelf to take with me back to my usual study place. I know there are no science books in this library that will have up-to-date information about modern physics, but at least it will get my mind back into a studying mode.

But when I get to my secluded little study place, I see a "RESERVED" sign on the table. What does it mean? I've never seen a reserved sign on any table in this library.

Although I really like this little secluded table, I guess I'll have to find another place.

But now I see Julie coming through the stacks toward me. I take it as a good sign that she's smiling.

When she arrives, I point at the sign.

She does her usual little chuckle, and says, "It's reserved for you. I was hoping you'd show up today, and I didn't want anybody else taking your study place."

She reaches out to take my hand, and now she's not smiling. "Ever since I got the stuff you left for me, I've been worried about you, Curt. And I've missed you. I was so mad at my father for not letting me come here to see you that I . . . well, never mind that now. You're back, and that's what's important."

I squeeze her hand, and I like it that she doesn't pull it away. The only thing I can think to say is, "Yes, I'm back. But don't blame your father. He . . . well, he was just protecting you."

"Yeah, protecting me as if I was still a child." She hesitates, and then lets go of my hand to show me what's in her other hand. "But look here. I just got the latest issue of our science journal. You have to look at it right away. It summarizes some of the new theories in quantum mechanics, just what we've been wanting. Why don't you look it over so you can explain it to me." She again does her little chuckle, and then adds, "Assuming you think my little brain can understand it."

"Don't say things like that, Julie. You have a fine brain. And besides, I've been realizing the only reason everybody thinks I'm some sort of genius is just because I remember everything I read."

"Well, that's what a genius brain does, isn't it? I've been reading about genius. Trying to read about it, that is. The few books I can find that even mention the subject of genius just lists a bunch of child geniuses and describes their accomplishments. Like being good at math, or being chess champions. You never talk about math, except in the context of physics, and as far as I know, you don't play chess, do you?"

"I've read about chess, the rules and some of the main strategies of play. It's an interesting game, but it's still a game. I don't think I could keep my mind focused on a game long enough to get any good at it. I'd rather be reading."

Now she's smiling again. "Well, good. I'd rather have you studying, especially studying what I like to study. Well, I'd better get back to the desk, but I'll come back here as often as I can this evening to see how it's going."

"I would like that very much, Julie, but I promised Mr. and Mrs. Hansen I would join them for supper tonight at six-thirty."

"John Hansen? The rich builder guy?"

"Yes. He and his wife have been letting me stay with them since I got locked out of my apartment. Do you know him?"

"Everybody in this town knows John Hansen. He's even on the board of the local college, where I'm taking classes."

"Is that right?"

"Yes. Hey, if you're getting to know him, maybe he could get you into his college. You said you weren't getting much out of going to that high school."

"I don't think I could ask him something like that."

"Well, think about it anyhow. So, if you're going over there tonight, I guess we'll have to wait to study together at my house this weekend."

"And your father won't mind that?"

"I don't care if he likes it or not. I'm a grown up person, and I need to learn this stuff."

She waits for me to respond, but I'm not sure I'd feel comfortable going to her house again. I'm pretty sure her father would prefer it if I stayed away from her.

"Well, she says, "are you going to help me with this quantum physics stuff or not?"

"Yes, sure. I was just thinking we should find a better place to study. I wish you could study with me here, but I know you have to stay up at the front desk."

"Not during the day. And I don't have any classes tomorrow morning."

"Are you suggesting I skip school?"

"Well, you were the one that said you weren't getting much out of going to that school."

Is she challenging me to stop going to school and just study with her? Actually, I'd probably get a lot more education if I spent all my time here at this library. And if she'd be here too, why not? "Okay, what time?"

"My parents expect me to have breakfast with them before my father goes to work. So, let's say nine o'clock."

"I'll be here.. Can we leave this "reserved" sign here?"

"You bet. I'll make sure the morning staff knows about it. I'll tell them it's for me, studying for my college classes. Which is actually true, in a way."

"Okay, Julie. I'll be here."

"Good. Now you study this new journal, and we'll figure out what it means tomorrow morning. Together." She reaches out to squeeze my hand one last time before she hurries off to go back to her job at the front desk.

I sit down at my study table and open the journal. The table of contents indicates what Julie said, that this issue is about the latest research in quantum mechanics.

Turning to the first article, I see it's about Richard Feynman's work. He's fairly famous for his work on the atomic bomb and his theories about particle physics. The article discusses his path integral formulation. The article should be especially interesting as it says it has the potential to overturn some classical physics theories by proposing to a new way to compute quantum amplitude.

Another article mentions Freeman Dyson and his theories of quantum electrodynamics. and it also covers Dyson's analysis of Feynman's theories.

I look up from the journal to think about what I'm doing. I'm sitting in a fine library, studying exactly what I want to study, and not thinking about anything else. This is exactly what I've been needing, something to really challenge me and keep my brain occupied. The fact that I will also get to go over it here with Julie tomorrow morning makes it even better. Can it really have been such a short time ago since I got locked out of our apartment and just about froze to death in that boat shed in the park? And now, it suddenly seems as if I'm getting everything I could have hoped for.

Oddly, that thought suddenly gives me an uncomfortable feeling. When things go this well, it feels like you have a lot more to lose.

Forty

When it's time to head for the Hansen house, I hurry up to the front desk to say goodbye to Julie.

When I give her back the journal, she asks, "How is it? Will you be able to explain it to me?"

I try to think how to answer her question. "Well, the journal seems to make a lot of assumptions about the reader's prior knowledge of the subjects being discussed, more knowledge than either of us have, but we should be able to learn a lot just by trying to figure it out. And it will undoubtedly lead us toward what we should study next."

She smiles and again reaches across the desk to touch my wrist.

I'm liking more and more her tendency to do that, but before I can tell her that, we are interrupted by a library patron who has come to the desk to check out some books.

I tell Julie I have to hurry to the Hansen's for supper, and she leans forward to whisper, "Don't forget to ask him about taking some college courses."

I just say "Okay," and get out of the way of the impatient library patron.

It's cold and windy outside the library, but I'm a lot warmer now with a good stocking cap and gloves. I wrap the thick scarf around my neck, and that helps more than I would have expected.

As I get closer to the Hansens' house, I'm starting to worry about how I'm going to get past their big iron fence. If they don't know I'm outside, how will I get in?

When I get to their house, I go around to the back gate where I went in with Haru, but it's still locked. I won't be able to get in that way without a key. Did Mr. Hansen mean to give me a key and just forgot?

No, there must be another way in. I hurry along the fence until I get to the main front driveway, and sure enough, at this large gate, there's a button I assume must be some sort of door-bell. I press it, and it isn't long before the large gate creaks open. This must be how their delivery services are let in.

I go in though the gate, and I'm hardly inside when the gate starts creaking to a close behind me. Now what? The drive-way is also fenced, and I don't see any entry doors, only a garage with a wide door.

No sooner do I have that thought when the garage door begins to slide up to open. Inside, I see two large cars, and almost immediately Mr. Hansen comes running out between them. He hurries to me and puts his hand on my shoulder to lead me toward a door at the back of the garage.

"Damn, I'm sorry, Curt," says. "You were hardly gone this morning when my wife told me I'd forgotten to give you a key to the back gate. But I knew you'd figure out to come around here to the front driveway." He hands me a key. "This is the key to the side gate. We want you to be able to come and go anytime you want to."

I thank him and put the key in my pocket as he goes to push the button to close the garage door. So, they're not thinking of this as a temporary arrangement. I wonder what that means.

Mr. Hansen leads me up an inside stairway that leads to a hallway that I recognize as the one that will lead to his office. I wonder why he's taking me there.

He invites me to sit down on a chair next to his. He has a very serious look on his face.

He says, "Curt, I need to . . . well, I might as well just tell you. After you told me about the drug dealers and the disappear-ance of your mother, I decided to call the police to get more information. I talked to an Officer Flynn, the senior police officer that seems to be in charge of the case. I told him you were staying here with us, and he said that was good, but there were some things I should know about you. He said you'd gotten yourself involved with the wrong kind of crowd."

I start to object, but he holds up his hand.

"The officer said I should know that none of that was your fault, that maybe you were sometimes overly trusting of people. He said you were a good kid."

He stops talking and just sits there looking at me.

Is he waiting for me to say something? I'm not sure what he wants me to say. Was Officer Flynn warning him, or doing the opposite, encouraging him to help me?

But then he goes on. "The officer told me I should be careful of others that might claim to know you. When I asked him what he meant, he said there were some students from your school that are getting into illegal drugs."

I quickly interrupt to say, "I've never had anything to do with that, sir, except when Officer Flynn asked me ask around school to find out if any of that was going on."

"Yes, that's what the officer said. He said you had been a great help to him, and it would be very unfortunate if that had been what had cost the life of your mother. Those were the words he used, 'cost the life of your mother.' Now, you previously told us your mother had been kidnapped, but you did not say she was dead. I'm sorry to say it to you like that, but was the officer telling me something you didn't know?"

"I knew she had been kidnapped by foreign drug dealers, and I was told they might . . . " I can't seem to get the rest of the words out. I clear my throat, but it doesn't work. I'm determined not to start crying in front of this kind man, but I'm afraid if I go on, I will.

He reaches out and puts a gentle hand on my shoulder. He says, "I understand, Curt. As I told you before, I lost my mother to cancer when I was young." He pauses and then adds, "So, you didn't know she was dead?"

I clear my throat again and manage to say, "I was told she might be, but they hadn't found her body, so I hoped . . . "

He says, "I understand. Officer Flynn said they haven't found her body, and from the information they got from the cap-tured the captured drug dealer, they probably won't ever."

All I can manage to do is nod my head to show him I understand.

He still has his hand on my shoulder as he says, "All right, Curt. We won't need to talk about this again. But if you're going to live here with us, I want us to always be honest with each other. Therefore, I felt the need to tell you about that phone call I made to the police."

I again nod my head to show him I appreciate what he's saying, but I'm too overcome by him saying they want me to live here with them to be able to get any words out. But he's waiting for me to say something, so I manage a quiet, "Thank you, sir. It's been . . . really hard . . . lately."

He softly pats my shoulder, and says, "I understand. I felt completely lost, and very alone, after my mother died. And Curt, there's absolutely no need to thank me. Katherine and I both like having you here."

He glances as his wrist watch. "Now, Curt, let's think about supper. Katherine will be downstairs working with Mrs. Yoshida to prepare a nice supper for us. But we still have a few minutes to talk. How was school today?"

I try to get my mind out of the deep place I'm in, but I can only manage to say, "Fine." But then I wonder if I shouldn't be more honest with him, so I add, "But to tell you the truth, sir, I'm not getting much out of school. It seems like all they're teaching is what I've already learned from books, and if I point that out, they get irritated with me."

He smiles and says, "I bet they do. Sitting here talking with you, I have to keep on reminding myself I'm talking to a fourteen-year-old boy. But it seem like better teachers would appreciate your superior ability."

"Well, I suppose the teachers at the high school are all right. For most of the students anyhow. The other students don't, uh, read as much as I do."

"What you don't want to say out loud is that you're too smart for that school."

"Well, sir, I wouldn't put it that way. I know that they have to teach to the appropriate level of the class. It's just that I —"

"I understand. You're well above that level. What if we could get you into another school? There's a private high school in this town that I hear is very good. Do you think that would be a better fit for you?"

I think about that for a few moments, but then I feel I have to say, "A school with brighter students would be more enjoyable, but it would still be a school with a prepared curriculum. The problem is my mind seems to want to jump from one subject to another. My mind gets . . . I don't know what to call it. Dissatisfied, I guess. I often feel like I'm some kind of weird study machine that needs to gobble up more and more data."

"That's a funny image, my young friend. No wonder you aren't fitting in at a school where they just want you to quietly sit in straight rows and take lecture notes. I have to admit I wasn't a very good student in high school either. Got bored. I did better in college, and even better in graduate school."

"Now that you mention that, sir, my friend that I study with at the downtown library is a student at the local college, and she said she thought I would do better in a college environment where I could take whatever classes I needed."

"Perhaps she also told you I am on the board of that college."

Uh oh, does he think I manipulated the conversation to get to this point? But I need to remember the rule—always be honest with him. "Yes, she did, sir. But I didn't think I should bother you with my problems at school. And I didn't mean to take advantage of your position at . . . "

He smiles and again reaches out to pat my shoulder. "It's all right, Curt. In my line of work, I've learned you only get things by going after them. In fact, I'd advise you to be more aggressive in asking for what you want. So, do you want to do what she suggested, ask me if I can get you into the college?"

"Do you think that would be possible?"

"Well, in college, you have to chose a major area of study, and the curriculum for each major is also somewhat fixed." He hesitates and glances at his wall of books before turning back to me. "However, there is a new program we're just trying out. It's called Independent Study. It's a new type of major that can incorporate multiple majors. You'd have to form a committee that would approve your choices of classes."

"That sounds like exactly what I need, sir. Would it be possible for me to get into that?"

He again looks at his wall of books. Is he wondering if I would be capable of competing with other college students in something like that? I quickly say, "I think I could do it, sir. And I'd be willing to put in whatever time it took."

"Oh, I don't doubt you could compete. In fact, if you do get into college, you might still want to refrain from implying you know more than your teachers."

"Would that kind of thing also happen in college, sir?"

"I'm afraid it does. Teaching quality varies in every learning environment. I had a few run-ins with my . . . should we say, less competent university instructors until I learned it was better to just get along."

I'm glad he understands. To get where he is in life, he too must have been a standout student. His thriving company and the wall of books proves that. It may be why he's the first person I've ever met who really seems to understand the type of student I am.

"Well, I'll have to go to the Independent Study faculty administrator to find out what they would think of admitting a student into their program that doesn't have a high school degree."

He stands up and says, "But for now, let's go down and get some of the nourishment we need for our bodies. Mrs. Yoshida always prepares wonderful meals for us. We're very lucky to have discovered her."

I stand up and say, "Haru says the same thing about you, sir. I mean that they were lucky you found them after they got let out of that awful camp."

"Yes. When I first brought them in, I talked at length with Mrs. Yoshida about that camp. Since then, I've investigated the subject more and learned a great deal about what our government did to our Japanese-American citizens. It will eventually all come out, and mark my words, some reparations are going to need to be provided to them."

"Yes, Haru said it was a terrible time for them." I don't know what more I can say, so I remain quiet as we walk downstairs to the dining room. Even though I know they were not killing people in the camps they created for the West Coast Japanese-Americans, it's hard not to compare them to the concentration camps I've read the Nazis created for the Jews and others in Europe. In both cases, the people were sent there against their will, and in both cases, they were surrounded by barbed wire fences and guards with guns.

Forty-One

The next morning, at breakfast, Mr. Hansen tells me he called the professor at the college who is in charge of the Independent Study program. He says I should come back here today for lunch, so we can go to the college to talk to him.

After we finish breakfast, I go out through the door of the basement pool room, and then I use my new key to let myself out through the back fence gate.

It's early, so Haru hasn't come out of his house yet to head for school.

That's good, because I don't want to explain to him that I'm not going to school today, and if anybody asks him where I am, he can honestly say he doesn't know.

As I hurry downtown to the library though some early morning wind-driven light snow, I can hardly wait to see Julie again. I'm eager to get deep into the new physics journal with her.

Once inside the library, I hurry back to our study place, sure she will be there waiting.

But she isn't. Instead, her father is sitting in my study chair.

I duck back out of sight before he sees me. What is he doing here, and where is Julie? He is the last person I would want to see right now when things are going so well. I don't want to have anything to do with the world of crime and violence he represents.

I almost feel like going right back out into the snowstorm.

But I know I can't do that. I have to confront whatever this is.

I go down the aisle between the bookshelves toward him, and as soon as he sees me coming, he stands up.

At least he's smiling.

As soon as I get to him, he holds out his hand. "Good to see you again, Curt. Julie will be here soon. She had to finish up some things at home. Sorry, but when her mother needs help with something, Julie responds."

I shake his hand and say, "Is that why you're here?"

"Not exactly. When she told me she was meeting you here to study, I remembered you always study back here, and I decided . . . well, I thought I should come and tell you Mr. Hansen called me yesterday. Although I don't know him personally, everybody in this town knows of him, and it was a surprise when they told me he was on the line. The first thing he told me is that you've been staying with them."

"Yes. For the past few days. After my mother disappeared, I got locked out of our apartment."

"I see. Well, that's why he was calling me. About your mother, that is. He wanted to know what it was all about. I told him what we know. And this morning I felt like I should come here and tell you he was checking on you. Not checking *up* on you, just checking on you. I got the feeling he and his wife are concerned about you. He wanted to know what caused your mother to be kidnapped."

"Yes, Mr. Hansen told me he'd called you."

"Oh, did he? I'm glad to hear that. Anyhow, I couldn't tell him much because we don't actually know much. I assume the reason they took your mother is because of your association with that Pan character. Beyond that, we don't know why they are so violent. The FBI tells me there have been a lot of drug-related killings, some in this country, but especially down in Columbia. Anyhow, Mr. Hansen was very sympathetic when I told him your mother is dead."

I'm determined to keep my voice steady and respond to him in the same way he's talking to me. "And you're sure now? That she's actually . . . dead?"

"Well, the FBI seems sure of it. The haven't found her body, but they say normally, with this gang, people disappear and their bodies are never found. They asked us to drag the lake, and we did that. No bodies were found, so they may be burying their victims out in the woods somewhere."

He's waiting for me to respond, but I don't know what to say, and I don't think I can keep up this sort of calm-sounding way of talking about my mother.

Finally, he must have realized it's hard for me to talk about her in this way, because he says, "I'm sorry to have to be talking to you about this again. I understand how hard this must be for you." He shakes my hand again and turns to leave. But then he turns back. "Oh, by the way, the FBI tells me that Pan guy is back in Puerto Rico. They're keeping an eye on him and his mother down there."

After he leaves, I sit in my chair to think about what he told me. So, the FBI is saying victims of the drug gang are not usually found. Therefore, I may never know for sure what happened to her.

But I am glad to hear Pan has left this country, just like he said he would. It'll be good to be rid of him and all the trouble he caused me, but I guess I'm glad to hear he and his mother are safe in Puerto Rico. I hope he stays out of this country from now on, but I'm not sure he will.

I look down the aisle between the book shelves, hoping to see Julie coming, but so far, there's no sign of her.

Looking at all those books tells me what I should do: I should get up and grab a few of those books, any of them, and bury my mind in whatever they have to offer. Better to study something not at all important than to let my mind go too deeply into what Officer Flynn was just telling me about my mother.

But no sooner do I get up and start looking through books on the shelf when I see Julie coming. Thank goodness! Now we can talk about physics. I want to think about that and nothing else.

When she gets to me, she gives me a hug.

She's never done that before, and although it surprises me, I completely welcome it and hug her back.

She points to the table and says, "Well, are you ready to get really deep into physics? Some of the stuff in this journal is way over my head."

We sit down, and she puts the journal on the table.

"Before we get started, Julie, I should tell you your father was here."

She looks surprised. "What? He was here?"

"He was waiting for me when I got here. He told me you'd be a little late."

"Oh, Curt, I'm sorry I was late, but my mother wanted me to . . . well, never mind about that. Are you saying my father came here just to tell you I might be a little late?"

"No, he came here to tell me Mr. Hansen had called him."

"Hansen called my father? Why would he do that?"

"I told Mr. Hansen my mother had been kidnapped. I guess he wanted to know more about that."

"Oh, right."

She's looking very sad, so I think she's trying to think what to say to make me feel better.

I quickly say, "You don't have to say anything, Julie. I know you care, and that's enough for me. If they never find her body, I'll just have to accept that she's gone. When something bad happens, we still have to go on with our lives, don't we?"

Now she has tears in her eyes. She says, "I had an argument with my mother today. What you said made me think about what if she was gone. I . . . I mean you've had such a hard time. It made me realize I have such an easy life. I don't know how you, well . . . how you . . . "

I reach out to touch her hand. "It's all right, Julie. Maybe we should just study this journal."

She wipes her eyes with the back of her hands, and says, "Right. Exactly right. We're here to study."

I open the journal and again turn to the article that summarizes the history of theories and discoveries in the field of quantum mechanics.

It goes all the way back to the beginning of the twentieth century when the first double-slit experiments showed that matter can display characteristics of both classically defined waves and particles, illustrating the probabilistic nature of matter at the sub-atomic level.

It also discusses Einstein and the photoelectric effect, and points out Marie Curie's contributions.

I say, "You probably knew Marie Curie was the first woman to win a Nobel prize, but did you know she was the first person to win it twice?"

"I didn't know that. Good for her. For her studies of radiation?"

"No, in chemistry. For her discovery of radium."

"Oh. I did know that in the academic world she was repeatedly discriminated against for being a woman."

"Right. She was almost barred from the Nobel ceremony. They accused her of having a sexual relationship outside of the institution of marriage."

That gets a quick laugh out of Julie. "Good thing we are well past that kind of attitude these days."

I start to say "are we?" but change my mind and decide to stick to physics. "Uh, right. Too bad she had to die so young."

"Yes, from her exposure to radiation."

I turn my attention back to the journal article and point out a paragraph about Niels Bohr. "There is also a note about how Niels Bohr proposed a new way of visualizing the atom. That was way back in nineteen thirteen, and that seems to me to be about where the import of modern quantum physics starts to be more universally felt. His quantum theory, with its more modern description of the atom, is now often referred to as 'old quantum theory.' This note also mentions Max Planck and his description of radiation as consisting of quanta with specific energies, and the math of that is now referred to as Planck's constant."

I realize Julie is staring at me, so I stop talking.

She says, "This is all pretty easy for you, isn't it?"

"Well, these early discoveries are pretty straightforward. Soon, we're going to get into the more modern theories that are, uh, harder to get your mind around."

"Okay, that's what I want to learn about. The modern theories. What does it say about that?"

"Well, moving ahead, we of course have to look at Heisenberg's formulation of the quantum uncertainty principle."

"Yes, I've heard of that, but I don't know what it is."

"Well, Werner Heisenberg used mathematical analysis to show that it is not possible to predict the value of a subatomic quantity with all certainty. But what got people's attention was his description of the observer effect That is, measurements of certain systems cannot be made without affecting the system. It goes all way back to the double-slit experiment, suggesting that measurements of that experiment changed the outcome."

"You mean just by watching the experiment we might change the outcome?"

"Well, by measuring it. There have now been many experiments that fact."

"And what about quantum entanglement? I've been hearing about that. Wasn't it supposed to have upset Einstein?"

"Quantum entanglement, described experimentally, is when particles share a quantum state that can't be described independently of each other."

"Meaning, what affects one, affects the other."

"Correct. Most importantly, it doesn't matter how proximate the particles are to each other. What concerned Einstein was that it implied instant interaction between the particles, even at a distance, and that seemed to violate the supposed speed limit of light. He said it meant the accepted description of quantum mechanics must therefore be incomplete."

"What do you think?"

"Well, I'm nowhere near advanced enough to have a coherent opinion, but I think I would have to agree with Einstein that there is something wrong with the way we're looking at it. In any case, the correct way of looking at it has not yet been formulated, so in the meantime, quantum entanglement is the best way of describing the phenomenon."

"This is great, Curt. We're going to have such fun learning about all this stuff. I wish we could just live together and study all the time." She stops and seems to be having trouble deciding what to say next. Finally, she says, "But of course, now you've found a much better place to live, with the Hansens."

"Yes, and I have some news about that. We might be able to take classes together at the college. I did what you suggested and talked to Mr. Hansen about my possibly taking classes there, and he said there's a new Independent Study program that he might be able to get me into. We're going there this afternoon to meet with the professor who is in charge of that program."

"That's wonderful news, Curt. What time do you go?"

"After lunch."

She looks at her wrist watch. "Well, it's almost noon now, so shouldn't you be going?"

I jump up. "Oh no, I always lose track of time when we get into this physics stuff. I'd better hurry."

She reaches up to take my hand and says, "Okay, go. We can pick this up again tomorrow. I sure hope you get into that program. I know you aren't getting much out of your high school classes."

I give her hand a last squeeze and hurry toward the library's front door.

Forty-Two

Out into the cold wind, I pull on the nice warm red stocking cap Mrs. Hansen gave me. As I start down the sidewalk, I'm just pulling on her warm red gloves when I notice a dark sedan parked at the curb.

I almost turn and run back into the library, but then I stop myself. There are lots of large black cars in this world, and none of them are likely to do me any harm. The time for being worried about dark cars are over. I should just hurry to the Hansens' house, and not worry so much.

When I get to the house, I use my key to get in the back gate and hurry in to the dining room. Thankfully, I'm not too late; Mrs. Yoshida is still in the kitchen organizing the lunch she's made for us.

I join Mrs. Hansen at the table, and she asks how my morning went. I tell her it went well, that my study partner and I read a new science journal that has articles about quantum mechanics.

She says, "Quantum mechanics? What's that?"

"Oh, it's an emerging field of physics research that's attempting to describe the properties of matter at the atomic and subatomic scale."

She smiles. "Okay. Maybe I shouldn't have asked."

"Well, it may sound complicated, but it's actually very interesting."

She's still smiling. "To you maybe. Edward has been telling me about your remarkable intelligence. He tells me the two of you are going over to the college this afternoon to see about you taking classes there."

"Yes, ma'am. And I'm very grateful."

As soon as Mr. Hansen joins us, Mrs. Yoshida serves us a fine meal of mixed green salad followed by a big bowl of rich vegetable and chicken soup.

By the time I finish eating, I'm completely full. It makes me wonder how both Mr. and Mrs. Hansen stay so thin. I think if I ate this much for lunch and then did it again at supper, it wouldn't take me long to get fat.

No sooner have we finished eating when Mr. Hansen pushes back from the table and tells me we'd better get on the road to the college.

On the way, riding in his big car with seats that feel as plush as a living room sofa, Mr. Hansen is telling me not to be nervous, but they're going to give me some kind of test.

I tell him the truth, that I'm not nervous; in fact, I'm looking forward to it.

At the college, I don't get to meet the professor in charge of the Independent Study program. Instead, Mr. Hansen goes to meet with him while an older woman with gray hair leads me into a room where she sits me down at a small table. She doesn't say anything, but from her sour look, I wonder if she's puzzled about why someone as young as me might be here taking a test at this college.

As soon as I'm seated, she gives me the test. She says I have one hour, and she starts a stopwatch. Then, she goes to sit at a desk at the front of the room to watch me.

The test is in booklet form, so I look through it before beginning. It's simply a set of questions, most of which are multiple choice, but some are true or false. Most of the questions seem to be testing my memory of things I've supposedly learned, but others seem to be testing my reasoning ability. There are a few math word questions, but they look pretty straightforward.

I finish the test in well under the specified hour, but I take the extra time to go over all my answers. I think I got them all right.

When the hour is up, the woman stands up and tells me to put my pencil down.

I do that, and she comes to pick up the test booklet. But then she surprises me by giving me another test booklet. She again says I have one hour.

This test is completely different. It seems to be a test of abstract reasoning and logic, and there are a lot of different types of questions. The first one is pictorial, a sequences of geometric designs which requires me to then pick another geometric design that would be next in the sequence. All them are pretty easy. I'm surprised such an easy test could actually be used to indicate a person's intelligence.

The next set of questions is also pictorial, but different. It's comprised of sets of boxes with symbols like circles, squares, triangles, and hexagons inside and requires me to pick from other similar sets of symbols would best fit into the initial set. Interesting, but again, pretty easy.

The last set of questions is the most interesting, and the easiest. It shows me sets of diagrams that look like abstract flowers, with some petals colored and others left white. It then asks me select which other flower-type design would fit best into the set.

When I finish, I realize that although Mr. Hansen was worried I'd be nervous about going to a college where they'd test me, the tests were not hard, and actually kind of fun.

Once again, I use the extra time to go over my answers, but I can't seem to find any I would change, so when the woman tells me to put down my pencil, I get up and take the test to her.

She accepts it without a word and tells me I can leave.

Out in the lobby, I'm told to wait, but after only a few minutes Mr. Hansen comes in. He says, "Well, how did it go?"

"Fine. Actually, the tests were kind of fun."

"Apparently, they must have been quite easy for you. The professor in charge of the program said they gave you a tough battery of tests, and after he quickly looked over your answers, he thinks you did very well. In fact, the phrase he used was 'remarkably well.'"

I'm glad to hear that. Although I wasn't worried, I couldn't be sure how they would react. I say, "I've never taken tests like that before There were several different kinds, and that made it really fun. I like figuring things out."

"The professor said they gave you a traditional IQ test and then a new type of logic and reasoning test that somebody back east has been working on." He pauses and then looks into my eyes. "But you think you did well on them?"

"Yes, I'm pretty sure I did."

Driving back to his house, he keeps asking me questions about the test. For some reason, he seems worried. He says, "Were there any especially hard parts?"

I answer him honestly, telling him the test seemed very easy, and I think I answered all of the questions correctly.

He says, "All of them? You didn't come across even one question that you weren't sure of?"

"No. They all seem pretty straightforward."

"Well, okay. Now we'll just have to wait for the committee to meet and see if they all will agree to let you into the program. I'll keep after them to hurry it along so you can get in by the start of the next term which is coming right up."

"If they let me in, I think I'd like to study physics and philosophy."

"Not engineering?"

I think he was hoping I would follow in footsteps. I quickly say, "I liked those engineering books of yours I read, but I mostly like the underlying concepts, especially those that have to with the physics of engineering. Force and materials and stresses. I'd like to keep on learning about those aspects of engineering."

"Good, good. I think I could help you with that." He chuckles. "Actually, it might be you that in some cases helps me. There are new things coming along all the time. We can learn about them together."

That last comment makes me wonder if maybe he's been wishing he had a son to pass his business on to. It is possible he's thinking I might be that son?

He's quiet for a few more moments, then he pulls over to the side of the road. "Curt, there's something important I want to talk to you about."

He looks out the car's windows.

I also look out. There is a whisper of snow in the air, and where we are parked overlooks a patch of forest. The winter trees seem bare and stark without any leaves on them, and there are patches of snow on the ground wherever the tree trunks provide shade.

Mr. Hansen turns to look at me. He's not smiling. "What I'm about to tell you is very confidential, Curt. My company has received a very large government contract to participate in the rebuilding of Japan's infrastructure. The project is already under-way, but it's turning out to be a monumental task. Because of the devastating bomb damage the Japanese cities suffered during the war, we've going to have to basically start from scratch. It's turn-ing out to be a design project as much as a rebuilding project. Anyhow, the reason I'm telling you this is because this summer I'm going to have to go over there to look over the situation with my top engineers, and I'd like you to go with me."

"Me? I mean yes, sure, I'd love to go with you, but will they allow that?"

"We will be traveling on military transport planes, and no, they might not like the idea of a young lad accompanying me. They probably wouldn't understand how helpful you could be. But if you were my son, and part of my company, they wouldn't be able to say no."

He's throwing so much at me all at once, it's taken me completely off guard. His company got a big government con-tract in Japan, and he wants me to accompany him there? And not on as part of his company, but also as his son? For the past few days, I'd been thinking he was treating me like a son, but to actu-ally *be* his son?

He reaches out to touch my arm. "Oh, I'm sorry, Curt. That caught you off guard, didn't it? Sometimes I do tend to blurt things out. Let me explain. A while back, the doctors told Kather-ine she won't be able to have children, so since then, adoption is something Katherine and I had been talking about. I told her I wanted a son that could become part of my company, a son I could talk to about . . . all kind of things. And then, last night, after you read a few of my engineering books and immediacy understood what was important about them, the underlying concepts as you said, I had the thought if only you could have been my son. I mentioned that to Katherine, and she also said it was nice having you there. And then, when I heard your mother was dead and you that you no longer had anybody . . . well, you see that I mean."

I do see what he was saying. And I realize what it could mean for me, what an unimaginable change it would mean for my life. But it would also mean I would have to accept as fact that my mother is really gone.

"I can see you're thinking about it, aren't you Curt? And that's all I want you to do. For now. My planned trip to Japan is months away, and so far all Katherine and I have done is investigate the adoption process. Just think about it for now, and later the three of us can sit down and talk about it."

I'm not sure what to say. And I'm not sure what he wants me to say. Of course it's a great opportunity, to go from being a destitute illegal immigrant to being the adopted son of the town's most affluent family. I can't say that to him, but I do need to say something. He's waiting. "I'm very grateful, sir, I mean that that you would want to . . . to take me into your family."

"Okay, fine. We don't need to talk about it any more right now. Let's wait and see how this special college Independent Study thing works out. But from what they said, I think you're in."

Epilog

It's the first week of June, and I'm in summer recess from my Independent Study college classes. I have a brand new last name, Hansen, instead of the name Smith, which never was my real name anyhow. I also have a brand new adopted father and mother. They have been extraordinarily kind to me, and I love them very much.

My father and I just boarded a military plane, and we are on our way to an Air Force base in California. From there, we will board a huge military transport plane to make the long trip to Japan.

My father has been showing me aerial pictures of Tokyo, and I can see that our company's rebuilding task is going to be formidable. There's very little left of the central part of the city.

Although many of the railroad tracks still appear to partly exist, the few surviving locomotives are the old coal-fired type.

We've decided our first task will be to help the government rebuild the transportation infrastructure. Part of that will be to transition the entire rail system to electricity.

Japan is rapidly building new electrical energy generating plants to facilitate it. Once the new transportation system is compete, Japanese workers will be able to quickly and efficiently get to their places of work. My father believes establishing a nationwide efficient transportation system will be the quickest way to help Japan recover, and I agree with that concept.

I've brought along the physics and philosophy textbooks for my upcoming fall semester classes at the college. Assuming I get some breaks from our work in Tokyo, I'll be able to get a head start on my fall classes. There are some amazing new developments in quantum mechanics—which is my study specialization—and I want to keep on thinking about what those new developments will mean for the future of physics, and the world.

Haru was surprised when he learned I was going to the country of his ancestors. He said I was crazy to want to set foot in such a primitive country. Of course, he was kidding me, as usual.

Julie was not at all happy when she learned her study partner would be leaving for the entire summer, but she realized it was a great opportunity for me. In the end, she kissed me and told me to bring her some funny little Japanese souvenir. I promised I would.